## "Come dance with

Trey's eyes twinkled brightly as he pulled Debra to the dance floor and into his arms. She leaned closer to him.

Trey smiled down at her. His hand on her back was strong and masterful as they took off across the dance floor. "You look amazing tonight," he said.

"Thank you," she replied, hoping he couldn't hear the loud thunder of her heartbeat. She wanted to dip her head into the hollow of his throat, feel his body scandalously close against hers. "Your speech was pretty amazing, too."

He laughed. "We'll see about that by the campaign donations that appear in the next few weeks. If nothing else, it seems that everyone has had a wonderful time tonight. My only regret is that I haven't had a chance to dance with you before now."

She raised her head to gaze up at him, and in his blue eyes she saw what she felt—desire and want and everything that shouldn't have been in those blue depths.

Dear Reader,

It's always exciting to kick off a new series, and The Adair Legacy promises to have it all—hot heroes, strong heroines, plenty of secrets and danger all set against a background of politics.

The Winston family is extraordinary, with a strong mother and three brothers who share not only a family bond of love, but also enough dysfunction to crank up the intrigue.

I loved writing the story of eldest brother Trey, a strong man with a dream, and Debra, his mother's assistant, who threatens everything Trey believed he'd wanted in his life. I hope you enjoy reading their story.

Thanks and keep reading!

Best,

Carla Cassidy

# HER SECRET, HIS DUTY

—

## Carla Cassidy

HARLEQUIN® ROMANTIC SUSPENSE

Special thanks and acknowledgment to Carla Cassidy for her contribution to The Adair Legacy miniseries.

Recycling programs
for this product may
not exist in your area.

ISBN-13: 978-0-373-27866-4

HER SECRET, HIS DUTY

Copyright © 2014 by Harlequin Books S.A.

**Printed in U.S.A.**

## Books by Carla Cassidy

### Harlequin Romantic Suspense

### Silhouette Romantic Suspense

Other titles by this author
available in ebook format.

---

## CARLA CASSIDY

is a New York Times bestselling and award-winning author who has written more than one hundred books for Harlequin. In 1995 she won Best Silhouette Romance from *RT Book Reviews* for *Anything for Danny*. In 1998 she won a Career Achievement Award for Best Innovative Series from *RT Book Reviews*.

Carla believes the only thing better than curling up with a good book to read is sitting down at the computer with a good story to write. She's looking forward to writing many more books and bringing hours of pleasure to readers.

# Chapter 1

"Impossible." The single word escaped Debra Prentice's lips in disbelieving horror as she stared at the three separate pregnancy tests lined up like little soldiers on her bathroom vanity.

Not one, not two, but three tests and each showing a positive sign. Undeniable results that her brain tried to absorb.

Pregnant. There was no question now that she was pregnant. She'd wondered about it when she was late with her period, but had written it off as stress. She'd been late in the past.

Pregnant. How was it possible? Even as the question formed in her mind, memories of a single night six weeks ago gave her the answer.

An unexpected encounter, too many drinks and a mad dash to a nearby hotel room where she'd found complete abandon with a man she had no business being with at all.

Her cheeks burned as she remembered the awkward morning after. Gazes not meeting as they both hurriedly dressed and then the humiliating ride in a cab from the hotel to her front door. And now this, the icing on a cake that should have never been baked in the first place. Pregnant.

A glance at the small clock in the bathroom forced a gasp from her. If she didn't hurry she'd be late to work, and in all the years that Debra had worked as personal secretary and assistant to Kate Adair Winston, she had never been late to work.

She got up and tossed the tests into the trash, then gave herself a quick glance in the bathroom mirror. The slim black pencil skirt she wore didn't display a hint of her current condition but the red tailored button-up blouse only emphasized the paleness of her face, a paleness that the results of the tests had surely created.

Her light brown hair was already attempting to escape the twisted bun she'd trapped it in earlier, but she didn't have time to fix it now.

She left the bathroom, deciding that she couldn't, she wouldn't think about her pregnancy right now. She had a little time to figure things out, but right now she had to get her brain in work mode.

She pulled on a black winter coat and grabbed her purse, then left her two-story townhouse and headed for her car parked at the curb. There was parking behind the townhouse, but she rarely used it, preferring the convenience of curbside parking instead.

The January air was bracing, hovering right around

the freezing mark. Thankfully the sky was bright blue and she didn't have to worry about snow or sleet.

The townhouse was located just off Glenwood Avenue in the uptown district of Raleigh, North Carolina. It was Debra's pride and joy, bought two years ago after years of renting. She loved the area, loved the fact that she could paint walls and hang pictures without getting a landlord's approval. It was cozy and filled with all the colors and textiles she loved.

Once inside the car she checked the clock. It was just after seven, but she still had to maneuver morning traffic to get to North Raleigh where the Winston Estate was located.

Every morning in the capital city of North Carolina the morning rush traffic was bad, but on this Wednesday morning it seemed particularly heavy.

Or, maybe it was the racing of her thoughts that made the ride feel longer and more difficult than usual. Even though it was unplanned and unexpected there was no doubt in her mind that she would keep the baby. For her, that decision was a no-brainer.

She would just need to keep the father's identity to herself for the rest of her life. She would let the people close to her assume that the baby was Barry's, the snake-in-the-grass boyfriend who had broken up with her on the night she'd been in that restaurant bar, the same night she'd done something completely out of character.

But, there was no question in her mind who the father was because she hadn't been pregnant when she and Barry had broken up and she was pregnant now. There had only been that single night of utter madness to account for her current condition.

She steered her thoughts away from the pregnancy as she approached her workplace. The impressive Winston Estate was located on two acres of lush, meticulously manicured grounds.

Built in 1975, the six-bedroom, nine-bath white-and-red brick house also boasted a beautiful swimming pool, a backyard area around the pool big enough for entertaining and a small guest house where Kate's security, a Secret Service detail, worked from.

The front entrance boasted a large black iron gate that was opened only when security and Kate allowed. The entire estate was fenced in except for a side entrance through which staff and service vehicles came and went.

Debra turned into the access entrance and waved to Jeff Benton, part of the security team that kept Kate and her family safe when the former vice president was in the house.

Debra pulled into a parking spot specifically for staff and hurriedly got out of the car. She entered the house through a side door that led into a large, empty mudroom and then into the huge kitchen where at the moment fresh coffee and cinnamon were the predominant scents.

None of the help was in the large, airy room that had the latest cooking equipment, but Sam Winston, Kate's thirty-three-year-old middle son, sat at a small table next to a window with a cup of coffee before him.

"Good morning, Sam," she said tentatively. Since Sam's return from overseas where he'd served in Army Special Forces, he'd been distant, at times downright unpleasant, and she never knew exactly what to expect from him when they happened to run into each other.

He looked up from his coffee, his blue eyes dark and unreadable. "Morning," he replied and then shifted his gaze back into the depths of his cup, obviously not encouraging any further conversation.

Debra passed through the kitchen and entered the main foyer. As always, her breath was half stolen from her by the beauty of the black-and-white marble floors and the exquisite winding wooden staircase that led up to the second level.

Beyond the foyer were Kate's official office and a doorway right next to it that led to Debra's much smaller office. She knew that Kate didn't usually go into her office to begin her day until sometime after eight, but that didn't mean Debra didn't have things to do before Kate made her official appearance.

Debra's office was small but efficient with a desk that held a computer, a multifunctional printer and memo pads. A wooden five-drawer file cabinet sat nearby on the right wall. The other wall was a white dry-erase area that took up the left side of the room, where she kept track of Kate's ever-busy, ever-changing social calendar with dry-erase markers in a variety of colors.

She closed the door, took off her coat and hung it in the tiny closet that stored extra paper and printer supplies and then sat at the desk and powered up her computer.

There was only one personal item in the whole room. It was a framed picture that hung on the wall, a photo of Debra with a Parisian street vendor who sold hot croissants and coffee from a colorful cart just down the block from the U.S. Embassy in Paris.

Debra had lived in Paris for the two years that Kate had served as U.S. ambassador to France. It had been an amazing experience for Debra. She'd learned some of the language, wandered the streets on her time off and breathed in the local ambiance.

When Kate's time in that position had ended and it was time to return to the states, Debra hadn't wanted the usual souvenirs of a picture or a miniature statue of the famous Eiffel Tower.

She'd wanted a photo of herself and Pierre, the charming Frenchman who had begun her mornings with a bright smile, a hot croissant and a cup of steaming café au lait. A fellow staffer had taken the photo and Debra had brought it into a local craft store to have it enlarged and framed.

The time in France had been wonderful, but that was then and this was now. Pregnant. She was pregnant. She couldn't quite wrap her mind around it yet, but she knew one thing for sure, once the baby was born her life would be irrevocably changed.

She shoved the thought away and instead focused on her morning work. It took twenty minutes to go through her emails, deleting spam that had managed to get through the filter, marking messages to forward to Kate and answering those that didn't require her boss's attention.

Once the email was finished, she moved to the file folder on her desk that held a stack of invitations for Kate. As a former U.S. ambassador and vice president, Kate was invited to hundreds of events each week.

As Debra looked at each one, she made a list of who, what and where for each event that required a response in the next week or so. The social calendar Debra kept on the wall was an ever-morphing, color-coded animal that required constant attention.

There were rumors that Kate was being groomed to run for president in the next election and she was already being courted by special-interest groups and powerful party movers and shakers.

So far she hadn't mentioned her plans to anyone, but Debra suspected the idea of becoming the first female president of the United States was definitely appealing. Kate had a reputation as a loving mother, a family-oriented person, but Debra knew she was also a woman of great convictions about how the country should move forward in the coming years.

It was just after eight when a familiar soft knock sounded on Debra's door. She grabbed her memo pad and left her desk. It was their routine; Kate knocked to let Debra know she was now in her office and it was time for a morning update.

At fifty-eight years old, Kathleen Adair Winston was an attractive woman with short, stylish light brown hair and blue eyes that radiated honesty, kindness and intelligence. Debra had worked for her long enough to know that she also possessed a will of steel, a slight streak of stubbornness and a love of her family that was enviable.

This morning she was dressed in a pair of tailored navy slacks and a pale blue blouse that emphasized the bright hue of her eyes. Her jewelry was tasteful, a wedding ring despite the fact that she was a widow and a silver necklace with matching earrings.

"Good morning, Debra." Her smile was warm, and adoration for the woman who had been her boss since she'd been a college graduate swelled up inside Debra.

"Good morning to you, Kate," she replied and took the chair opposite the large ornate desk where Kate sat. "Did you sleep well?"

"I always sleep well," Kate replied. "It seems the days are too long and the nights are far too short for my taste."

Debra nodded and smiled and then got down to business. "I have several pressing things we need to discuss this morning," she said.

It took nearly forty-five minutes for Debra to update Kate and get confirmation or regrets on the invitations that required answers.

When they had finished that particular task, Kate leaned back in her chair and sipped the coffee she must have carried with her into the office. "You look tired," she said. "Did you not sleep well last night?"

Debra stared at her in surprise. Did it already show somehow on her face? Did newly discovered pregnancy make a woman look tired the day she realized she was pregnant?

"Nothing to worry about," Debra said, pleased that her voice sounded normal. "I did do a lot of tossing and turning last night. I think it was indigestion, but I'm sure I'll sleep fine tonight."

"Anything in particular on your mind?"

Debra smiled with a forced brightness. "Yes, I'm wondering along with the rest of the world if my boss intends to make a run for the presidency."

*Deflect,* she thought. She had always been good about making the conversation about other people rather than about herself.

"Your boss still hasn't made up her mind," Kate replied ruefully. She turned in her chair and stared at the wall that held an array of family photos. Most of them were of Kate with her three handsome sons.

"Although I know I need to come to a decision in

the next couple of weeks. It's a long, arduous process to begin a campaign, but the men who have already thrown their hats in the ring are not what the country needs right now. I do believe I'd do a better job than any of them, but I also realize the price I'd be asking my family to pay if I decide to become an official candidate," she said as she turned back to look at Debra.

"You'll make the right decision," Debra said confidently. "You always do. Either way, you'll do what's best for both your family and the country."

Kate flashed her the bright smile that had been her trademark both when she'd served her four years as vice president and as a beloved ambassador to France. "You're the special secret in my pocket, Debra. There are days that your efficiency and loyalty are responsible for my very sanity. Thank goodness you possess the organizational skills that keep me on track."

"I have a feeling you'd be just fine without me, but I love what I do, and now I'd better get back to my office and take care of the RSVPs on these invitations." Debra stood. "You'll let me know if there's anything else I can do for you. You have nothing on your calendar for the day so hopefully you can give yourself a break and just relax a bit."

"Maybe." Kate stood and carried her coffee to the window that looked out on a lovely garden.

Debra left the room aware that Kate didn't know how to relax—until she made up her mind about the next presidential election, she would worry and stew, weigh pros and cons, until she made a final decision about what her future would hold.

Debra didn't even want to think about her own future. She knew that the first thing she needed to do was see a doctor. She'd try to schedule an appointment with her gynecologist for the weekend to confirm what she already knew.

In the meantime, day by day—that's how she would have to take things right now. She'd scarcely had time to process the reality of her condition.

Eventually her pregnancy would show and she'd have some explaining to do, but until that day came she had to focus on her work.

She remained at her desk until just after eleven when Kate used the intercom to call her back into her office. Debra grabbed her notepad and reentered Kate's office, only to stop short at the sight of the ridiculously handsome man seated in the chair she had vacated earlier.

Trey Winston was not only incredibly handsome with his rich dark brown hair and striking blue eyes, he was also the CEO of Adair Enterprises, the family business, a rich and powerful man who was well liked by his employees and friends. He was also the father of the baby Debra carried.

"Here we are," Kate said as Debra entered the room. She gestured her assistant to the chair next to Trey's. Trey offered Debra a faint, rather uncomfortable smile.

Uncomfortable. That's the way things had been for him whenever he saw Debra after the crazy one night they'd spent together—a night that should never have happened.

He'd been at the popular bar/restaurant celebrating the close of a big business deal and she'd been there commiserating a breakup with her boyfriend. The two of them had somehow hooked up, shared too many drinks and then had continued to make the mistake of heading to a nearby hotel and having hot, passionate sex.

He hadn't been too drunk to know what he was doing and neither had she, but he should never have allowed it to happen at all.

He'd spent the past six weeks putting it out of his mind, trying to pretend that it had never happened. Unfortunately, trying to forget had been difficult.

His mother would kill him if she found out. Kate would give him a motherly smackdown to end all smackdowns if she believed he had taken advantage of her assistant, a young woman he knew his mother loved and trusted.

"Trey has just informed me that I'm not the only political beast in the family," Kate said once Debra was seated next to Trey. "He's thinking about running for the Senate."

Debra looked at him in surprise and then quickly averted her gaze back to Kate. "I'm sure he'd make a fine senator."

"You know that and I know that, but what we need to do is see how much support he would be able to get behind him," Kate replied.

Trey could see the wheels turning in his mother's head. Of all the people in his life, Trey trusted his mother more than anyone. He'd been flirting with the idea of entering politics for some time and finally felt the time was right now.

"What do you have in mind?" Debra asked.

Her voice was sweet and soft, but Trey had memories of husky moans and sighs of pleasure. He also couldn't help but notice and remember the fresh, clean scent of her, so unlike the cloying perfumes most of the women in his social circle wore.

"A fund-raiser dinner party." Kate's words snapped Trey back to the matter at hand. "And we'd need to get it scheduled and on the calendar in the next two weeks."

"Two weeks?" Debra sounded horrified as she stared at Kate. "But that's impossible."

"Nonsense. Nothing is impossible," Kate replied confidently, "especially if you're in charge. You've set up these kinds of things a thousand times for me in the past, Debra."

"But not in less than a month," she protested.

Trey watched the interplay between Debra and his mother, knowing no matter how the conversation went the dinner would get done in two weeks' time. Kate usually got her way and Debra was one of the most efficient women Trey had ever known.

"I'll have Haley step in and do most of the work you normally do for me," Kate said, mentioning one of her senior interns. "That will free you up to work closely with Trey to get this done. I recommend you both go into the sitting room right now and figure out a specific date and a venue. Let's get this thing rolling."

Trey could tell that this was probably the last thing on earth that Debra wanted to do. He could see her reluctance as she slowly stood from her chair, in the small crease that darted across her forehead.

He wasn't exactly thrilled by the idea of working closely with his one-night stand, either. But, he also knew that if anyone could pull this event off on time and with flair, it was Debra Prentice.

They could work together, he told himself as he followed her slender frame into the informal sitting area at the back of the house. All they had to do was continue doing what they had been doing for the past six weeks: pretend that crazy night they had shared hadn't happened.

"I didn't realize she was going to pull you into this," he said as she sat in one of the plush, comfortable beige chairs and he sank down on the sofa opposite her.

The family sitting room was large, with floor to ceiling windows on one side and comfortable, yet attractive furnishings. A bar was located at the back of the room and doors led out to the patio and pool area.

It was in this room that the family had often come together to discuss problems or simply to enjoy each other's company and catch up on busy lives.

"My job is to do whatever Kate needs done and since this is important to you, it's important to her." She stared down at her notepad. "The first thing we need to do is find a venue. With less than a month lead time that might be a problem. Do you have any place specific in mind?" Her vivid green eyes finally made contact with him.

"I was thinking maybe the Raleigh Regent or the Capital Hotel," he suggested. "Both places are popular for such events."

"That's the problem." That tiny crease deepened again across her forehead. "I'm fairly sure that the Capital Hotel ballroom will be impossible to get at this late date. I'll check with the Regent and see what's available. Last I heard the ballroom was undergoing some renovations and I'm not certain if they are complete or not. I'm still not sure I'm going to be able to make this happen so soon. I'm assuming you want a Saturday night?"

"Or a Friday night would be fine," he replied. He

watched as she made several notes on the pad. Debra Prentice wasn't a knockout kind of woman, but she also didn't play up her pretty features. She wore little makeup and her hair always looked as if it had been tortured into a position at the back of her head that it couldn't possibly hold.

Still, he knew that her light brown hair was incredibly silky and that she had a cute, perfectly proportioned figure that had fit perfectly in his arms. He knew how her eyes sparkled while in the throes of passion and exactly how her lips tasted.

"Trey?" Her eyes held a touch of impatience, making him realize she must have tried to get his attention while he'd been lost in thought.

"Sorry. What was the question?"

"How many people are you expecting to invite?"

"Two hundred or maybe two hundred and fifty," he replied.

"Pick a number," she said with a light edge to her voice. "I need a specific number to tell the event planner when we settle where this is going take place."

"Two hundred and fifty," he said firmly.

She nodded. "I'll need the guest list from you as soon as possible. Invitations will have to go out in the next couple of days or so. Thank goodness it's January and there isn't much else going on around town." She wrote a couple more notes on her pad and then met his gaze again. "I think that's all I need from you to get started. By the end of the day I'll have a list of dates and places for you to consider."

She stood as if dismissing him, her body instantly poised to run back to her little office.

"Then tomorrow let's make arrangements to see

some of the venues together," he said as he also stood. "And I'll want to be with you when you speak to the event planner. We'll need to pick the menu and make decisions on a number of other things."

It was obvious he'd surprised her. She'd probably just assumed everything would be left up to her. But Trey freely admitted that he was something of a control freak. He couldn't run Adair Enterprises and be as successful as he'd been without being detail oriented and on top of every element in his life.

"I just assumed..." Her voice trailed off.

"This is important to me, Debra. Assume that I'll be at your side every step of the way until this dinner party is over."

Her eyes widened slightly and then she gave him a curt, professional nod. "Then I'll call you later this evening and we'll make arrangements for tomorrow."

She left the sitting room and Trey sank back into the chair, his thoughts a riot inside his head. He'd taken over the running of the family business when his grandfather had died. Walt Winston had mentored Trey and instilled in him the need to be the best that he could be.

It was Walt who'd wanted to see Trey in politics. The old man had even made a list of women he thought would be an asset in his quest for public office. At thirty-five years old, Trey knew it was time for him to marry. He also knew he'd make a more attractive candidate if he had a wife by his side.

With that thought in mind he'd dated dozens of women over the past year and finally eight months ago he'd begun to see Cecily McKenna exclusively.

Although he wasn't madly in love with Cecily, he knew she'd make the perfect wife for him. She was a thirty-three-year-old heiress. Articulate, charming and beautiful, Cecily also possessed a fierce ambition not just for herself, but for him, as well.

He knew there were rumors swirling of an imminent engagement between him and Cecily, rumors he suspected Cecily had started herself. He smiled inwardly. He wouldn't put it past her.

He looked up as Sam came into the room. "So, word has it that you're joining the ranks of the sex-scandal-ridden, fake and crooked politicians of the world." Sam threw himself into the chair that Debra had vacated.

It was obvious his brother was in one of his foul moods. "Actually, I'm hoping to do something good for the people of North Carolina."

"That's my big brother, the overachieving perfect son."

Trey drew a steadying breath. He knew the man seated before him with the scowl on his handsome face wasn't the brother, wasn't the man who had left here to serve his country.

"Sam, why don't you talk to me?" he asked softly. Sam had spent three months imprisoned overseas and months in a hospital recovering from the severe torture he'd endured while a prisoner. He had since been deemed unfit to return to duty and had been mad at the world ever since.

"I don't need to talk to anyone," Sam growled and got up from the chair. "I'm fine just the way I am."

Trey watched helplessly, troubled for his brother as Sam left the room. Sam was a powder keg, but he refused to speak about his time in prison or what had been done to him. The scars he carried were deep and dark and Trey wished he'd share some of the horror with somebody…anybody who could help him heal.

Unfortunately, Sam wouldn't be fixed until Sam wanted to be fixed and at the moment he appeared to be perfectly satisfied being angry.

Trey checked his watch and stood. It was time for him to get back to his own office. Now that he'd pretty much made up his mind to run for Senator, he didn't want to just run, he wanted to win.

He also needed to call Cecily. He hadn't even told her yet that he'd made up his mind to begin the process of gaining support and throwing his hat in the ring. She would be beyond thrilled. She'd been telling him for months that he was what the state needed, that he could do great things.

As he left the house he found himself wondering what Debra thought of his decision to run. Did she believe he was capable of doing great things?

*Who cares what she thinks?* he asked himself. All he needed from her was her skills at pulling together an event that would provide him a solid foundation on which to begin to build his campaign.

*Chapter 2*

Debra had suffered a crush on Trey Winston from the very first time she'd met him years ago. She'd always known he was out of her league, but her crush had never really diminished over the years.

She couldn't help the fact that her heart always leapt a bit at the sight of him, that she often grew tongue-tied and clumsy in his presence. Even sharing the single night that they'd had together hadn't changed her attraction to him; instead it had only deepened her feelings for Trey.

But, it didn't matter what she felt about him because she knew that she was the last woman on earth he would ever want to have a public relationship with. He had his future neatly planned out with Cecily McKenna by his side.

As she drove to the Regent Hotel to meet both him

and the hotel manager to discuss the event, she couldn't halt the tingling nerves that fluttered through her veins at the thought of working with him so closely.

She knew he'd probably marry Cecily, a gorgeous heiress who had the social savvy and political chops to be an asset to him.

Debra also knew that she would be a definite liability to Trey. She'd been born out of wedlock. Her father, who had been a married CEO of a Fortune 500 company at the time, had never acknowledged her existence personally. In fact, Debra had been raised by her mother to never mention her father's name, to never expect anything but a monthly support check in the mail from him.

When her mother died right after Debra's graduation from college, she had met with her father for the first and the last time. She had requested one thing from him—she wanted him to use his influence to get her a job in the political arena, specifically with Kathleen Adair Winston. As one of Kate's top contributors to her political campaign when she'd run for vice president, he had been instrumental in her attaining her position with Kate.

That's the only thing Debra had ever asked from the man who had never been anything but a name on a check, but he hadn't even managed to follow through on that. In recent years, there had been whispers of scandals within his company and talk of her father having some shady dealings.

Debra could crush on Trey all she wanted, but she knew she would only be an embarrassing one-night stand and right now a valuable tool to use to achieve his dreams. She would work her butt off to help him in his bid for a seat in the Senate. She wanted him to have his dream and she'd also do the best she could because Kate had asked her to.

She parked in front of the prestigious thirty-story hotel and looked at her watch. She was twenty minutes early for their ten-o'clock appointment so she remained in the car with the engine running and warm air blowing from the heater vents.

She'd been surprised when she'd called the hotel and discovered that the ballroom was available on a Friday night two weeks from now. Two weeks. Jeez, Kate must think she was some kind of magician.

But there had to be some magic at work for the ballroom not to already be booked, Debra thought.

Her hand fell to her stomach, caressing the place where she knew eventually there would be a baby bump, a bump that could potentially destroy Trey's future plans.

Politics thrived on scandals and any of Trey's adversaries would turn a simple night between two consenting adults into something ugly to use against him. Everyone knew he'd been seeing Cecily so that one-night stand would be a testimony to a lack of morals on both their parts. He would be painted with the same brush that had darkened his father's Senate term.

Debra knew that neither of them lacked a moral compass. The night had simply gotten away from them, both of them making mistakes in judgment.

He would never know about the baby, although it broke her heart that she felt like she was somehow repeating a history she'd never wanted for any child of her own.

She loved the baby, despite the circumstances of the conception. She would be the best mother she could and maybe eventually she'd meet a man who wanted her and her child enough to form a family unit.

She checked her watch once again and then cut the car engine. She grabbed her purse with her electronic notepad inside and then got out of the car. She'd power dressed today in a stylish dark brown skirt and suit jacket with a beige blouse. Brown pumps adorned her feet and tiny gold hoop earrings were her only jewelry.

Drawing in several deep breaths as she walked to the hotel entrance, she shoved all thoughts from her mind except what needed to be here to do her job well.

She still couldn't believe how lucky they had been that the Regent's ballroom was available on a Friday night two weeks from now. Two weeks was the mere blink of an eye in planning the kind of event they intended to have.

Whenever possible, Debra used the hotel's event planner, but the Regent had a new woman working in that position, somebody Debra had never worked with before. It wouldn't take long for Debra to discern if the woman was adequately prepared to do the job they needed and if she wasn't then Debra would bring in an event planner of her own.

Debra knew she had a reputation as being sweet and accommodating, but she could be a vicious shark when it was necessary to get what was best for the Winston family.

She went to the reservation desk and asked for Donald Rasworth, the hotel manager. She smelled Trey before she saw him, the expensive scent of a slightly spicy cologne that had clung intimately to her skin the morning after their wild, impetuous encounter.

She turned and nearly bumped into him. "Oh. You're here," she said.

He smiled. "Aren't I supposed to be here?"

"Yes, but I just didn't know that you were here… That you'd actually arrived…"

Thankfully she was rescued from her inane ramble by a tall slender man who approached them with a hand extended and a wide smile of welcome on his face.

"Mr. Winston," he said as he grabbed Trey's hand in a shake. "It's a pleasure to meet you, sir. We're hoping here at the Raleigh Regent that we can meet all your needs for whatever event you want to plan."

Trey turned to Debra and introduced her. "This is the person you need to please," Trey said. "She's our special weapon when it comes to planning these things."

"I understand you have a new event planner. Will she be joining us?" Debra asked.

"Stacy Boone and yes, she should be joining us at any moment." He looked around the lobby, as if expecting the woman to be hiding behind a potted plant or an elegant column. "While we wait for her why don't I go ahead and take you to our main ballroom and let you have a look around."

One demerit for the late Stacy Boone, Debra thought as she followed behind the two men. Trey was clad in a navy suit with a matching shirt, and she couldn't help but notice that he looked as good from the back as he did from the front.

Broad shoulders, slim waist and long legs, the man was definitely eye candy even without his confident stride and the aura of power that radiated from him.

A vision of his naked body flashed in her brain, causing her to stumble over a bump in the carpet that didn't exist. Trey turned in time to put a hand on her shoulder to steady her. "Okay?" he asked with concern.

"I'm fine," she assured him quickly. It was a relief when he dropped his hand from her. He was a warm and friendly man, a toucher by nature, but she didn't want him touching her in any way. It evoked too many memories she definitely needed to forget.

They had just reached the ballroom's double doors when a young blonde in a pink dress and high heels to heaven came rushing in. She carried a messy pile of paperwork and a smile of apology. "Sorry I'm late." Her gaze landed on Trey and admiration filled her eyes. "I'm so sorry I'm late."

Donald introduced the woman as Stacy, not only his new event planner but his favorite niece, as well. *Uh-oh,* Debra thought. She didn't have any real problem with the nepotism, but Stacy looked very young and definitely had the aura of an airhead about her.

Even Trey looked slightly troubled as he said hello and then exchanged a quick glance with Debra. Debra returned a reassuring smile to him. She'd know within an hour if Stacy was up to the job or not and if she wasn't then she'd be out and Debra would be working with somebody she knew could help her get this job done right.

Stacy led them into the ballroom and set her papers on a nearby table. "You're lucky you called when you did. Most people don't know yet that we just recently finished the renovation of the ballroom. New lighting, carpeting and wall covering. We also have the ability to remove the carpeting, which is actually big squares, in order to lay down a fantastic dance floor."

"I like that," Trey said with enthusiasm. "Dinner and dancing."

"That means we'll have to hire a small orchestra," Debra said as she stifled an inward groan. She'd been so flustered yesterday when she'd initially met with Trey they hadn't talked about the budget for this affair.

"Then we'll hire an orchestra," he replied breezily. "I want people leaving that night feeling good about their evening and me. Dancing after dinner definitely has to happen," he replied.

"Then we'll make it happen." Debra pulled her tablet out of her purse and made notes to add to the computer file she'd started for Trey's dinner party.

Stacy pulled a paper form from her stack and gestured for the three of them to sit at the single table just inside the room. Debra took off her coat and flung it across the back of her chair while Trey took off his overcoat and did the same.

As they began talking about the basic logistics, the date and time and how many would be attending, Stacy took notes and Trey leaned back in his chair and looked around the room, making Debra wonder what thoughts were tumbling around in his head.

Was he thinking about the dinner and maybe writing, in his head, the speech he'd give that night? Or perhaps he was mulling over how difficult the Senate race would be. The incumbent Senator William DeCrow was seeking another term and he was known to be a down and dirty fighter.

Thankfully, Trey had no dirt from his past or present that could be thrown on him, as long as nobody ever knew about their night together, as long as nobody ever knew about the baby she carried he should be fine.

Stacy might have flown in like an airhead, but when it got right down to business, she appeared to be savvy and eager to please, a perfect combination for getting things done properly.

"I can email you a variety of menus first thing tomorrow," she said to Debra after they'd both signed a contract to rent the ballroom for the date. "And are we doing a cash or an open bar?"

"We'll serve wine with dinner, but set up a cash bar," Debra replied. Trey leaned forward and opened his mouth as if to protest, but Debra didn't allow him.

"Cash bar," she said firmly. "This night is supposed to be about you beginning to build a support base, not about a bunch of drunks who won't remember what you said in your speech the next morning."

"And people never drink as much when they have to pay for it out of their own pockets," Stacy added.

"Okay, then I guess I'm outvoted on this topic," he replied and once again leaned back in the chair.

"Let's talk about room setup," Stacy said.

Debra and Stacy began to discuss placement of tables and the dance floor that Trey wanted. As the two women spoke, Debra was acutely aware of the scent of Trey's cologne, the warmth of his body far too close to hers.

Somehow, someway, she needed to get over the silly, schoolgirl crush or whatever it was she had where he was concerned.

Even though the night they'd shared was burned indelibly into her brain, she doubted that it had crossed his mind after he'd put her in the cab to take her home the next morning.

Trey Winston was off-limits, always had been and always would be. He had no interest in her other than using her as an effective weapon to achieve his ambitious desire of becoming the next senator of North Carolina.

She'd told herself she would do whatever she could to help him because of her devotion to Kate, but the truth of the matter was she'd do it because she cared about him enough to want to see him get everything he wanted in life.

Trey tried to keep his gaze off Debra and Stacy as they went over the initial planning stages. The two women were polar opposites. Stacy looked like a fashion doll with her bleached blond hair and black-fringed blue eyes. Her pink dress hugged her body in all the right places and she would instantly draw the gaze of any man who was breathing.

Debra, on the other hand, flew just under the radar in her brown suit and with her hair pulled back into a messy knot at the back of her head.

And yet it was Debra who kept drawing his gaze. She had the loveliest eyes he'd ever seen, so big and so green. Her slightly heart-shaped face expressed each and every emotion she felt.

As the two women talked, Debra displayed both earnestness and an underlying will of steel. She listened to Stacy's ideas, tossing some while accepting others.

He knew Debra was his mother's go-to woman, practically Kate's right hand, moving behind the scenes to keep his mother's life in order and running as smoothly as possible six days a week.

He also knew that the night they had met up in the bar, Debra had been upset about a breakup with some guy named Gary or Larry, or something like that.

Initially, he'd just wanted to console her, but he was in such good spirits about his own business deal, it wasn't long before he had Debra laughing and the surprising sparks had flown between them.

Debra was a constant at the Winston Estate, but he suddenly realized he knew virtually nothing about her personal life or who she was when she wasn't Kate Winston's assistant.

Did she like to dance? What was her favorite kind of music? Did she have any hobbies? How did she spend her evenings and Sundays?

He frowned and stared up at an elaborate crystal chandelier. He shouldn't be wondering about Debra's personal life. It… *She* was none of his business. Just because they'd hooked up for one night didn't mean anything at all.

He knew without doubt that it was a secret neither of them would speak of to anyone else. He trusted Debra. Her loyalty and love had always been with the family.

Still, she had stunned him with her passion, delighted him with her abandon that night. Granted, they'd both been buzzed on champagne, but neither of them could claim inebriation to the point of a lack of consent.

He knew he shouldn't even be thinking about that night. It had been a foolish misstep on both their parts. Instead he should be thinking about Cecily and her excitement when he'd called her the night before and told her about the dinner party and his decision to enter the race.

"Then I guess we're done here for now." Stacy's perky voice brought him back to the present. "I'll email you the various menus and a couple of tentative table and floor plans first thing in the morning."

Debra nodded and stood. "And I'll get back to you on exactly what we want for a speaker's podium and maybe a head table."

"Sounds like a plan," Stacy replied and also got to her feet. Trey followed suit, rising and taking Debra's coat from the back of her chair to help her into it.

Even her coat smelled of that fresh scent that had dizzied his senses when he'd held her in his arms. She quickly slid her arms in and stepped away from him with a murmured thanks.

Trey pulled his coat on and at the ballroom doorway they both said goodbye to Stacy, who scurried off in one direction while Trey and Debra headed back to the lobby and the front door.

They stepped outside into the bracing air. "It's after eleven. Do you want to go someplace for a quick lunch before you head back to the office?" he asked.

He could tell that he'd surprised her by the look on her face. "Oh, no, thanks. I really need to get back to work. All I need from you is a guest list as quickly as possible so that we can get the invitations out."

"I'll work on it this afternoon and how about I drop it by your place this evening? That way you'll have it first thing in the morning to start working on. I've got business meetings tomorrow that will keep me at Adair Enterprises for most of the day. You'll be home this evening?"

"Yes, I'll be home by six-thirty or so."

He shoved his hands into his coat pockets, noting how the brisk breeze whipped a pretty pink into her cheeks. "How are things with Larry?" It was the first time either of them had made any mention of what had transpired six weeks ago.

"It's Barry, and things are fine. He's gone and I'm happy. He was nothing but a creep."

"You seemed pretty upset about the breakup," Trey replied.

The pink in her cheeks was definitely brighter now and he had a feeling it had nothing to do with the weather. "I was mostly upset because I intended to break up with him that night and he beat me to the punch and broke up with me first." She looked toward her car and shifted from one foot to the other, as if wishing for an immediate escape route.

"Okay then, I guess I'll see you later this evening. Shall we say around seven?" he asked.

She nodded. "That would be fine." With a murmured goodbye she made her escape, hurrying away from him as if unable to get out of his presence fast enough.

He frowned as he headed for his own car. He found it impossible to discern what Debra thought of him. In all the years he'd known her, he'd never been able to figure out if she actually liked him or not. The night of sharing a bed and hot sex hadn't changed the fact that he didn't know what to think about her or what she might think about him.

And it irritated him that he cared. He got into his car and tried to push thoughts of Debra Prentice away. He had so many other things to focus on, like how he intended to continue to run the successful Adair Enterprises at the same time he launched a campaign.

Grandfather Walt would be proud of him. The old man was probably dancing with the angels at Trey's decision to enter the world of politics. Running the family business and politics had been what the old man had wanted for him.

Trey knew he had a good chance of winning. He didn't lean too far left or too far to the right. His politics were middle-of-the-road. He'd already proven his business acumen in the success of Adair Enterprises and he knew he'd made a reputation for himself as a hard worker and decent man who was willing to compromise when it was necessary.

In the course of doing business, he'd made enemies, but he knew that his opponents would have a hard time slinging mud at him.

He'd always been the good son, the firstborn who had excelled in college, had taken the family business into a new level of success and had never done drugs or slept with married women. He'd never taken pictures of his body parts and put them online.

In fact, he'd worked hard to keep his nose clean for just this time. Walt had wanted this for him since Trey was old enough to understand the world of politics and now Trey wanted it for himself.

He knew Cecily would put more pressure on him now for the announcement of their engagement. She would reason that an engaged or newly married candidate only made a man more appealing to the masses. It suggested stability and commitment, considered good character traits by voters.

She was right, but he wasn't ready yet to pop the

question to her. Maybe he'd ask her to marry him once the dinner party was finished. The event would be his first real step in declaring himself ready to be a serious contender and at the moment he needed all his energy and attention focused on that.

The main office of Adair Enterprises was located in downtown Raleigh, but they also had offices in Seattle and factories in Durham and Iowa.

The company had been started by his mother's grandfather in the 1930s as a shipping company for tobacco and local farmers to get their products across the country.

When Walt had taken over, the business had evolved into shipping containers and then to plastics and Trey had transformed it once again into a company also known for computer systems.

One of the strengths of the business was in its ability to be ever-changing with the times, and Trey prided himself on not only being a visionary, but also smart enough to hire equally driven and bright people to work with him.

As he walked through the glass doors of the building he was instantly greeted by security guard Jason Ridgeway. "Good morning, Mr. Winston."

"Morning, Jason. How are Stella and the kids doing?"

"Great, everyone is great."

"Billy's broken arm healing all right?"

Jason nodded. "The cast is due to come off sometime next week. I swear that kid is going to age me before my time."

Trey laughed. "Just keep him out of trees," he said and then with a wave headed to the bank of elevators that would take him to the top floor of the building and his personal office.

The elevator opened into a spacious airy reception area and Rhonda Wilson sat behind the large, modern reception desk. Rhonda was part beauty, part bulldog, the perfect final gatekeeper to Trey.

In her mid-fifties, Rhonda was tall and broad shouldered. She could be exceedingly pleasant and was fiercely devoted to Trey, but she also could tear a new one in any reporter or the like who tried to breach Trey's privacy.

"Good morning, boss," she greeted him with a pleasant smile.

"It's almost twelve," he replied. "Hopefully you're going to tell me I have nothing on my calendar for the rest of the afternoon?"

"You have nothing on your calendar for the rest of the afternoon," she repeated dutifully. "Although you do have a ton of phone messages on your desk."

"As usual," he replied as he took off his coat. "Could you order a roast-beef sub for me and keep everyone out of my hair for the next couple of hours?"

"No problem." She picked up the phone to call the nearby restaurant Trey often ordered his lunch from as Trey went into the inner sanctum that often felt more like home than his huge new mansion just outside the Raleigh beltline.

His personal office was the size of a large apartment. Not only did it boast a desk the size of a small boat, but also a sitting area complete with sofa and chairs, a minibar and a bathroom that had both a shower and sauna, and a large walk-in closet.

There had been many nights when working on an

intricate deal that Trey had slept on the sofa and then awakened the next morning to shower and dress for another day of mergers or hiccups that needed to be solved.

He tossed his coat on the back of the sleek leather sofa and then took his place at his desk and powered up the state-of-the-art computer system that allowed him to monitor every area of the business, video chat with managers in other parts of the country and stay on top of each and every problem that might arise.

Today he did a cursory check of emails to make sure there were no major issues at any of the plants or offices. He quickly flew through the phone messages, setting aside the ones he intended to return later and then pulled up his list of contacts and began to work on an invitation list for the dinner.

He wanted his friends and business associates there, but he knew it was even more important that invitations went to labor-union leaders, local and state government officials, and political backers who could bring both clout and campaign contributions.

He started his list but found himself distracted by the anticipation of going to Debra's place later that evening. He'd never been to the townhouse she'd bought, but he remembered her excitement over no longer having to rent and being a real homeowner.

He knew the silkiness of her skin, the smooth slide of her body against his own. He knew the contours of her body intimately, but he couldn't imagine how her home would be decorated.

What definitely confounded him was the fact that even though it wasn't quite noon yet, he couldn't wait for seven o'clock to come.

* * *

Kate Winston stood at her office window. It was just after six and Debra had left to go home. Business was officially ended for the day, but it would still be twenty minutes or so before dinner was served.

A softness filled her as she thought of Debra. In many ways Debra had taken the place of the daughter nobody knew she'd had, the baby girl who had died at birth. Kate had only been seventeen when she'd given birth and after learning the baby did not survive, she had fallen into a deep depression that she'd believed would last forever.

She'd been sent away to school, where she pretended that she was just like all the other debutantes with nothing to trouble her except which dress to wear to what event, but she'd never quite gotten over the heartache of the loss of the baby girl.

It was only when Buchanan Winston had entered her life that Kate discovered a new reason for living. She had fallen head over heels in love with Buck. She'd not only given him three healthy sons, but had also supported him in his political aspirations that began on a local level and eventually ended in the Senate.

It was during the Senate election that she'd found out that Buck had been having affairs for most of their marriage. Her heart had been broken and she'd threatened to leave him, but he'd told her if she left he'd declare her an unfit mother and seek to gain full custody of their children.

Afraid of his power and influence, Kate had stayed and played the role of supportive wife, and then, like a bad cliché, Buck had died in one of his mistress's arms.

He'd had one year left in his term as senator and Kate had stepped in to fill his shoes.

She'd discovered she loved politics and had run for a term of her own the next year. After that had come a four-year stint as the first female vice president of the United States. Her party had lost the next election and now she had people whispering in her ear about running for president when election time rolled around again.

She wanted it. But her decision about running for the most prestigious and powerful position in the world was tempered by other elements besides her own desire.

She'd made many friends in her years of public service, but she'd also made enemies and she didn't have just herself to worry about when the election got dirty, and elections always got dirty.

Moving away from the window, she thought of her sons and how the decision to run for president might affect each of them. Trey would be all right. He was a strong man and already preparing himself for the battle arena of politics.

She worried about Sam. He'd come home so damaged and unwilling to seek help from either family members or professionals. He was a loose cannon at the moment and she was concerned how the bright spotlight of a national campaign might affect him.

Then there was Thad. Her youngest, Thaddeus had turned his back on the family business and had made a modest life for himself in Garner, North Carolina. He worked for the Raleigh Police Department as a crime-scene investigator.

He led a quiet life alone and would hate having any role in the world she loved. Maybe she should just flip a coin to come to a final decision, she thought ruefully.

She only knew two things for sure. She believed with all her heart that she was the right person for the job, that she would be far better for the country than the front-runners who had already begun the political dance of becoming elected.

The second thing she knew with certainty was that some of the enemies she'd made over the years were utterly ruthless and would do everything in their power to destroy her and anyone she loved, not only politically, but personally, as well.

# Chapter 3

Debra arrived home, hung her coat in the hall closet and then raced around like a mad woman to make sure her living room/dining area and the kitchen were spotlessly clean.

She was by nature a neat and tidy woman, so there was little to do, but with the thought that Trey would be seeing her home for the very first time she wanted everything perfect.

She fluffed the red-and-yellow throw pillows on the black sofa twice and dithered over lighting several of the scented candles she normally lit in the evenings. She finally decided against it, not wanting him to believe that she was in any way attempting to create an intimate, romantic setting.

At six forty-five she sat down on the edge of the sofa and told herself she was acting completely ridiculous.

Trey probably wouldn't even take a step into the small, gleaming hardwood-floor foyer. He'd meet her at the door, hand her the list of names he'd prepared and then leave with his mission accomplished.

The last thing Trey Winston cared about was sitting around and chatting with his mother's assistant. Debra had eaten on the way home from the estate and had put on coffee, which now filled the air with its freshly brewed scent.

The coffee wasn't for him. She always made coffee or hot tea when she got home from work, especially at this time of year when outside the cold knocked on every window and attempted to seep into every crack.

She was thankful that the townhouse seemed well insulated and she loved to keep the thermostat low and build a nice fire in the stone see-through fireplace that was between the living room and kitchen.

There were no flames in the fireplace now. Again, she didn't want Trey to get any ideas that she had any thought about another encounter with him. The last thing she wanted was to come off as some pathetic one-night stand who didn't understand exactly what she'd been.

She'd changed out of her suit and into a pair of comfortable jeans and a mint-green fleece sweatshirt. She hadn't even bothered to check herself in a mirror as she'd left her upstairs bedroom to come down here to wait for Trey's appearance.

She jumped when the doorbell rang, nerves jangling discordantly through her as she got up from the sofa and hurried to answer.

Her breath caught slightly in her throat as she opened the door and he smiled at her. Trey Winston definitely had a killer smile, all white straight teeth and warmth. "Hi," he said.

"Hi," she replied.

His smile widened, crinkling the corners of his eyes. "Are you going to invite me in?"

"Oh, of course…if you want to come in… I mean you don't have to if you don't want to."

"Thanks, I'd love to come in." He swept past her, trailing the bold scent of his cologne as she quickly closed the front door and followed him into her living room.

He shrugged out of his coat and slung it across the back of one of the two chairs that faced the sofa as if he'd done it a hundred times before. He'd changed clothes, too. Instead of his usual suit, he was dressed in a pair of casual black slacks and a white polo shirt that hugged his shoulders and chest as if specifically tailored for him.

"Is that fresh coffee I smell?" he asked.

"Yes, it is. Would you like a cup?" To say that she was shocked to have him not only actually in her townhouse, but also asking for a cup of coffee was an understatement.

"I'd love a cup," he replied.

She motioned him to the sofa. "Just make yourself comfortable and I'll bring it in here."

"I don't mind sitting in the kitchen," he said as he followed at her heels. His gaze seemed to take in every nook and corner of the room. "Nice place."

"Thanks, I like it." She was grateful when he sank down at the round wooden table with its centerpiece of a crystal bowl with red and yellow flowers.

The kitchen was her favorite place to spend time.

Located at the back of the townhouse, the windows looked out on a lush flower garden she'd planted last spring, although now there was nothing to see but dormant plants and the redbrick tiers of the flowerbeds.

Above the butcher-block center island hung a rack with gleaming copper-bottomed pots and pans. The counters not only held the coffeepot but a variety of small appliances she used on a regular basis on the weekends.

"You like to cook," he said as he looked around with obvious interest.

"On the weekends," she replied as she reached with slightly nervous fingers to get two of her nicest black mugs down from the cabinet. She swallowed hard as she nearly dropped one. *Get a grip,* she commanded herself.

She poured the coffee and managed to deliver both cups to the table without incident. "Sugar? Cream?"

"Black is fine," he replied.

She sank down onto the chair opposite him, wondering how it was possible that his mere presence diminished the size of her kitchen and sucked up the energy, making her feel slightly lightheaded, as if she was suffering from a lack of oxygen.

"What kind of food do you like to cook?" he asked, his big hands cradling the coffee mug.

"Anything…everything, whatever sounds good. I try to do a new recipe every weekend on Sunday. Last week it was chicken *malai* curry, an Indian dish. The week before that was spicy cherry pork stir fry."

"Sounds delicious and adventurous," he replied, his head cocked slightly to one side and his gaze intent on her as if trying to see inside her head.

She forced a dry laugh. "*Adventurous* isn't exactly

an adjective that is normally used when describing me." She mentally begged him not to mention the night they'd spent together, a night that had been out of character for both of them. She'd definitely been adventurous and bold then.

"Efficient and driven. Sweet but with a touch of barracuda," he replied. He took a sip of his coffee and then set the mug back down. "That's how I would describe you. I was impressed with how you handled the negotiations today with Stacy."

"Thanks. We'll see how well I did when I get the menus and floor plans from her in the morning," she replied, beginning to relax. "And we never discussed what your budget was for the event."

"Whatever it takes to do it right," he replied.

"Everything needs a budget, Trey," she admonished. "If you can't stick to a budget, then how can the voters trust you with their tax dollars?"

"Okay." He named an amount that was adequate and yet not too extravagant. "We'll use that figure as our budget. What do you think about my decision to run for senator?"

She looked at him, surprised he would care one way or the other what she thought about it. She took a sip of her coffee, unwilling to give him a quick, flippant answer.

"You've always been successful at whatever endeavor you've undertaken," she said thoughtfully. "You have all the qualities to be a great senator, but have you considered how you're going to juggle the running of Adair Enterprises with the responsibilities of being a state senator? Not only does the job take a lot of hours and work, but campaigning will be a huge commitment of both time and energy."

"I know, but I'm lucky that I have good people working with me at Adair Enterprises and they will step up to cover whenever I can't be at the business." He took another drink. "Has Mom given you any hint as to whether she's going to take up the challenge and run for president?"

Debra smiled. "Your mother shares a lot with me, but this is one decision she's keeping pretty close to her chest. I know there is pressure on her from a variety of places to run, but I have no idea what she's going to decide."

"She should go for it. She'd be great for the country. Not only is she strong and intelligent, but she's more than paid her dues and she's smarter than any of the other schmucks who are making noise about running."

"You're preaching to the choir," Debra replied with a smile. "She'd have my vote in a minute."

He returned her smile and suddenly the nerves jumped through her veins once again. "This is nice," he said as his gaze swept the room and lingered on the fireplace. "I'll bet it's quite cozy in here when the fire is lit and you have something exotic cooking in the oven or on the stove."

"It is nice," she agreed. "Buying this place was the best decision I've ever made."

He finished his coffee and when he set the mug down on the table and looked at her, something in the depths of his eyes caused her to tense warily.

"Debra, about that night…"

"What night?" she said quickly. "I have no idea what you're talking about." She pled with her eyes for him to take it no further. She didn't want to have a discussion about a night that shouldn't have happened. A hand automatically fell to her lap, as if in an attempt to hide the secret she carried.

"I'm your mother's assistant and I'll do everything I can to help you reach your goal of becoming a North Carolina state senator," she said softly. "And that's really all we have to discuss."

He held her gaze for a long moment and then gave a curt nod of his head and stood. "Thanks for the coffee, Debra, and all your hard work."

"No problem. One more thing, did you bring me the list of names of people you want to invite?" She got up from the table.

He snapped his finger and grinned at her. "I knew there was a reason I stopped by here. The list is in my coat pocket."

Together they left the kitchen and went back into the living room where he grabbed his coat from the back of the chair and put it on. He reached into one of the pockets and pulled out the printed list.

"Thanks," she said as she took it from him. "I'll get the invitations ordered tomorrow and have them addressed and mailed by the end of the next day. Do you want to look at the invitations before they go out? I was thinking something simple and elegant."

"I trust your judgment."

"You can trust me in everything," she said pointedly, hoping her words were enough to put him at ease about that damned night they'd spent together.

He'd probably wanted to mention it to her to assure himself that she had no plans to take it public. She could probably make a little extra money selling the story to the tabloids.

She could only imagine the salacious headlines if the information got out that he'd slept with a member of his mother's staff while practically engaged to a wealthy socialite. But he had nothing to worry about where she was concerned.

"You have absolutely nothing to be worried about," she said to reiterate to him that the secret of their unexpected tryst would remain just that—a secret.

"Then I guess I'll leave you to the rest of your evening," he said, and they walked together toward the front door.

"I'll get in touch with you sometime tomorrow, as soon as I get the things emailed over from Stacy," she replied, grateful that they'd broached the subject of their night together without really talking about it.

"This dinner party is an important first step and together we're going to make it amazing," he said. He gave her one last devastating smile and then stepped out the front door and disappeared into the gloom of a cloudy twilight.

Debra locked the door behind him and leaned against the door. Curse that man. She could still smell the heady scent of his cologne, feel a lingering vibrating energy in the air despite his absence.

She shoved herself off the door with a muttered curse and carried the list of names he'd given her into the small chamber just off the living room that served as her home office.

She placed the list on her desk next to her computer and then left the room and returned to the kitchen. She placed Trey's coffee mug in the dishwasher and silently cursed him for even making her think about that night.

Her body flushed with heat as she thought of how he'd slowly caressed each and every inch of her skin. His kisses had driven her half out of her mind with desire and she knew making love with Trey Winston was an experience she'd never, ever forget.

What bothered her more than anything was the knowledge that even knowing it was wrong, even with the unexpected result that had occurred, she'd do it again in a hot minute.

Trey wasn't sure what he had hoped to accomplish by bringing up the night he'd spent with Debra after all this time. Over six weeks had passed and they'd spoken numerous times since then without ever mentioning what had transpired between them.

So, what had he wanted to say to her tonight? What had he wanted her to say to him? That she'd liked being with him? That he'd been a pleasing lover?

He mentally scoffed at his own thoughts. As terrible as it sounded, he probably just wanted to double-check that she didn't intend to go public with their misdeed, but even thinking that did a disservice to the woman he knew that Debra was. He knew how devoted she was to the family. She would never do anything to hurt any of them in any way.

Instead of heading home to his mansion, he decided to drop in and visit with his grandmother in the nursing home. As he drove his thoughts continued to be filled with Debra.

She'd looked cute as a bug in her jeans and green sweatshirt. He'd never seen her in casual clothes before and the jeans had hugged her long legs, shapely legs that he remembered wrapped around him.

He tightened his grip on the steering wheel, realizing the skies were spitting a bit of ice. January in Raleigh could be surprisingly unpredictable. It might be cold with a bit of snow or ice, or it could be surprisingly mild. Occasionally they got a killer ice storm, but thankfully nothing like that so far this year.

The weather forecast that morning had mentioned the threat of a little frozen precipitation, but nothing for travelers to worry about. Slowing his speed a bit, his thoughts went back to Debra.

Her townhome had surprised him. He'd expected the furnishings to be utilitarian and rather cold, but stepping into her living room had been like being welcomed into a place where he'd wanted to stay and linger awhile.

The living space had been warm and inviting, as had the kitchen, as well. He thought of the stark formal furnishings in his own mansion and for a moment entertained the idea of hiring Debra to do a bit of decorating transformation.

It was a silly thought. If he worked his plan to achieve his ultimate goal, then Cecily would be moving into the mansion and she'd want to put her own personal stamp in place there, although he doubted that Cecily would have the taste for warm and inviting. She'd want formal and expensive. She'd want to create a showcase rather than a home.

He punched the button on his steering wheel that would connect him to phone services. He gave the command to call Cecily on her cell and then waited for her to answer.

"Darling," her voice chirped through the interior of the car. "I was wondering if I was going to hear from you today."

"Between work at the office and planning this dinner party, I've been swamped." He could hear from the background noise on her phone that she wasn't at home. "Where are you now?"

"At a Women's League meeting. I'm already not-so-subtly campaigning for you, Trey."

He smiled, certain that she was doing just that. "You know I appreciate it."

"You'd better," she replied with a laugh. "Rumor has it your mother is seriously considering running for president. We'll let her have that position for two terms and then *we'll* be ready to move into the White House."

Trey laughed. "One step at a time, Cecily. This dinner party will let me know if I can get some of the big hitters in town behind me in order to achieve the first step in the process."

"You can take it one step at a time, but I'm already envisioning what the White House Christmas tree will look like," she replied with a laugh. "Oh, gotta go. I'll talk to you tomorrow."

She ended the call and Trey shook his head. Cecily McKenna was like a force of nature, unstoppable and powerful and completely in his corner. She would make a perfect ally and support as a wife.

He pulled into the parking lot of the Brookside Nursing Home, an upscale establishment where his grandmother, Eunice, had resided since Walt's death.

When she'd lost her husband she had spiraled into a depression so deep nobody seemed to be able to pull her out. Trey knew one of the most difficult decisions his mother had made was to move her own mother here instead of keeping her living at the estate. But Eunice needed more than what Kate and the family could provide.

After several months of residency Eunice had appeared to rally from her depression. She seemed quite content where she was, in a small apartmentlike set of rooms with an aid who stayed with her twenty-four hours a day.

He nodded to the security guard on duty outside the front door and entered into a small lobby with a couple of elegant chairs and a front desk.

"Good evening, Mr. Winston," Amy Fedder, a middle-aged woman behind the reception desk greeted him. He was a frequent visitor and knew most of the people on staff.

"Hi, Amy." He walked to the desk where there was a sign-in sheet and quickly signed his name and the time he'd arrived. "Have you heard how she's doing today?"

"I know she had dinner in the dining room and earlier in the day she joined a group of women playing bingo."

"Then it sounds like it's been a good day for her," he replied, a happiness filling him. He adored his grandmother. "Thanks Amy, I'll see you on my way out." He left the front desk and headed for the elevator, which would take him to the second floor where his grandmother's little apartment was located. It amused him that her place was in what the nursing home called the west wing.

There were only forty residents at any given time in Brookside and almost as many staff members. The nursing home catered to the wealthy and powerful who wanted their loved ones in an upscale environment with exceptional care and security. Every member of the staff had undergone intense background and security checks before being hired and there was a front door and a back door, both with an armed security guard on duty at all times.

He got off the elevator and walked down a long hallway, passing several closed doors before he arrived at apartment 211.

He knocked and the door was answered by Serena Sue Sana, a tall beautiful African-American woman who went by the nickname of Sassy. She was of an indeterminable age, but Trey guessed her to be somewhere in her mid-sixties.

"Mr. Trey," she greeted him, her white teeth flashing in a bright smile. "Come in." She opened the door wider. "Ms. Eunice will be so happy to see you." She leaned closer to him. "She's had a good day but seems a bit agitated this evening," she whispered.

He nodded and walked into the nice-size living room with a small kitchenette area and doors that led to the bathroom and two bedrooms, one large and one smaller.

His eighty-six-year-old grandmother was where she usually was at this time of the evening, her small frame nearly swallowed up by the comfortable light blue chair surrounding her.

Her silvery-white hair was pulled up neatly into a bun atop her head and her blue eyes lit up and a smile curved her lips at the sight of him. "I know you," she said, her affection for him thick in her voice.

"And I know you," Trey replied as he walked over to her and planted a kiss on her forehead.

"I'll just go on into my room so you two can have a nice private chat," Sassy said.

"Before you go, would you make this television be quiet?" Eunice held out the remote control to Sassy.

"I'll take care of it," Trey replied. He sat in the chair next to Eunice and took the remote control and hit the mute button as Sassy disappeared into the small bedroom and closed the door behind her.

"I love Sassy to death, but she likes to watch the silliest television shows," Eunice said. "And sometimes I just like to sit and visit with my favorite grandson."

"I'll bet you say that to all your grandsons," Trey said teasingly.

She giggled like a young girl. "You might be right about that." Her blue eyes, so like Trey's mother's, sparkled merrily.

"I heard you played bingo this afternoon," Trey said.

Her smile instantly transformed into a frown. "Did I...? Yes, yes I did, although I didn't win. I never win." She leaned closer to him. "That woman from downstairs in 108 always wins. I think the fix is in."

Trey laughed and leaned over and covered her frail hand with his. "You don't have to win all the time."

Her eyes flashed and her chin jutted forward with a show of stubbornness. "Adairs always win," she said, her voice strident as she pulled her hand back from his and instead worried the edge of the fringed shawl that was around her shoulders.

"That's what we do," she muttered more to herself than to him. "We win."

"Speaking of winning, have you talked to Mom lately?"

She frowned again in thought. "She called yesterday…or maybe it was the day before." She shook her head with obvious agitation. "I can't remember. Sometimes I can't remember what happened when, except I have lots of memories of when you boys were young. You three were such a handful. But sometimes my brain just gets a bit scrambled."

"It's okay," Trey said gently. "I was just wondering if she told you that I'm considering a run for the Senate."

Eunice's eyes widened. "No, she didn't tell me." Her fingers threaded through the shawl fringe at a quicker pace. "She never mentioned that to me before."

"Then I guess she didn't tell you that we think she's also considering a run for the White House," Trey said.

Eunice appeared to freeze in place, the only movement being her gaze darting frantically around the room as if seeking something she'd misplaced and desperately needed to find.

"Grandma, what is it?" Trey asked.

She stood from her chair and began to pace in front of him, her back slightly bent from the osteoporosis that plagued her. "No. No. No." The word snapped out of her louder and more frantic with each shuffled step of her feet.

Trey stood in an attempt to reach out and draw her back into her chair, but she slapped his hands away and continued to pace.

"This is bad news…. It's terrible, terrible news." She stopped her movement and stared at him, her eyes wide with fear. "You shouldn't do this. She shouldn't do this. Pandora's box, that's all it will be."

"What are you talking about? Grandma, what are you afraid of?"

Her eyes filled with tears as she looked at him in horror. "Secrets and lies," she said in a bare whisper.

## Chapter 4

*It has to be here,* Debra thought frantically as she searched the area on top of her desk. The early morning sun drifted through the office window, letting her know it was getting later and later.

She moved file folders and papers helter-skelter, her heart pounding in her ears as she looked for the missing paperwork. It had to be here, it just had to be.

She distinctly remembered putting the guest list that Trey had given her next to her computer the night before, but it wasn't there now.

She was already dressed to go to work and had come into the office to grab the list before leaving her place. In a panic she now fell to her hands and knees in the plush carpeting, searching on the floor, hoping that it had somehow drifted off the desk, but it wasn't there, either.

She checked the wastebasket to make sure it hadn't fallen into it somehow during the night. Nothing. No list magically appeared.

Half-breathless from her anxious search, she sank down at her desk chair. *Think,* she commanded herself. After she'd placed it on the desk the night before had she come back in here for any reason and mindlessly placed it elsewhere?

No, she was certain she hadn't reentered the office again last night. After Trey had left she'd watched a little television and then had gone upstairs to bed. She had not come back into the office.

Was it possible she had sleepwalked and moved the list?

She couldn't imagine such a thing. As far as she knew she'd never sleepwalked in her life. Besides, she would have had to maneuver herself not just out of her bed, but also down the stairs and into the office all the while being unconscious in sleep.

Impossible. Utterly ridiculous to even entertain such an idea, but the darned list didn't get up and walk away on its own.

Granted, she'd been unsettled after Trey had left. Maybe she had wandered in here and taken the list someplace else in the house before she'd gone to bed.

With this thought in mind, she jumped out of the chair and raced through the lower level of the house. Her heart pounded in an unsteady rhythm as she checked the kitchen counters, the living-room coffee table and any reasonable place she might have put the list, but it was nowhere to be found.

The thought of calling Trey and asking him for another copy horrified her. She was organized and efficient. She didn't lose things. So how had she lost such an important piece of paper?

After a run-through of the entire house yielded no results, she finally returned to the kitchen, defeated and knowing she needed to get on the road or she'd definitely be late to work.

She hurried to the refrigerator and opened the freezer to take out a small package of chicken breasts to thaw for dinner and stared at the piece of paper that was slid between them and a frozen pizza.

She grabbed the paper, saw that it was the missing list and hugged it tight to her chest in relief. Hurriedly yanking out the chicken breasts, she set them in the fridge and then raced for the front door, grabbing her purse and coat on the way out.

As she waited for her car to warm up, she folded the guest list and tucked it into her purse, then pulled her coat around her shoulders. She tried to ignore the rapid beating of her heart that still continued, the frantic beat that had begun the moment she'd realized the list was missing.

Heading toward the Winston Estate, she wondered if somehow between last night and this morning her brain had slipped a cog. Had she been so flustered by Trey's visit that she'd mindlessly placed the list in the freezer?

It was crazy. It was insane, but she couldn't ignore the fact that she was the only person in the house who could have put the list in the freezer.

Maybe it had something to do with hormones. She had called her doctor to make an appointment for the weekend. Was it possible that pregnancy hormones made you lose your mind? She'd be sure and ask her doctor.

As if to make the day worse, Jerry Cahill was on guard duty as she pulled into the side entrance. The tall, sandy-haired Secret Service man gave her the creeps. He seemed to have some sort of a weird crush on her and had asked her out twice. Both times she'd politely declined but one time last month she'd thought she'd seen him standing on the sidewalk in front of her place and staring at her townhouse.

He stopped her car before she could pull into her usual parking space and motioned for her to roll down her window. "Hey, doll, running a little late this morning, aren't you?" He leaned too far into her window, invading her personal space.

"Maybe just a few minutes," she replied.

Jerry had hazel eyes that should have been warm in hue, but instead reminded her of an untamed jungle animal that could spring at a vulnerable throat at any moment.

His breath smelled of peppermint and the fact that he was close enough to smell his breath freaked her out just a little bit.

He held her gaze for a long moment and then stepped back and tapped the top of her car. "Well, I just wanted to tell you to have a good day."

She rolled up her window and parked her car, feeling revulsion just from the brief encounter. Jerry Cahill might be a Secret Service agent, but that didn't make him any less of a creep.

She hurried into the house to find Maddie Fitzgerald, head housekeeper, and Myra Henry, head cook, seated at the small table enjoying a cup of coffee together.

"Good morning, Ms. Debra," Maddie said. Her plump cheeks danced upward with her smile. With red hair cut in a no-nonsense style and her perpetual optimism, Maddie had been around long before Debra. She'd not only been the first person Kate had hired, but she'd helped Kate raise the boys and was intensely devoted to the Winston family, as they all were to her.

"Good morning, ladies," Debra said. She smiled at Myra and drew in a deep breath. "Is that your famous cinnamon rolls I smell?"

"It is. If you want to get settled into your office I'll bring you a couple with a nice cup of coffee," Myra said.

"That sounds heavenly," Debra replied. "Thanks, Myra."

She kept her smile pasted on her lips until she reached her office where she hung up her coat and then sank down at her desk. She opened her purse and retrieved the list that Trey had given her.

She'd just set it next to her computer when Myra arrived with a steaming cup of coffee and two large iced cinnamon rolls on an oversize saucer.

"Those look too sinful to eat," Debra exclaimed as she eyed the goodies.

Myra grinned at her. "I make them special, no calories so there's no guilt."

"Yeah, right," Debra replied with a laugh.

"Enjoy," Myra said and left the office.

Debra took a sip of the coffee and then got to work typing up the list of names Trey had given her so she'd have a hard copy on her computer. Once it was in the computer she wouldn't have to worry about losing it again.

She was still troubled twenty minutes later when she had the copy made and leaned back in her chair and drew a deep breath.

"Crisis averted," she muttered aloud to herself. She picked up one of the cinnamon rolls and took a bite, but her stomach was still in knots because of the morning trauma.

Or was it morning sickness?

She couldn't think about being pregnant now. She'd think about it after she saw her doctor. Right now she had work to do, not only did she have to pick invitations to be printed and addressed and mailed, there was also the matter of finding a good orchestra to hire for the night of the dinner. Once she got information from Stacy she'd need to meet with Trey to make some final decisions.

It would be easy for her to feel overwhelmed, but Debra knew the way to get things done was focus on one item at a time and not look too far ahead.

Kate's morning knock came at eight-thirty and Debra instantly got up to join her boss in her office.

"Good morning, Kate," Debra said as she sat in the chair opposite the desk.

"And a good morning to you," Kate said with a fond smile. "I've already given Haley the things that needed to be taken care of for me this morning. One thing I love about interns is that they're so eager to please. What I want from you is an update on you and Trey's visit to the Regent yesterday."

For the next half an hour Debra filled Kate in on what had transpired at the hotel and where they were in the planning stages.

"I know you're pulling everything together quickly," Kate said. "If you need more help, let me know and I'll assign an assistant for you."

"Actually, I think Stacy, the hotel event planner is

going to be all I need. She seemed to understand exactly what we want, what we need for a successful evening for Trey. I'm expecting her to get me a floor plan and some menu options sometime this morning. That will tell me how good she is at her job."

"Do you think he's ready for this?" Kate asked.

"I think he's more ready than anyone could be," Debra replied. "I know he's saying that this dinner party is just to dip his toes in the water to see what kind of support he might have if he decides to run, but I believe he's already made up his mind. His head is definitely already in the game."

Kate nodded. "That's what I believe, too, and Trey never does anything halfway."

"He'll make a wonderful senator," Debra said, unable to keep the passion of her belief out of her voice. "He'll bring new life and new hope to the people of North Carolina."

Kate nodded. "I know my son. Even if he decided to be a garbage man he'd be the best in the business. He always does everything well."

"He's a chip off the old block," Debra replied with a smile.

Kate laughed. "Get out of here and get to work on helping my son. I won't need anything from you today. I know the time constraints you have to get the details of this dinner party under control are incredibly tight, so get to it."

By the time she got back to her office she'd received a number of emails from Stacy. The young event planner had sent several different seating plans and three menus with prices. Even though she'd had to pull teeth in order for Trey to come up with a budget, Debra intended to negotiate hard to keep costs low and quality high.

She was an old pro at this, having set up dozens of such events in the past for Kate. Despite what Trey had said, budgets always mattered, and it would reflect poorly on his business acumen to not bring the dinner party in as reasonably as possible.

If you wanted the taxpayers to back you, then you had to show a willingness to work within budgets, she thought.

Gathering the emails all together, she knew what she needed now was for she and Trey to have another meeting and make more decisions. She picked up the phone to call him at Adair Enterprises.

The receptionist connected her to him immediately.

"Good morning, Debra." His deep smooth voice was like a physical caress through the line.

She returned the greeting, although what she wanted to do was tell him about her frantic search for his list that morning, the ridiculousness of finally finding it in the freezer and that Myra's cinnamon rolls had made her slightly queasy.

Trey told her he intended to come to the house around two and they would meet then to hammer out any decisions that needed to be made. Then they disconnected.

Debra leaned back in her chair and for the first time in years wished she had a best friend. Her entire adult life had been built surrounded by the Winston family. There hadn't been time for friends outside of the intimacy of the family members.

Certainly her childhood hadn't been conducive to making friends. She'd never invited anyone to her home, afraid that her classmates might see her mother drunk or hungover. Once she started working for Kate, the work and the family had taken precedence over anything and everyone else.

That had been part of her problem with dating Barry. There had been little time to really grow any meaningful relationship. Although ultimately he'd broken up with her because he told her he wasn't getting what he needed from her, she'd already intended to break up with him because she'd figured out he was getting what he needed from his married secretary. The jerk.

Maybe it was best that she didn't have a best friend, she thought as her hand fell to her lap and she caressed her lower belly.

Perhaps she would be tempted to share too much with a best friend, and a secret wasn't a secret if two people knew about it. And Debra knew better than anyone that she had a secret that had the potential to destroy a career before it began.

Trey had been disturbed since he'd left the nursing home the night before. His grandmother had become quite agitated before he'd left, frantic as she continued to whisper about secrets and lies.

Sassy had finally come out of her room to deal with the older woman. She'd given Eunice a mild sedative and by the time Trey had left, Eunice had fallen asleep in her chair.

Sassy had assured him that she'd be fine, but as Trey drove to the Winston Estate, he couldn't help the worry that had been with him since the visit the night before.

He'd always been close to his Adair grandparents and had mourned deeply when Walt had died. Now he was both concerned and confused about his grandmother and after meeting with Debra he intended to speak to his mother about the issue.

The front door of the estate was opened by housekeeper Maddie, who always greeted him as if it had been months since she'd seen him. "And aren't you looking just fine today," she said as she took his coat from him. "You know I've always liked you in a nice blue suit, it makes those eyes of yours downright beautiful."

Trey laughed. "You've been charming me since I was a baby, Maddie, and the years haven't changed anything a bit. I'm assuming Debra is in?"

"Holed up in that little office of hers as usual."

"Would you tell her that I'm here and that I'll meet her in the sitting room?"

"I'd be happy to. Tea or coffee? Maybe a plate of cookies?" she asked, knowing his weakness for sweets.

"Coffee and what kind of cookies?" he asked.

She smiled at him slyly. "Does it really matter?"

He laughed. "No, it doesn't, not as long as Myra baked them. Okay, a couple of cookies would be good." He was still smiling as he entered the informal sitting room where the afternoon sun flooded through the floor to ceiling windows at one end.

The weather system that had brought the little bit of icing the night before had moved on, leaving behind blue skies and sunshine.

Trey sank into one of two beige easy chairs in front of the windows, enjoying the warmth of the sun on his back. Within seconds Myra entered the room, carrying with her a tray that held a small coffeepot, two cups and a plate of oatmeal-raisin cookies he knew would be soft and gooey, just the way he liked them.

"Thanks, Myra," he told the cook, who nodded and then left him alone in the room.

He poured the coffee into the two cups and thought about having coffee in Debra's townhome the night before. She was bright and sweet and easy to be around. Last night as he'd sat in her kitchen he'd felt more relaxed than he had in months and he thought it had not been just the cozy surroundings, but also her company.

She didn't seem to have one high-maintenance bone in her body. He found her blushes charming and the fact that she cooked something special and new just to please herself each Sunday intriguing.

He had nearly destroyed the nice interaction between them by attempting to bring up the night they had spent together, but she'd made it clear that she didn't want to discuss it and was more than a bit embarrassed by the whole affair.

He should feel embarrassed about it, too. Still, he couldn't help but admit that he was looking forward to seeing her again. He tried to tell himself that it had nothing to do with any feelings he might have for her. Granted, he'd more than enjoyed his one night with her, but he knew where his duty, where his future lay and it definitely wasn't with Debra.

The subject of his thoughts entered the room. Clad in a pair of tailored black slacks and a white blouse, she looked all business as she offered him a curt smile.

"I had Myra bring in some cookies and coffee," he said as she sat in the chair next to him. "It's been my experience that every important decision should be made over a good cookie."

She smiled and set a handful of papers on the coffee table next to the silver tray of refreshments. "No cookies for me, and no coffee. I've been trying to cut down on my caffeine."

As always whenever she was around he was aware of the scent of her, that fresh, clean fragrance that stirred something deep inside him. What kind of perfume did Cecily wear? For the life of him he couldn't seem to bring it to his mind whenever Debra was close to him.

"So, what have we got?" he asked, slightly irritated with himself and the crazy tug of attraction he felt for a woman who had no place in his future plans.

She leaned forward and grabbed the small stack of papers. "Stacy sent me these this morning. The first three are various floor plans, including an area for an orchestra and dance floor and the table arrangements." She handed them to him.

He tried to focus on the papers in his hands and not on how the brilliant sunshine streaming through the window made her light brown hair sparkle as if lit by a thousand fireflies.

She got up from her chair and moved to the back of his where she could lean over to see which plan he was looking at. "Do you want to hear my thoughts about each one?" she asked hesitantly.

"Absolutely. You're the expert at these kinds of things."

She leaned closer, so close that if he turned his head he'd be able to place his lips on the long length of her graceful neck. He narrowed his eyes and stared at the piece of paper on top.

"I don't like this one because she's got the orchestra and dance floor both on the same side, which makes the room look uneven and off-balance," she explained.

He cast her a quick sideways glance and noted the

long length of her sable eyelashes, the skin that looked bare and beautiful and like smooth porcelain. His fingers tingled as he remembered stroking that skin.

"This is the plan I think works much better," she said, leaning farther over him to take the papers from his hand and shuffle them around.

He stared back down again, wondering what in the hell was wrong with him. Tonight he had a date with Cecily, the woman who was the front-runner to be by his side for the rest of his life and yet all he could think about at the moment was the soft press of Debra's breasts against his back as she leaned over him, the sweet fresh scent that eddied in the air whenever she was near.

"See how the orchestra is on the left side, but the dance floor is in the center, right in front of the head table? The tables all seat eight and that means with a head table of eight and two hundred and fifty guests we'll need thirty-one tables."

"This looks fine to me," he replied and released a small sigh of relief as she straightened up, returned to her chair and gave him a little breathing room from her.

"I figured you, Cecily, your mother, your brother Sam, the governor and his wife, Thad and his guest would comprise the people at the head table," she said.

"Thad won't come." Trey thought of his youngest brother. "There's no point in even inviting him. He has his own life and has no interest in this." He fought back a touch of hurt as he thought of the distance between himself and Thad that had grown bigger and deeper with each year that passed.

"Then we'll put the mayor and his wife at the head

table," Debra replied. "They probably should be there anyway."

Trey nodded, still attempting to regain control of the swift desire that had momentarily taken ahold of him with her nearness.

"This is the invitation I thought would be nice." She handed him a black-and-white invitation, bold and slightly masculine. "If you approve it I've got the printers standing by and I can have them in the mail by tomorrow morning."

He looked at her in surprise. "Hand addressed?"

"Absolutely." The brilliant green of her eyes was filled with quiet confidence.

"But won't that take you half the night?"

She shrugged. "It takes however long it takes. They should have gone out a month ago. They definitely have to go out tomorrow."

He handed her back the invitation. "It's perfect. You can start the printers."

"And now we move on to the menu issue."

It took them almost an hour to go through the variety of menus Stacy had presented, along with the suggested price per plate.

"Don't pay any attention to the prices," Debra said. "There's no way we'll pay what the hotel is asking." This time there was a gleam of challenge in her eyes that he found very hot.

They spoke for another half an hour about food, finally settling on what he'd like to see served. He was almost disappointed when she told him that was all she had to discuss with him today and that she'd be back in touch with him the first of next week to talk about decor and silverware and dish choice.

They left the sitting room and as she disappeared into her office and closed the door, he poked his head into his mother's office, but she wasn't there.

Instead, her head intern, Haley, was filing folders in the file cabinet. "Hi, Trey," she said, a bright smile on her youthful face.

"Hey, where's the boss?" he asked.

"She mentioned a bit of a headache and went up to her room a little while ago. Is there something I can help you with?" Haley asked with the overeagerness of a young woman wanting to prove her worth.

"No, thanks, I think I'll just head up to check on her." With a wave of his hand he headed for the wooden spiral staircase in the entry that would take him to the bedrooms located on the second floor. He could have used the small elevator located just beneath the stairs, but he preferred the exercise of walking up.

When he reached the top of the stairs he continued down the long hallway, passing bedrooms and baths on either side and finally reaching his mother's doorway at the end of the hall. He knocked and heard her say, "Come in."

When he opened the door she was seated in one of the two plush white chairs that formed a sitting area complete with fireplace and French doors that led to an upper-deck patio. At the far end of the room her white-canopied bed was visible through double doors that could be closed at night.

She smiled in surprise. "I didn't expect it to be you. I thought it might be Myra—she's bringing me up some hot tea. Would you like me to ring her to bring you a cup, too?"

"No, thanks, I just had coffee with Debra." He sank

into the chair next to hers. "Are you doing okay? Haley said you had a headache."

She waved a hand as if to dismiss the idea. "Just a little one. I decided to escape the office and come up here to do a little thinking away from everyone else and any distractions."

"Have you come to a decision?"

She shook her head. "No, and I think that's what's giving me my headache. How did things go with you and Debra? Weren't you two getting together to talk about menus and such?"

"I just finished up with her. She'd definitely on top of things. We've now settled on the floor plan and a tentative menu for the evening." He paused a moment and then continued. "She's going to get the invitations out tomorrow and find an orchestra, but I really didn't come up here to talk about all that. I stopped last night and had a visit with Grandma."

Kate sat up a little taller in her chair. "How was she doing? I'm planning on visiting her this Sunday."

Trey frowned. "To be honest, I'm a little worried about her."

"Worried how?" Kate leaned forward and rubbed the center of her forehead as if he'd definitely made her head ache a little more.

"Maybe now isn't a good time to talk about it," Trey said sympathetically.

At that moment a knock sounded at the door and Myra entered with a tray holding a cup of tea and sugar and lemon wedges. She placed it on the dainty table between the two chairs. "Is there anything else you need?" she asked Kate first and then looked at Trey who shook his head.

"We're fine, Myra, thank you." She waited until Myra had left the room and then stirred a spoonful of sugar into the cup of green tea. She squeezed a lemon slice and placed the wedge on the side of the saucer. "Now, where were we?"

"I was saying that if you have a headache, then maybe we should have this conversation another time."

"We'll have it now," Kate replied and lifted her cup to her lips.

"Okay, she seemed fine when I first arrived. She'd eaten dinner in the dining room and had played bingo during the day, but Sassy told me when I arrived that she'd been a bit anxious throughout the evening. Initially the visit went fine, but when I mentioned to her my plans for the Senate and your possible plans to run for president, she went crazy."

Kate lowered her cup with a frown. "What do you mean by that? Went crazy how?"

"She starting pacing and screaming no and muttering about secrets and lies. I mean, she was so upset Sassy had to give her a sedative. I'm not even sure she knew who I was when she was having her tirade." Trey paused to draw a breath, to get the strength to tell his mother what really worried him. "I think maybe she's getting dementia."

Kate's forehead creased with pain, but Trey had a feeling the pain was less physical and more emotional. "She is eighty-six years old, Trey. Maybe her mind is starting to slip a bit."

"Yeah, but all that stuff about secrets and lies? What could she possibly be talking about?"

Kate took another sip of her tea and when she placed the cup back on the saucer she released a deep sigh.

"Trey, I know how fond you were of my father, but to be honest, he wasn't a very good husband and he definitely wasn't the greatest of fathers."

"What do you mean?" Trey couldn't imagine the man who had mentored him as being anything but a wonderful man. Walt had shown Trey infinite patience, had spent hours talking to him, leading him in learning the family business and encouraging Trey's natural competiveness and ambition.

"You probably don't know that my mother miscarried three sons before she finally had me. My father never let her forget that she had been unable to give him what he wanted most—a son. He was verbally abusive both to my mother and to me. The one thing that seemed to transform him was your birth. He saw you as the son he'd never had. I imagine some details of my mother's tumultuous relationship with my father are coming to play in her mind."

Trey studied his mother, thinking about what she'd just said. Was it possible that Eunice's breakdown had merely been her replaying portions of her own past in her mind? She'd told him she remembered the days of old but had trouble remembering what had happened the day before.

"And you're sure there's nothing more to it?" he asked.

Kate averted her gaze from his and rubbed her forehead once again, as if attempting to ease a much bigger headache than she'd professed to have suffered earlier. "I'm sure I don't want to talk about it anymore. My mother is old and who knows what goes on in her mind anymore."

"Then I'll leave you to drink your tea in peace and

quiet," he replied. He got up from his chair and left her room.

If he'd been troubled before about how his grandmother had reacted to the news that he was running for senator and his mother might be seeking the presidency, the conversation with his mother certainly hadn't eased his concerns.

Was Eunice really suffering from the onset of dementia or working through issues she'd had with her husband? Or were there secrets and lies someplace in the family history that might be dangerous to both his own and his mother's political future?

# Chapter 5

The ring of the phone awakened Debra. She jerked up, scattering envelopes not just across the kitchen table but also to the floor.

A quick glance at the kitchen clock let her know it was after eleven. The phone rang again and she jumped up from the table and frowned as she saw that the caller ID indicated a private number.

She grabbed the cordless phone from its base. "Hello?"

Nobody spoke, but Debra was certain somebody was on the line. "Hello?" she repeated. "Are you there?"

Silence, although the line remained open and the faint sound of somebody breathing sent a chill up her spine. "Is this some sort of juvenile prank phone call?" Debra asked and was rewarded by a click.

She hung up the phone, unsettled by the call but

grateful that the ring had awakened her. She still had envelopes to finish up addressing and apparently had accidentally fallen asleep in the middle of the process.

The hot cocoa she'd fixed earlier was now cold in the pot. She poured herself a cup and set it in the microwave to warm and then returned to the kitchen table where she'd been working.

As she sat back down at the table she remembered the dream she'd been having while she slept. It was more than a dream, it had been a memory of a conversation she'd had with her mother when Debra had been about ten years old.

Debra had wanted to know why she didn't have a daddy who lived with them. Why she was never, ever allowed to talk to her father or see him.

Debra's mother, Glenda, had tried to explain to Debra that her father was an important man and that he had another family he lived with and Debra would be a bad girl if she ever tried to contact her father because she would destroy his life.

As she grew older Debra had recognized that the truth of the matter was that her mother had been far more enchanted with the generous support checks that came every month than she had probably ever been with the wealthy married man she'd slept with that had resulted in Debra.

The support checks had allowed Glenda to not have to work, to continue to have a party-girl lifestyle that had ultimately killed her in a drunk driving accident the summer after Debra had graduated from college. Those support checks had stolen Debra's childhood as she'd tried to take care of a mother who was drunk most of the time.

The dream had created ancient memories of rejection, the wistful hopes of a little girl who had just wanted her daddy to want her back. The pang of wistfulness the dream had evoked still lingered in the depths of her heart.

And she was about to place a child of her own in the very same position.

*No, it won't be the same at all,* she told herself as she dropped down to her knees to retrieve the envelopes that had fallen to the floor when she'd jumped up to answer the phone.

She gathered the envelopes and then sat back down at the table and took a drink of her cocoa. Glenda hadn't been much of a mother, preferring her booze and men to spending much time with her lonely daughter.

Debra would be better than that. She would make sure her child knew the depth of her love. She'd love her son or daughter so madly, so deeply, that he or she wouldn't feel the absence of a father figure.

Besides, there was a chance that eventually Debra would meet a man and marry and then the baby would have a stepfather. She could still create a family unit.

The phone rang again. Debra frowned and once again got up from the table. And again the caller ID displayed a private number. "Hello," she snapped into the receiver.

Silence. Just like the call before.

"Stop calling, you jerk," Debra said and slammed down the phone. She unplugged it from the wall. If anyone important needed to get ahold of her, they'd use her cell phone. Her landline seldom rang and usually it was only sales calls. Anyone who knew her always called her on her cell.

Once again she sat at the table and rubbed her eyes wearily and then took another drink of her cocoa. She hadn't meant to fall asleep. She needed to get the last of the invitations stuffed and addressed before morning.

She knew that most people in Kate and Trey's positions hired professional calligraphers to do the hand writing, but early in her employment with Kate, Debra had taken classes so that she could develop the skills so that nobody would have to be hired. It was just one effort a young new employee had done to try to make herself as indispensable as possible.

It was well after midnight when she finally finished. Exhaustion weighed heavily upon her as she climbed the stairs to her bedroom.

The townhouse had a guest bedroom and bath and a master suite upstairs with its own large bathroom. Debra stumbled into the bathroom and quickly shucked her clothes.

It had been a ridiculously long day. After her meeting with Trey she'd contacted the printers who were standing by to get the invitations done. They'd been delivered to her at the estate right before she'd left to go home for the day.

She'd also made a doctor's appointment for the next day, deciding to get that off her mind instead of putting it off.

Too tired to think about a shower or bath, she pulled on her nightgown and headed for her king-size bed.

The last thing she did before tumbling into bed was unplug the cordless beside her, not wanting her sleep disrupted by any further obvious prank phone calls.

Despite the late night her alarm went off at six and although her desire was to linger beneath the sheets and the navy-and-peach-colored spread, she got up without hitting the snooze button.

After a long hot shower and getting dressed, she plodded down the stairs, feeling almost as exhausted as she'd been when she'd finally gone to bed.

She plugged her phone back in, rechecked the caller ID and was surprised to see that the blocked calls she'd received the night before didn't show up there. Neither did any other calls show up in the history.

*Odd,* she thought as she leaned against the counter and waited for her teakettle of water to boil. Maybe her machine was on its way to answering machine heaven. It was certainly old enough to die a natural death.

She'd decided to skip the coffee this morning, knowing that she should have as little caffeine as possible in her condition, and instead stick to a nice hot cup of tea and maybe a couple of crackers. Although she didn't feel nauseous yet, she remembered the uneasy roll of her stomach the day before when she'd thought about food first thing in the morning.

The neatly addressed invitations were ready to go in a large tote bag on the table. They would be picked up by a special mail carrier at ten that morning from Debra's office.

She went to the cabinet that held her favorite mug, a pink Support the Cause mug that was her go-to vessel for either hot tea or cocoa.

The mug wasn't in its usual place. She frowned at the conspicuous empty spot in the cabinet. Where was her mug? She felt a déjà vu from the morning before when she'd had the frantic hunt for Trey's guest list.

Although she hadn't used the mug for a couple of days, she walked over to the dishwasher that was full of clean dishes and checked for it there. There was no sign of it.

As the teakettle whistled, she moved it off the burner and then grabbed a teabag and another mug to make her tea.

Still, the mystery of the missing mug bothered her. On impulse before sitting down, she walked over to the refrigerator and checked the freezer, grateful that she didn't see the familiar pink cup nestled uncomfortably next to the frozen pizza.

She sat at the table and drank the hot tea and nibbled on a couple of saltines, wondering if she was slowly losing her mind. First the list yesterday and now the mug today. Maybe she hadn't even really gotten those phone calls last night. Maybe she'd only imagined them and that's why they didn't register on the telephone caller identification.

Despite the fact that it was Saturday, she had a doctor's appointment that afternoon at two. Maybe she'd ask her doctor if pregnancy could make a woman go stark raving mad.

She left her house by seven, deciding to go in a little early since her plans were to leave early for her appointment. She still felt tired. Thankfully tomorrow was Sunday and if she felt like it she could sleep until noon.

When she'd initially taken the job with Kate, she'd known it was a six-day-a-week job, that the hours were often unpredictable and could include evenings, but she hadn't cared. As far as she was concerned, working for Kate wasn't just a job, it was her passion.

As she pulled up to the side entrance of the gate she was relieved to see Secret Service Agent Jeff Benton on duty. He waved her on through with a cheerful smile.

At least this morning she didn't have to start her day with another creepy encounter with Jerry Cahill. She got out of her car and noticed that several of the agents stood in front of the carriage house. Even from the distance she recognized Robert D'Angelis, Daniel Henderson and Jerry Cahill. She figured it was a morning meeting of assignments and knew that on most Saturdays the senior Secret Service man, Robert, gave Kate a security update.

Myra was pulling a tray of golden biscuits out of the oven as Debra came into the house. "Mmm, those look yummy," she said as she greeted the cook.

"Ms. Cecily is joining Ms. Kate for brunch this morning," Myra explained.

"Oh, that's nice." Debra was surprised by the tiny flair of jealousy that winged through her. Of course Cecily and Kate would be growing close, fostering the beginning of a relationship that would probably be a lifelong one. By the time the election happened, Cecily would be Kate's daughter-in-law. Trey was smart enough to know that being married would make him a more enticing candidate.

"I've got biscuits done and I'm about to make that cheesy egg casserole that Ms. Kate loves. I've also prepared little fruit cups."

"Sounds delicious, I'm sure they'll enjoy it."

"Would you like a little plate of your own?" Myra asked.

"Thanks for the offer, but no, thank you. I already had some breakfast this morning," Debra replied.

As Myra busied herself cracking eggs into a large bowl, Debra carried her purse and the large tote of envelopes to her office. Once there she took off her coat and then sat at her desk, fighting against the unexpected jealousy that had momentarily filled her as she thought of Cecily McKenna.

She had no right to feel jealous. She had no right to wish things could be different, because it was just a waste of energy.

Instead of examining the unusual emotion, she shoved it aside and turned her computer on, knowing that she needed to get all her work done early this morning in order to head out around one for the doctor's appointment. She was lucky that her doctor saw patients on Saturday.

What she needed to get together for the morning were table dressings that were available for the dinner party that would now take place in just a little under two weeks' time. She wanted to have a list of tablecloth colors and dinnerware options for Trey on Monday. They also needed to discuss how the head table would be dressed and what kind of centerpieces he wanted for each of the tables.

Details, details. A successful event was always in the minutia of the details and Debra wanted this particular dinner party to be perfect, not just because she was in charge of it, but because it was for Trey.

The special mail courier arrived and Debra was grateful to hand him the tote of invitations, knowing that they would go out today and probably be received by invited guests by Monday or Tuesday at the latest. The RSVPs were due the following week. Debra was expecting very few regrets.

She and Stacy had exchanged half a dozen emails when a knock fell on her door and Cecily poked her head in. Cecily McKenna was a beautiful woman. Her hair was raven-black, cut short and chic, and her eyes were doe-brown. Her features were classically elegant, and when she smiled it gave her face a warmth that was instantly inviting.

"Hi, Debra. I just wanted to stop in before meeting with Kate and let you know how much I appreciate everything you're doing to help Trey."

"No problem, we're all working toward a common goal," Debra replied, hoping her smile hid her unease at the unusual visit.

"I wanted to give you my personal thank-you," Cecily replied. "This isn't just important to the family and staff and me, but I think it's important for all of the people of North Carolina. Trey is the right man for this job and the dinner party is the first step in assuring that he's considered a legitimate contender."

Cecily released a tinkling burst of laughter. "Listen to me babbling on. You know that about Trey already."

"He's definitely got my vote," Debra replied. As she saw the stylish black slacks, gold blouse and tasteful necklace and earrings that Cecily wore Debra felt downright dowdy with her hair in a messy knot at the back of her head and the olive-green skirt and blouse she'd bought two seasons before off a clearance rack.

At that moment Kate called to Cecily. "Oh, gotta go. It was nice seeing you again, Debra. I'm sure we'll be seeing a lot of each other in the future." With another one of her warm smiles, Cecily stepped back and closed Debra's door.

Debra released a deep sigh. Everything would be so much easier for her if she hated Cecily, if Cecily was snarky and egotistical instead of nice. Things would be so much easier if Debra truly believed that the beautiful woman was all wrong for Trey.

But Debra knew Cecily was the right woman to be at Trey's side. She was bright and articulate, she came from a stable wealthy family and had influential friends and she appeared to genuinely love people, just like Trey.

Yes, they would make a perfect power couple. It would only be so much easier if in the past three minutes Debra hadn't realized that she wasn't just crushing on Trey Winston…but that she was in love with him.

Trey got a phone call from Debra at noon. "We need to get together on Monday to finalize the rest of the details for the dinner party," she said. "Is that doable for you?"

"Actually, Monday isn't good for me," he replied. "I'm going to be tied up in meetings all day long. What about tomorrow? What's on your Sunday menu?"

He knew he'd surprised her by the long silence that followed the question. Hell, he'd surprised himself with the question. What was he thinking?

"Actually I was going to try a recipe for bourbon barbecue pork chops," she said tentatively.

"Sounds delicious. Could I maybe wrangle an invite from you and we could talk about the business end of things over dinner?" Somewhere in the back of his mind he wondered what in the hell he was doing. It was obvious he wasn't thinking rationally at all.

He already had dinner plans with Cecily for this evening, there was no reason for him to eat dinner with Debra tomorrow night to discuss work issues. And yet he didn't take back his words. He was surprised to realize he didn't want to.

"Around six?" she asked hesitantly.

"Works for me," he agreed.

When he hung up his phone he didn't want to consider what he looked forward to more: an elegant fine dining experience with the beautiful Cecily or a smoky bourbon barbeque dinner with his mother's personal secretary/assistant?

Maybe the pressure of having made up his mind to run for senator already had him cracking up. Maybe he was already seeking some form of escape from the crazy world he was about to enter, and somehow, someway, Debra felt like an escape.

The minute he hung up the phone Rhonda buzzed him to let him know that Chad Brothers, an experienced campaign manager, had arrived.

Dismissing thoughts of Debra, he rose as Chad walked into the office, extending his hand to the man who looked more like a professional wrestler than a savvy political expert.

"I hope you called this meeting for the reason I want it to be," Chad said after he shook Trey's hand and took a seat in the chair in front of his desk. He leaned forward, his bald head gleaming in the sunshine flowing in through the windows.

"You know I've been kicking around the idea of running for the Senate—" Trey began.

"I'd be happy to," Chad replied before Trey had gotten his entire sentence out of his mouth. "And you know I'm the man who can help get you where you want to go, but if we agree to work together, then we need to get busy right away."

"I've already set up a dinner party that's taking place a week from next Friday night." Trey shared the details of the dinner and dance event with the man he trusted to run a fair and honest campaign.

Chad was not only fair and honest, he was also tenacious and brilliant when it came to putting in place a political machine. He was also an old friend that had shown his loyalty to the Winston family for years.

The two men chatted for a little over two hours, talking about plans and tossing out ideas back and forth. Trey found the meeting invigorating and he was in a great mood when he left the office at six for dinner with Cecily at La Palace, a French restaurant where the food was excellent, but equally important was that most of the mover and shakers of Raleigh could be found there on a Friday or Saturday night.

He was meeting Cecily at the restaurant as she was coming from a charity event she'd attended that afternoon for an anti-domestic abuse initiative.

He was eager to tell her about his meeting with Chad. She'd be ecstatic to hear that he'd be working with a man who had the reputation of running an election both effortlessly and with winning results.

Trey had only been inside the restaurant a few minutes when Cecily arrived. As always when she entered a room, men's heads turned in her direction. Tonight she looked particularly beautiful in a red dress that was just tight enough to showcase her dynamite figure, but not so tight as to be tasteless.

"Darling," she said as she air-kissed near his cheek. "I hope you haven't been waiting for me long."

"Not long at all," he replied. "And our table is ready," he said as the host nodded at him.

Trey placed a hand in the small of her back as they were led to a table by the front windows of the restaurant. They were coveted tables in the world of power, places to sit and eat where you could see and be seen.

The host took their coats and the minute he departed a waitress appeared with menus and the wine listing. Trey ordered them each a glass of white wine and ordered their meals. As they waited for their food to arrive Trey told her about his meeting with Chad.

"So, it's really going to happen," she said, her brown eyes sparkling with not just excitement but that shine of an ambition that resonated deep inside him.

"It's really going to happen," he agreed. "The dinner-dance party will be the official kickoff of my campaign. I've got to write a rousing speech and then I'll officially declare my bid for Senate and hope that the money and the support follow."

"You know it will." Cecily clapped her hands together and then reached across the table and grasped one of his hands with hers. "I'm so excited for you, so excited for us." She released his hand and picked up her wineglass.

"You know it's going to be a crazy ride," he warned her. "It isn't just about parties and fun. It's going to be long days and longer nights, nasty rumors and traveling from city to city, never knowing when or where we'll see each other again."

He saw the flash of disappointment in her eyes, there only a moment and then gone. He knew she'd probably expected a proposal, but he just wasn't ready to take that step right now. He intended to marry only once in his life and he wanted to be absolutely certain when he proposed.

"You know I'm in this for the long run, Trey," she said softly.

"I know," he replied somberly. "I just need to get things moving, get plans together in my head. Once we get beyond the dinner party and a press conference to announce my official declaration, we'll see where things shake out."

"Of course. I understand," Cecily replied smoothly as if that quick look of disappointment that he'd seen in her eyes had only been a figment of his imagination. "And whenever you're not with me, I'll be working to help achieve our goals."

Their food was served and for the remainder of the meal Cecily talked about the charity auction she'd attended that afternoon and her plans to immediately begin to form a Women for Winston coalition.

As she talked and they ate, Trey's mind drifted, first to all the things that would need to be done to achieve his ultimate goals, and secondly to the dinner he would be having the next night at Debra's.

A business dinner, he reminded himself, a dinner that he'd invited himself to. He should be focused on the beautiful woman across from him, a woman who would add her ambition to his own to see that he reached his goals, followed his duties as his grandfather had wanted for him in public service.

Trey had always been so clear on where he was going and who would be at his side when he arrived there… until that night almost seven weeks ago. That night had somehow thrown him off his personal game, awakened yearnings inside him he hadn't known he possessed.

He mentally shook himself and focused on Cecily,

the woman who was right for him, a woman his grandfather and his mother would have handpicked to be at
his side as he traversed through the murky waters of
politics.

## Chapter 6

That morning the pink mug had been front and center in the cabinet where Debra would have sworn it hadn't been the morning before. The mystery of the mug's reappearance had set a discordant tone for the beginning of the day.

Yesterday afternoon Dr. Gina Finnegan had confirmed what Debra already knew, that she was about six and a half weeks pregnant. After Dr. Finnegan had done the blood work and physical, discussed vitamins and handed Debra a pamphlet about pregnancy, Debra had asked about forgetfulness being a part of the condition.

"We've coined a term for it here in the clinic," Dr. Finnegan had said with a laugh. "Pregnesia...the condition of absentmindedness that comes with all the hormonal changes due to pregnancy. Don't worry, most of my patients tell me it goes away by the second trimester along with any morning sickness you might be suffering."

Dr. Finnegan had set her due date around the third week of August. A summer baby, Debra had thought. It would probably be a long, uncomfortable July but it would be worth it. By summer's end she'd have a precious bundle of joy to love.

As she sliced potatoes for a cheesy scalloped dish to go with the pork chops, she tried not to think about the evening ahead, an evening where she'd be sharing dinner, sharing private time and conversation with Trey.

It was a cold gray blustery day and she'd built a fire in the fireplace despite her concern that it might look too romantic. There was nothing she liked better than a roaring fire on a wintry day while she worked in the kitchen and she'd decided she didn't care what he thought, it was just a good day for a fire.

It was just before five and both the potatoes and the pork chops would take about an hour to cook. The table was already set for two with her good black-and-red dinnerware and she had a salad made and in the refrigerator.

The smoky bourbon barbecue sauce smelled like heaven and half of it was in a saucepan ready to be reheated and poured over the chops when they were finished cooking. The other half of the sauce was marinating the meat.

All she had to do was put the two baking dishes into the oven and then take a shower and dress for Trey's arrival at six. She had all the paperwork ready for him to look at to make the final decisions on the setup of the ballroom and that's what the meeting was all about.

It had been *his* idea to do it over dinner. *It was strictly a business dinner,* she reminded herself over and over again throughout the day.

Once they went over those last final details there would be no reason for her to meet with him again until possibly the night before the event.

She would be there the night of the dinner, not as a guest, but she'd arrive at the hotel at least an hour or so before things got started to make certain that everything had been handled properly, that the evening was set perfectly for Trey's special night.

Fifteen minutes later she stood beneath a warm spray of water, far too eager for the night to come. It was wrong of her to want to see Trey, to see him seated at her table across from her. It was wrong of her to want to hear his deep, smooth voice talking just to her. More than anything it was wrong on every level for her to want him again.

He belonged to Cecily. They were so right together. Debra might carry his baby, but nobody would ever know that. She would never screw up his dreams by telling him about her condition because she knew he was the kind of man who would have to do something about it and that something would destroy all of the goals he had for himself.

He was a Winston, bred for business and politics. He deserved to have winners surrounding him. He deserved to have a winner as a wife and that woman was Cecily. He definitely didn't need a mousy, efficient woman like Debra in his life.

By the time she dressed in a pair of jeans and a long-sleeved navy fleece shirt, she felt as if she had all of her emotions under control. They would enjoy a good meal, discuss business and then he would leave.

Once the dinner party at the Regent was finished, she would see him only rarely when he came to visit his mother. Even then it was possible they wouldn't run into each other often at all.

Her emotions remained cool and calm until six o'clock when her doorbell rang. She answered and with a slightly nervous smile invited him in. She took his coat and hung it in her foyer closet, noting that he had dressed casual, as well.

Trey Winston wore a suit like he'd been born in one, but he looked equally as hot in a pair of slightly worn, tight blue jeans and a navy-and-white-striped sweater that emphasized the broadness of his shoulders.

"Something smells delicious," he said as he followed her into the kitchen where she gestured him to a chair at the table.

"Let's hope it tastes as good as it smells," she replied. As with the last time he'd been sitting in her kitchen, she felt as if the walls closed in and got smaller with his very presence in the room. He emanated such energy, commanded all the space around him.

She was grateful she'd done most of the work ahead of time because she suddenly felt clumsy.

"Let me help," he said, and jumped out of his chair as she opened the oven door to take the baking dishes out of the oven.

"Okay, knock yourself out," she replied and handed him two pot holders. She'd nearly tripped just carrying the salad from the refrigerator to the table. "You can just set the pork and potatoes on top of the hot pads here." She pointed to the two awaiting pads on the counter.

She stepped back and watched as he maneuvered the two large dishes onto the counter next to the oven. He smelled so good and as he moved his sweater pulled tightly across his broad shoulders. She averted her gaze, not wanting to care about the way he looked or remember that scent that he'd worn when they'd hooked up on that fateful night.

He pulled the tin foil off the dishes and sighed in obvious delight. "This all looks amazing."

"Wait for it," she said as she pulled the saucepan of bubbling sauce from the stovetop and poured the last of it over the pork chops. "There's enough bourbon in here I'm not sure we'll need before-dinner drinks," she said jokingly. "We'll be half-snookered by the time we finish eating the sauce." She flushed as she remembered that half-snookered was what had put her in the condition she was in.

"Why don't we just bring our plates over here and dig in straight from the baking pans?" he suggested. "No need to be formal on my account."

"Okay," she agreed, grateful that she didn't have to attempt to take the two hot dishes to the center of the table. That was just a disaster waiting to happen.

"Other than cooking, did you have a busy day or were you able to rest up a little on your day off?" he asked as he grabbed the two red-and-black-patterned plates from the table and rejoined her by the stove.

"Actually, I managed to sleep a little later than usual and then I cleaned a bit. I even managed to work in a little reading so it was a fairly restful day."

She waited for him to snag one of the thick pork chops along with a large serving of the cheesy potatoes. "What about you? Busy day?" she asked.

"Not too bad at all. I feel like today was the calm

before the storm. Chad is already busy working to fill every minute of my schedule."

She smiled. "But everyone in town knows he turns out winners." Chad was a household name in the city of Raleigh among the political crowd.

Trey carried his plate back to the table while she served herself, eternally grateful that she didn't drop a chop on the floor or dribble cheese potatoes down the front of her.

Once they were both seated and Debra took out the salad and dinner rolls, they both dug in. "These pork chops are to die for," he exclaimed after his first bite.

She smiled with pleasure. "Thanks, I was hoping they would come out tasty."

"Do you generally invite people over to share in your Sunday culinary delights?"

"Barry used to occasionally join me but since we broke up, never. I cook for myself because I enjoy it and it's the one hobby I have time for one day a week."

"Between your work for my mom and now for me, we've been keeping you too busy."

"Not at all," she protested. "I love my work. I adore your mother and I can't imagine doing anything else. I'm doing what I always wanted to do." *Except for being a mom,* she thought. That would soon be added to the things she loved.

With the thought of motherhood, the sight of Trey so masculine and handsome across from her and with a flash of sudden visions of their hot and wild night together all swirling around in her mind, she attempted to grab a roll from the center of the table and bring it to her plate, but nearly dropped it to the floor.

"That was a close one," he said with a grin.

She flushed. "Lately I seem to be suffering episodes of extreme clumsiness. So if I happen to flip a chunk of lettuce or a cherry tomato across the table at you or drop a roll in your lap, please don't take it personally."

"Will do," he said with a cheerful smile.

"So, are you all geared up to work with Chad? I've heard he's a rough taskmaster."

He laughed and shook his head ruefully. "I'm ready for whatever Chad brings. He has some great ideas and I'm excited to have him on my team."

All that was important to Debra was that she keep her secret. What was important was that Trey maintain his pristine reputation because for him the sky was the limit.

She had to keep her pregnancy as far away from Trey and his campaign as possible. She knew what his adversaries would do to him if they knew he'd slept with his mother's assistant and now that assistant was pregnant.

They would massacre him.

Dinner conversation remained light and pleasant and the meal was better than any Trey had ever enjoyed in a five-star restaurant.

Afterward he helped her clear the table and she suggested they drink her special mint hot cocoa in the living room where she had all the paperwork ready for him to make some final decisions about the ballroom decor.

As they sat side by side on the sofa with the paperwork on the coffee table in front of them, he realized he wasn't ready yet to talk business. What he wanted to talk about was her.

"You know, you've worked for my mother for years and yet I realized the other day that I know so little about you and about how you came to work for Mom. Did you grow up here? Are your parents still alive? I've never heard you mention anything about family."

She leaned back against the black sofa, the dark background making her hair look lighter and her large eyes more green than ever. "Yes, I was born and raised right here in Raleigh. My father is alive, although I've only spoken to him once in my entire life." Her eyes darkened slightly.

He leaned toward her, sensing pain trapped someplace deep inside her. "And why is that?"

Her beautiful eyes darkened even more and a crease danced across her brow. "My father is a highly successful businessman who is married and has two children who are just a couple of years older than me. My mother was his mistress for about six months before she got pregnant. He tried to pay her off to have an abortion, but I think my mother thought that I'd be worth more if I was alive, so she had me and she and my father came to an understanding."

"An understanding?" Trey fought his desire to move closer to her, to take one of her hands in his and offer her some sort of support. While her story was not completely uncommon, especially in the world of politics and successful, egomaniacal businessmen, that didn't make it any less ugly.

She gave a curt nod. "My father would financially support us as long as my mother and I never mentioned his name, never went public and ruined not only his image, but also his happy marriage. For me, my father was a once-a-month check in the mail that kept a roof over our heads and food on the table."

"That stinks," he said softly.

Her lush lips curved up slightly in a wry smile. "Yeah, it did. But what's equally as bad is that the support money allowed my mother the freedom to continue her party-girl lifestyle."

She paused to take a drink of her cocoa and eyed him somberly over the rim of the cup. "Having an alcoholic mother made me grow up pretty fast. She died the year I graduated from college in a drunk-driving accident. She was the drunk driver." She set her cup back down and Trey couldn't stand it any longer, he reached out and took one of her hands in his.

*Cold and small,* he thought as he held tight in an attempt to warm it. "I'm sorry, Debra. I'm sorry that's the life you were dealt."

She squeezed his hand and then pulled hers away. "They say what doesn't kill you makes you stronger, and in this case maybe it was true. I realized early on that I would not be following in my mother's footsteps. I studied hard and during my free time I watched on television whenever Congress was in session. That's when I first saw your mother, when she was serving out the last of your father's term. I fell in love with her politics, with her style and strength. I researched everything I could about her and when I was ready I went to my father and told him all I'd ever ask of him was for him to somehow arrange for an interview for me to intern for your mother."

She paused and drew a deep breath. It was the longest monologue Trey had ever heard from her. "And so he got you an interview with Mom," he said.

"No, he said he'd do what he could do, but I knew by his dismissive attitude that he wasn't going to do anything. So, I began a writing campaign to Kate. I wrote to her once a week, telling her why I'd be perfect working for her, what I would bring to the table as a valuable employee. I quoted bits and pieces of her speeches and told her why they had resonated with me." She smiled. "I think she finally decided to interview me to cut down on her mail. Anyway, she took me on and I've never looked back since then. I don't have any family but I feel like after all these years your mother has become my family."

Trey had a feeling there was a lot of ugliness in her early life that she'd left out of her story. Having an absent father and being raised by an alcoholic mother had to have been more than just a little difficult.

"So, the truth of my past is that I'm just the illegitimate daughter of an immoral businessman, who, rumor has it, is doing some shady business, and an alcoholic mother who wound up killing herself in an accident of her own doing," she finished. There was no bitterness in her voice. It was just a simple statement of facts.

"Those are just the circumstances of your birth and early life, but that doesn't begin to describe who you are now," Trey said, unable to hide his admiration for her. "I was lucky, I had a great role model in my mother, but my dad certainly tarnished the family name with his many affairs."

"The pitfalls of public service," she replied. "Sometimes I think most of the men in Washington have women on the side. A lot of them eventually get caught with their pants down, but a lot of them never get caught."

"I won't," he said firmly. "I mean I shouldn't have with you. I'm a one-woman man and when it comes time for me to marry, I won't cheat. I saw what my mother went through when the scandal about my father broke. I saw how his lies and cheating broke her heart. Besides, despite what happened between us, I believe in monogamy—one man, one woman and a family."

"Your mother rode out that scandal like the strong lady she is and went on to become vice president," Debra replied. She eyed him soberly. "And I believe you're cut from the same moral cloth as she is and that's why you'll be a great senator, a man who others will admire."

For several long seconds their gazes remained locked. Trey had never wanted a woman as badly as he did Debra at this moment and he was certain he saw a spark of desire in the depths of her eyes, as well.

She was the one who broke the gaze with an uncomfortable laugh. "We'd better get focused on the work. After all, that's why you're here, to pin down all the final details on your dinner event."

"Of course," he replied, still fighting the intense desire she had stirred inside him without even trying. Why didn't he feel this mind-numbing desire to touch, to taste, to make love to Cecily whenever he was with her? What was it about Debra that shot such heat through his veins and made his mouth hunger for hers?

He focused on the papers Debra shoved at him, papers showing tablecloths and dishes, silverware and glassware, but they were all a blur as he heard the snap and crackle of the fire in the fireplace, smelled that dizzying scent of Debra and imagined making love to her on the bright red throw rug in front of the warmth of the fire.

"Trey?"

He turned and stared at her and snapped out of his

momentary vision of her naked and gasping beneath him. "Yeah, I think we definitely want classic white tablecloths." He placed the paper with tablecloth colors to the side and stared at the dishware.

She leaned toward him, only making his concentration more difficult. The plates all seemed to blur together on the page, making it impossible for him to form a coherent decision.

"I think maybe the white plates with the black rims might be nice," she offered after a moment of silence from him. "They look bold and masculine. It wouldn't be a choice I'd usually make, but since this night is all about you, I think they'd be perfect."

"Done," he replied and moved on to the silverware page. What should have been easy decisions had become difficult with her seated so close and muddying his thoughts.

"These," he pointed to a set of plain silverware with tapered ends and moved on to the last page. "And these glasses." He set the paperwork down and reached for his cup, hoping a jolt of cocoa would wash all the inappropriate thoughts of her out of his mind.

"Good," she said with a wide smile as she gathered the paperwork together and set it on the end table next to her side of the sofa. "Now all we have left to talk about are the centerpieces and whether you want an official podium or not."

"Not," he replied immediately. "I figure my speech is only going to be about fifteen minutes long and I'll deliver it from my place at the head table."

"Okay, then I'll make sure we have a cordless microphone ready for you to use," she replied. "And the centerpieces?"

"I'll leave that to you, maybe something in black and white and crystal, but I don't want anything big and ornate. It's irritating to sit at a table and try to talk to somebody across some big plant or fancy centerpiece that is three feet high."

She laughed and again a burst of desire washed over him. She had a beautiful laugh, rich and full-bodied. He picked up his cup again, needing to keep his hands busy so they wouldn't reach out for her.

Other than that single moment when he thought he'd seen a spark of want in her eyes, she'd given him absolutely no indication that she'd be open to having anything to do with him other than on a business level.

He knew that he was here now only because he'd invited himself. Knowing her history with her mother, he was sure the last thing she'd want for herself was to become another quick hit for him on his way to his future.

And he didn't want that, either. She deserved better than that and it was completely out of character for him to even think of such a thing. It didn't fit with his vision for his future, it didn't speak to the kind of man he thought himself to be, the man he wanted to be.

It was bad enough that they'd already made a mistake, sleeping with her again would only compound the error. He turned his attention to the dancing flames in the fireplace.

"I've got five fireplaces in my house and have never burned a fire in any of them," he said.

"It's one of my guilty pleasures," she replied. "I order a cord of wood in the fall so that I can enjoy a fire whenever I want to through the winter, although I rarely burn one during the week. How's Cecily doing?" she asked, as if reading his thoughts and needing to mention the name of the woman he was certain to marry.

He turned his attention from the fire to her. "Cecily is fine. She's excited about what she jokingly calls my coming-out party. She knows I'm going to declare my intentions to run for the Senate on the night of the dinner and then hold a press conference to follow up. Which reminds me, I have one more guest to add to the list for that night."

Debra frowned. "It better be somebody important because I've almost finished a draft of the seating arrangements."

"It is somebody important. It's you. I want you to be there."

"Oh, don't worry, I'll be there well ahead of time to make sure that everything is in place for a successful night for everyone," she replied.

"That's not what I meant," he protested. "I mean I want you there as an invited guest."

"Oh, Trey, I don't think—"

"It's what I think that is important here," he interrupted her. "I want you there as my guest, Debra. It's important to me. You've done all the work, it's only right that you enjoy the fruits of your labor."

"I've enjoyed working on this project," she said, as if that was enough.

"That's nice, but it doesn't change the fact that I want you there in attendance through the entire thing. If you don't have anyone to bring as a guest, then we'll seat you next to Chad Brothers at one of the tables. He's already told me he's coming alone and you'll find him an entertaining companion who will regale you with stories of titillating political scandals and missteps that will make for fun entertainment."

He saw the hesitance in her eyes but pressed on. "Please, Debra. For me. Put on a fancy dress and your dancing shoes. I'll feel better giving my speech if I can look out and see your friendly face in the crowd."

"Okay, fine. I'll come." She said the words as if he'd placed a great burden on her, but her eyes glittered as if secretly pleased.

"Great. It's going to be a terrific night thanks to all your help. I know you got roped into this because of Mom, but I want to let you know how much I appreciate everything you've done to assure the success of the evening."

"It's been my pleasure," she replied, her cheeks dusting with a faint blush.

"And I imagine that once this night is done you'll just have time to barely catch your breath and Mom will announce."

One of Debra's light eyebrows shot upward. "Has she told you she's definitely going to run?"

"Not specifically, but she did mention that she's been invited to speak at a chamber of commerce Valentine's Day ball and I have a feeling that's when she'll make her big announcement."

"It's all so exciting," Debra said.

He nodded. "Exciting days for the Winston family. And now I should probably get out of your hair and let you enjoy what's left of your night off." He stood, oddly reluctant to go, and picked up his cup.

"Just leave that," she replied. "I'll take care of it."

He put his cup down and walked with her to the foyer where she pulled his coat from the closet. He shrugged it on. "Just think, in about two weeks' time you'll be the belle of the ball."

She laughed, that low and husky sound that stirred every sense he owned and surged desire through his veins. "I certainly doubt that, but I will enjoy being there."

"I think you underestimate yourself, Debra," he replied. She opened the door and he took one step out and then turned back to her, unable to halt the impulse he knew he'd later regret.

She gasped in surprise as he drew her into his arms and took possession of her mouth. She stiffened for just an instant and then melted against him, her mouth opening wider to invite him in.

She tasted just as he remembered, sweet and hot as their tongues met, moving together in an erotic dance of pleasure.

He wanted more from her, much more. He wasn't sure where his desire came from, but it burned through him like a white-hot fire. It was she who broke the kiss, stumbling back from him with wide eyes. She raised a hand and touched her lips and then dropped her hand to her side.

"You shouldn't have done that, Trey," she said, her voice trembling slightly and holding a faint touch of censure.

"Yeah, I know." Without saying another word, he pulled his coat collar up more tightly around his neck and stepped out into the cold night.

## Chapter 7

It had been a bad week.

Actually, it had been one of the worst weeks of Debra's life.

She felt as if for the past seven days she'd existed in the Twilight Zone. Not only had she had problems forgetting the unexpected kiss that Trey had planted on her the week before, but for the past week she'd felt as if some mysterious imp had entered her life to create utter havoc.

And the worst part about it was that she knew that she was the imp and felt as if she were slowly losing her mind.

As she pulled up Monday morning at the Winston Estate and saw that Jerry Cahill was on duty, she didn't see how things could get any worse.

She stifled a deep sigh as he stopped her car and gestured for her to roll down her window and as usual he leaned into the car and smiled. "Hey, Debra. Did you have a good day off yesterday?" He smelled of a cloying cologne and the ever-present peppermint. The mixed scents twisted a faint nausea in the pit of her stomach.

"It was nice and quiet, just the way I like it." In truth she had slept most of the day away and hadn't even bothered with cooking anything except the frozen pizza that had been in her freezer for months.

"I have just one question to ask you on this fine morning," he said.

"And what's that?" Dread added to the slight nausea rolling around in her stomach. She wondered what he would do if she just hit the button to raise her window while his head was still stuck inside her car.

She nearly giggled as a vision of her driving around town with him hanging off her car like an additional rearview mirror filled her head.

"Why won't you go out with me?" he asked, a twinge of impatience in his tone.

"It's nothing personal, Jerry," she fibbed. "I'm just too busy to date."

He frowned. "You were dating that other guy a few months ago."

"His name is Barry and he's gone because I didn't have time to date." There was no way Debra wanted to tell him that she'd never go out with him because something about him set her teeth on edge and made her feel icky inside.

"You know I could show you a good time," Jerry said.

"I'm sure you could," she agreed. "But I'm not dating right now. I'm completely focused on my professional life. And now I've got work to do, so if you'd excuse me..."

He jerked away from the car as she pulled forward. She wondered if she should say something to Kate about his forwardness, but then dismissed the idea. Kate was already busy working on her speech for the Valentine's Day night celebration and she had enough on her mind without handling a Secret Service man who was more than a little annoying, but certainly hadn't been particularly out of line.

He just wanted to date her and she didn't want to date him. End of story and no need to make a big drama out of it.

She parked her car and took a moment before getting out. She'd only been up for an hour and a half and already she was exhausted.

Of course, it didn't help that three nights in the past week her sleep had been interrupted by hang-up phone calls in the middle of the night. It didn't help that items kept disappearing and reappearing in her home, making her not able to trust her own sanity.

She'd read everything available on the internet about pregnancy. She understood her exhaustion and the bouts of nausea when food was the last thing she wanted in the morning. She understood a little bit of absentmindedness was normal, but surely nothing to the extent of what she had been experiencing.

Pregnesia, indeed. What scared her more than anything was the possibility that for some reason she was having a nervous breakdown.

Maybe she was working too hard. Maybe she'd reached her limits in trying to pull off the party for Trey and process her pregnancy, and now her mind was playing tricks on her because of exhaustion and stress.

She hoped that wasn't the case because if Kate followed through on deciding to run for president, Debra's workload would triple. Hard work had never stressed her before. She loved what she did, so what was the problem?

She grabbed her purse from the seat next to her and shot a glance out of her rearview mirror to see Jerry still staring at her with a frown. Ignoring him, she left the car, grateful that nobody was in the kitchen when she stepped inside.

She didn't feel like interacting with anyone at the moment. She just wanted to get to her office and close the door. Once she was behind her desk she leaned back in her chair and closed her eyes, playing over the disturbing events of the past week.

Absentmindedness was forgetting to return a phone call or that you'd put a load of clothing in the washing machine. It was not remembering to pull something out of the freezer to defrost for dinner.

It wasn't a crystal paperweight that disappeared from the top of your desk and then reappeared where it belonged two days later. It wasn't the dry cleaner's calling to tell you that the suit you'd brought in for cleaning was ready for pickup when you had no memory of taking anything to the dry cleaner's.

She was beginning to wonder if she was not only growing a baby in her belly, but maybe some sort of terrible brain tumor in her head, as well. She was starting to question her own sanity and the timing couldn't be worse for her to be going crazy.

Unexpected tears burned at her eyes and she swiped

at them, feeling foolish and overemotional. Darned hormones. Maybe she needed to start some sort of a diary or journal detailing the things that were happening to her, the things that made her feel as if she were slowly losing her mind.

She could take the journal in to her doctor when she had her next appointment in three weeks and maybe Dr. Finnegan could make sense of the things that Debra seemed incapable of figuring out at the moment.

At least she had something to look forward to tonight. After work she was going shopping for a gown to wear to Trey's party. Because her place was normally behind the scenes, she didn't have an adequate gown to wear as a guest and she was actually looking forward to shopping, which she rarely did.

She checked in with Kate and then worked until just after noon when she heard a knock on her door. The door opened and Trey filled the space. "Can I come in for a minute?" he asked.

"Sure," she replied and fought the sudden rapid beat of her heart. She hadn't seen him since the night he'd had dinner at her place, the night he'd kissed her like he meant it. That darned kiss, this darned man, had haunted her for the entire week.

He plopped down in the chair across from her small desk. "I just thought I'd check in and make sure everything was on schedule for Friday night."

"Everything is in place. Stacy has been like a bulldog getting things done." Debra shuffled several papers on top of her desk and pulled out one that displayed the centerpieces she and Stacy had agreed upon.

Short crystal vases that would hold an array of white and red flowers with silver and black sticks of onyx and crystal poking upward, the centerpieces were sophisticated, chic and short enough not to impede conversation across the table.

"Looks good," he replied and handed her back the paper. He frowned. "But you don't look so well."

"Gee, thanks, you sure know how to flatter a girl," Debra replied dryly. Self-consciously she tucked an errant strand of hair, that had escaped the knot at the nape of her neck, behind her ear.

"No, I'm serious. You look tired. You have dark circles under your eyes and your features looked strained with exhaustion." The worry in his eyes made the threat of tears rise up the back of her throat and burn at her eyes.

She swallowed hard to staunch her emotion. *Darned hormones anyway,* she thought. "I'm fine. I just haven't been sleeping very well, that's all. I'll catch up this weekend, once the dinner party is over and done."

"This has been too much on you, dealing with both my party and mom's work," he said with a guilty tone. "I should have taken a bigger role in putting together the dinner party or I should have seen that I was overworking you and gotten you an assistant."

"Don't be silly," she replied. "Haley has been a big help with Kate's work. I'll be fine and you did take on a big role in this process. I just need to grab a couple of hours of extra sleep this week."

His obvious concern touched her and she told herself that she'd better either get more rest or start wearing more makeup. She suspected it was the pregnancy and the worry about her mental state that was draining her energy, not the work she'd put in on the party.

"Is there anything else I can do to help?" he asked,

his tone gentle and filled with a caring that wasn't appropriate between them.

"I promise I'm fine," she said firmly. "You need to focus on your own health. You're about to enter months of a marathon race to get yourself elected. You'll be traveling all over the state and beyond, getting out your vision of what you want to see for the state of North Carolina in the future."

She wanted to tell him to go worry about the woman he was going to marry, not about a woman who had spent one night with him when they'd both been a little bit drunk and a lot stupid.

"I'm not your concern, Trey. You have bigger and more important things to focus on," she said.

His eyes turned a deep midnight-blue as he held her gaze.

Suddenly she was afraid he might say something, might do something that both of them would regret. "Go on, get out of here," she said, the words coming out more harshly than she intended. "I have lots of work to do and you are holding me up."

She held his gaze, as if daring him to do anything other than get out of her office. He finally sighed, raked a hand through his thick brown hair and stood. "Then I guess the next time I see you will be on Friday night at the party."

She nodded and stared down at her desk, as if already distracted. "See you then," she replied airily.

When he'd left, she once again leaned back in her chair and drew a deep steadying breath. She knew he felt something for her. Passion definitely, a caring certainly, but they were unacceptable emotions from a man who had far bigger fish to fry.

Her love for him was equally unacceptable and would remain unrequited. She had no illusions. She wasn't a dreamer. Trey would do what was expected of him, as he always had done in the past.

He'd choose a wife that would help him accomplish his ambitions and once his campaign kicked into full gear it would be Cecily at his side.

He wouldn't be around the Winston Estate much after that, and that was fine with Debra. Even though she carried his baby, she had to forget him. She had to emotionally separate herself from him.

Somehow, someway, she had to figure out how to stop loving Trey Winston.

Trey felt ridiculously nervous as he pulled up in front of Cecily's house to pick her up for the night's event. His tuxedo felt too tight, although he knew that it fit him exactly right. The evening air seemed too hot as he got out of his car, but in truth it was in the low forties.

Tonight was what he'd waited for. Tonight was his night to shine. Out of the two hundred and fifty invitations they'd sent out they'd only received eight regrets. It would be a full house and he was nervous as hell now that his moment had finally arrived.

Cecily's butler, John, met him at the door. "Good evening, Mr. Winston. Ms. Cecily will be down momentarily," he said.

In all the months that Trey had been seeing Cecily, she'd never been ready when he arrived to pick her up for any occasion. He stood patiently, knowing they had plenty of time as he'd made sure to build in waiting-on-Cecily time when he'd made the arrangements to pick her up.

At that moment Cecily appeared at the top of the staircase. She stood for just a moment, as if allowing him to appreciate how beautiful she looked in her silver formfitting gown and with her short dark hair coiffed to perfection.

"You look nervous," she said as she started down the stairs.

He grinned at her. "Does it show that badly?"

"Only to somebody who knows you as well as I do." Her ruby lips smiled as she reached him.

Up close she was utter perfection. Diamond earrings adorned her ears, sparkling as brightly as her brown eyes, and her makeup appeared effortless and yet enhanced her elegant beauty. She reached up and straightened his black bow tie. "Don't be nervous. You're going to be dynamite."

John held out her wrap for the evening, a silver cape that matched her dress. Yes, Cecily was perfection in heels. She would spend the evening at his side saying all the right things to all the right people.

It would be a good night for a proposal, he thought as he ushered her out to his car in the driveway. Yes, he knew Cecily was ready for the ring, but he hadn't bought a ring yet, and he had a feeling she'd much rather have a proposal be all about her instead of at the tail end of a party that had been all about him.

On second thought, it was a bad night for a proposal. Cecily would expect roses and him on bended knee, at least a five-carat ring and a band playing their song. Did they have a song? He frowned and tried to think of what it might be.

Proposing to her was going to be a lot of work, but he couldn't think about that now. He had a party to throw, people to persuade and a speech to give that would hopefully make campaign donations fall into his hands.

Tonight was the beginning of a long process and he knew with certainty that he was up for the battle. His nerves calmed the minute they were in the car and headed to the Raleigh Regent Hotel.

He knew his speech by heart, he knew that Debra and Stacy would have everything on point. The night was going to be a huge success, in large part due to Debra.

He didn't want to think about her right now, either. Thoughts of Debra confused the hell out of him and he needed to be clearheaded. Besides, the woman he intended to marry sat just beside him.

"You're very quiet," Cecily said.

"Just going over everything in my head," he replied.

"It's all going to be fine. Debra and Stacy have done a great job putting things all together and you always perform well. You'll charm everyone in the room."

"From your lips…"

She laughed. "Trey, honestly, for a man who has accomplished everything that you've done, you manage to have a humble streak in you that is quite charming." She paused a moment. "Is Sam planning on attending?"

"No. He told me he'd rather eat dirt than go anywhere tonight." Trey frowned. "I just wish we could get him to talk to somebody, to help him process everything he's been through."

"What about Thaddeus?" she asked.

"He sent his regrets also, as I figured he would."

She was silent for another long moment. "Will either of them become a liability to you as you move forward?"

"Not as far as I'm concerned. Sam is a war hero and

Thad is a respected crime-scene investigator. The fact that neither of them are particularly enthralled with politics shouldn't be an issue for anyone to use against me."

He frowned as he thought of his grandmother. Secrets and lies. What had she meant? Did she know something that could destroy them all?

Each time in the past week he'd tried to talk about his concerns with his mother, she'd insisted he needed to forget about his conversation with his grandmother and get on with his business of winning an election.

"I can't believe I haven't heard your speech yet," Cecily said.

He flashed her a quick smile. "Nobody has heard it. I wanted it to be all mine, with no input from anyone. If I can't write a fifteen-minute speech without help to excite people to get behind me, then I have no business being in politics at all."

"You're definitely bullheaded enough to be in politics," she replied teasingly. "Is your mother giving any kind of a speech?"

"No, just me. She's showing her support by being at my side, but we don't want to confuse what tonight is about, and it's about the state Senate race, not the next presidential race."

"You're a wise man not to let her steal any of your thunder," Cecily said.

For some reason her words irritated him. The last thing his mother would ever do was attempt to overshadow him or "steal his thunder," and the fact that Cecily's brain worked that way showed the cold, calculating streak he knew she possessed, but didn't show often.

Of course, it was that calculating, unemotional streak that would make her such a good wife. He would be able to depend on her to remove any emotion from any issue he might have to address if he became the next senator.

The Raleigh Regent Hotel was at the top of a fairly steep hill and Trey was thankful the weather was co-operating, not making it difficult for people to attend this special night.

By the time they reached the entrance of the hotel, any irritation he felt toward his beautiful passenger had passed and he couldn't wait to get inside and see the final results of all of his and Debra's preparations.

They were half an hour early, as Debra had requested them to be and as he handed his keys to the valet, his heart thrummed with restrained excitement.

As they walked into the lobby, there was an air of anticipation that he breathed in eagerly as he led Cecily toward the ballroom.

The doors were closed and an attendant stood at attention, obviously there to keep people out before the appropriate time for the festivities to begin.

He greeted Trey with a respectful nod of his head. "Mr. Winston, Ms. Prentice said to let you in as soon as you arrived." He opened the door and Trey and Cecily stepped inside.

"Oh, Trey," Cecily said and grabbed his hand. "It's all so perfect."

Members of the orchestra were already there, pulling instruments from bags and setting up on a raised stage on one side of the room. Black-and-white-uniformed waitresses and waiters scurried around the room, checking tables that already looked beautiful.

The dance floor gleamed with polish and the centerpieces with their pop of red were perfect foils against the white tablecloths and with the black-and-white dishes.

The head table was also on a dais and Debra had made the decision for it to be a table of nine, placing him in the center with four people on his left and four on his right. His mother and Cecily would sit directly on either side of him. The two most important women in his life, he thought.

Stacy came up to greet them. Clad in a plain black dress, with little makeup on her face, it was obvious she was here to keep things running smoothly with the staff and work behind the scenes.

"Everything looks great," Trey said after he'd made the introductions between the event planner and Cecily.

"It does look nice, doesn't it?" Stacy replied with obvious pride. "Of course, you can thank your assistant, Debra, for bringing things together. She's a tough taskmaster and a killer at negotiations."

"Is she here yet?" Trey asked.

"She's been here for about a half an hour. She checked everything out and then went to the office to sign off on some paperwork. She should be back here any moment now."

Trey nodded, hating himself for wanting to see her when he had the beautiful Cecily right by his side.

Stacy checked her watch. "We have about twenty minutes before people will begin to arrive. Debra wanted the two of you to stand at the doors and personally receive each guest as they arrive. We'll have hosts that will then see people to their assigned tables and on the tables are nameplates to indicate where they are to sit."

She flashed them a bright smile. "It should go relatively smoothly as long as you keep the initial greetings at the door to just a handshake and a welcome."

"Got it," Trey replied, his heart once again thundering in anticipation for the evening to come.

In just a little while he would take the place that his grandfather had groomed him for, he would begin to fulfill dreams long ago destined for him.

This was just the beginning and the excitement, the energy that flowed through him was one of challenge and there was nothing Trey loved more than a good challenge.

At five minutes before the doors were to open, the orchestra began playing soft dinner music and Cecily grabbed him by the arm, her eyes lit with a calm determination. She would perform brilliantly tonight, charming friends and adversaries alike.

His mother entered through the doors. Clad in a blue gown that emphasized the bright color of her eyes, she looked beautiful.

"Good luck tonight," she said as she pulled him to her for a hug. "And Cecily, you look wonderful on my son's arm."

"Thank you, Kate. We're all here for the same reason and it's going to be a wonderfully successful night for Trey."

At that moment the door opened once again and Debra walked in. Trey felt as if he'd been sucker punched in the gut as he took in her dazzling appearance.

The emerald-green dress she wore skimmed her body in silk from her shoulders to the tips of her silver high-heeled shoes. The neckline dipped just low enough to show a flirty hint of the tops of her breasts.

It was the first time since that crazy night they'd shared that he'd seen her with her hair down, rather than in one of her usual messy buns. It fell in soft waves to her shoulders, looking shiny and touchable.

Mascara darkened her eyelashes and a coppery pink lipstick colored her lips. Her cheeks grew pink and he realized he was staring at her as if she were the only woman in the entire room.

He also realized that this had been part of the anticipation he'd felt upon arriving at the hotel, the desire to see her all dressed up. He knew she'd look great, but he hadn't expected such beauty.

Everyone said hello to everyone else and then it was time for Trey and Cecily to stand at the door and greet the guests who had begun to arrive.

As Debra faded back near a large potted plant in the corner of the room, Trey swore that before the night was over he'd hold her in his arms. It was only right that he dance with all the women who had arrived without male companions. He told himself it was the gentlemanly thing to do, but deep in his soul he knew it was a simple decision of desire that he didn't want to try to justify or analyze.

He just wanted to hold Debra.

## Chapter 8

The night was going magnificently well. Trey had begun the festive evening with a short but rousing speech about his desire to make a difference in the state of North Carolina. He'd spoken with passion and enthusiasm that had resulted in the crowd being on their feet clapping and cheering when he'd finished.

Cecily and his mother had beamed and Debra felt the same pride and joy that she knew they must be feeling for him. Once the speech was given, dinner was served.

The servers moved like silent, efficient ghosts, filling glasses, placing plates with filet mignon and salmon without interrupting conversations.

Debra found Chad Brothers to be exactly the way Trey had described him, an entertaining dinner companion who had a big, bold laugh that escaped him often.

By the second course he'd declared himself madly

in love with her and wanted to hire her away from Kate to work for him. "Sorry, Chad," she said with a laugh. "No matter how many times you declare your undying love for me, my loyalty is with the Winston family."

"You cut me to my very soul," he declared with a mock look of dismay. "But I suppose I'll forgive you if you cut the rug with me when the dancing begins."

"I would be most delighted," Debra replied. "Though I have to warn you that I don't dance very well at all."

"Not a problem, I've got two left feet so we should be just fine together," he assured her with a charming smile.

Tonight she wasn't thinking about the fact that within another few weeks or so her pregnancy might be impossible to hide. She refused to dwell on the troubling events that had her believing herself half-crazy.

Tonight she wasn't anyone's assistant, she was simply a guest at a dinner party in a waterfall of green silk that made her feel sexy and carefree.

She'd refused wine at dinner, but felt intoxicated by the surroundings, the soft music and the fact that each time she glanced in Trey's direction she caught his gaze on her and her heart would beat a little bit faster.

He probably found it hard to believe that she could actually clean up so nicely, she thought. Still, she felt heady with knowing she had actually managed to turn a few male heads, that the event she'd worked so hard to put into place was going off without a single hiccup.

When the last dish had been removed from all the tables the band began to play a little louder and Trey and Cecily took to the dance floor.

"They make a nice couple, don't they?" Chad said.

Debra watched the couple gliding smoothly as if born

to dance together and couldn't help the wistful yearning that filled her. "Yes, they do," she replied.

"She'll make a perfect political wife," Chad continued. "She's bright and beautiful, but more importantly, she probably wants this more than Trey does. She knows the ins and outs of the game and she plays well with others when she needs to."

*Cecily plays well with others and I run with scissors,* Debra thought dryly. Chad couldn't know that with each compliment he gave Cecily, every time he mentioned what a perfect couple she and Trey made, he broke Debra's heart just a little bit.

Even though she knew that everything Chad said was right, that didn't mean that Debra couldn't wish that things could somehow be different.

But she knew her future, and there was no Trey in it anywhere. She would be a single parent raising a child alone unless she eventually met a good man she wanted to invite into her life, into her child's life.

Even without a man she would be fine and at the moment her love for Trey made it impossible for her to think of having any other man in her life.

There were moments when she ached with her love for Trey, but it was a love that would destroy him, destroy every plan he had for his future. It was a love she would have to lock deep in her heart forever.

By ten o'clock the cash bar was active and the dance floor was filled with couples enjoying the music. Small groups of people dotted various areas of the room, talking and laughing among themselves.

She saw Trey on the dance floor with his mother while Cecily danced with the mayor. Debra danced once with Chad and then gracefully declined two other men who approached her.

She was growing tired, and by eleven she'd found a spot at the edge of the room where a chair sat beneath a potted tree. She was content to hide out and just watch the rest of the evening unfold.

Another hour and it would all be over. The laughter, the music and the spirit of community that permeated the room would be finished and the tables would be broken down, chairs stored away to await the next big event.

After tonight there would be no more meetings with Trey. She wouldn't be surprised if this evening was followed fairly quickly by a public announcement of his and Cecily's engagement.

"Hiding out?"

The familiar deep voice shot a fire of warmth in the pit of her stomach. She turned to see Trey standing next to her. "Just watching the fun," she replied, and tried to ignore the slight flutter of her heartbeat.

"You look much too lovely tonight to be hiding out beneath a potted plant," he replied and held out a hand to her. "Come dance with me. I think they're playing our song." His eyes twinkled brightly.

"We don't have a song," she replied. The orchestra was playing a slow song and the last thing she wanted was to be held in his arms. The last thing she needed was to dance with him. Even as these thoughts flew through her head, she found her hand in his as he pulled her up from her chair.

She felt extremely self-conscious as he pulled her to the dance floor and into his arms. It was only then that she leaned closer to him. "I have two left feet, I can't dance," she whispered.

He smiled down at her. "You can dance with me." His words held such confidence that he made her believe if she was in his arms she could float across water.

His hand on her back was strong and masterful as they took off across the dance floor. "You look amazing tonight," he said and thankfully didn't mention that at that moment she stepped squarely on his toes.

"Thank you," she replied, hoping he couldn't hear the loud thunder of her heartbeat. She wanted to dip her head into the hollow of his throat, feel his body scandalously close against hers. "Your speech was pretty amazing, too. You had everyone in the room eating right out of the palm of your hand."

He laughed. "We'll see about that by the campaign donations that appear in the next few weeks. If nothing else it seems that everyone has had a wonderful time tonight. My only regret is that I haven't had a chance to dance with you before now."

She raised her head to gaze up at him and in his blue eyes she saw what she felt, desire and want and everything that shouldn't be in those blue depths.

She broke the eye contact and gazed over his shoulder. "I'm just glad it's finally over and I can get back to my regular work."

He stiffened slightly, as if perhaps hurt by her words. "I've enjoyed working with you," he finally said.

"And I've enjoyed working with you, too," she replied with forced lightness. "But now it's over and it's time for us each to get back to our own work, back to our own worlds."

Thankfully the music ended and she immediately dropped her hands from him and stepped away. "I'll just tell you good-night now," she said. "You'll be busy later telling your guests goodbye."

She turned and hurried away, leaving him on the dance floor as she returned to the chair beneath the potted plant. For just a moment as he'd held her in his arms and glided her across the floor, she'd felt as graceful as a ballerina, as beautiful as a fairy-tale princess.

It was a single moment in time that she would cherish for a very long time to come. By the time she was seated once again, Cecily was back at Trey's side, smiling up to him with a possessive confidence that Debra could only envy.

At midnight the orchestra stopped playing, indicating that the festivities were over. As people began to straggle out, Debra went in search of Stacy and found her in a small office just off the industrial kitchen.

The two women remained there, chatting about the evening and what a success it had been until everyone had left. "Come on, I'll walk you out," Stacy said.

As they reentered the ballroom Debra looked around. There was something almost sad about a ballroom with no people, an orchestra pit without music and a silky green dress going home all alone.

"You'll keep me and the hotel in mind for anything that comes up in the future?" Stacy asked as they reached the lobby.

"Absolutely," Debra replied without hesitation. "We worked very well together and I look forward to doing it again."

"Great." The two women said goodbye and Debra walked out into the cold night air.

She got into her car and waited for her heater to begin to blow hot air. Her exhaustion hit her like a ton of bricks. It had been a long night. It had been a long couple of weeks and now the letdown of it all being over made her realize just how tired she was.

Maybe she was crazy because she could have sworn Trey's gaze had been on her far too often throughout the night. And she must be crazy because she thought she'd seen desire in those beautiful blue eyes of his.

But that couldn't be right. She had to be misreading him. His life was mapped out before him by duty and responsibilities. He had a path to follow that didn't include her, but she couldn't get that spark in his eyes when he'd looked at her out of her head.

With the interior of her car finally warmed, she pulled out of the now-quiet parking lot and onto the outer road that would take her to the highway. Thankfully the weather had cooperated tonight, with a big full moon overhead and no clouds. A snow or ice storm would have been a potential disaster.

Eager to get home, she picked up speed as she went downhill, just wanting the comfort of her bed now. It had been a magical evening but she definitely felt as if she'd been turned into a pumpkin.

When she saw the red light gleaming in the night at the intersection coming up, she stepped on her brakes and the pedal slammed right to the floor.

With a sharp spike in her adrenaline that drove all tiredness from her body, she tried to pump the pedal, but there was no pump in it. It remained depressed to the floor as her car continued down the hill, picking up speed as it traveled.

The red light turned green just as she zoomed through

the intersection, now frantic as she realized she had no brakes at all and she was a long way from the bottom of the hill.

If she turned off the engine, then she would lose her ability to steer.

Frantic terror poured through her. She was going almost seventy miles an hour as she continued downward and there was no way to slow down. Several stoplights were between her and the bottom of the hill and although traffic was light, it wasn't nonexistent.

Panic crawled up the back of her throat and in desperation she yanked up the emergency brake, but nothing happened. In that instant, with another red light approaching, she realized the possibility that she might die. She was in a speeding bullet with no way to avoid some sort of impact.

As the red light came closer and her car careened down the hill, she gripped the wheel tightly and fought the impulse to close her eyes.

With the red light and the intersection imminent, she took one of her hands and laid on the horn, hoping to warn anyone else that might be coming that she was out of control. The horn blared, echoing inside her brain.

A hill was just ahead. If she could just make it to the hill then hopefully the car would slow down enough that she could maneuver it off the side of the road safely.

She was halfway through the intersection when she saw a car coming from the left. She turned her head, blinded by its headlights and braced. There was a squeal of brakes and then she felt the slam to the back left side of her car.

Instantly she went into a spin. The car swung around and around, dizzying her as she tried to control it, but the steering wheel careened wildly and with a gasp of resignation, she followed her impulse and squeezed her eyes closed.

The car came to an abrupt halt, crashing into something. As the airbag deployed, everything went black around her.

"The night couldn't have gone any better for us," Cecily said as Trey pulled into her driveway.

"It was a great time," he agreed. He parked his car in front of her door but didn't turn off the engine.

"You aren't coming in?" Cecily arched a perfect dark brow and looked at him with disappointment.

"I'm exhausted, Cecily. I think I'm going to head on home," he replied. It had been weeks since he'd had any intimacy with Cecily. In fact, he hadn't slept with her since he'd been with Debra. How could he make love to Cecily when he couldn't get the feel of Debra in his arms, the scent of her, out of his head?

"It's been weeks," Cecily said softly. "Are we okay?"

He forced a tired smile. "We're fine. I've just been so tied up with business and putting together tonight, I'm afraid my sexual drive has taken a temporary vacation."

She leaned over and placed a hand on his shoulder, her gaze soft with understanding. "Okay, I'll give you a pass for now. I know how hard you've been working to get things lined up between Adair Enterprises and starting the campaign. I just want to remind you that sex is a great stress reliever," she added flirtatiously.

He laughed, but wasn't a bit tempted. "I'll keep that in mind." He sobered as he looked at her. "I think what I need most from you right now is a little patience."

"I can give you that," she replied. "Just don't shut me out, Trey."

"That won't happen." He opened his door to get out and usher her to the front entrance, but she stopped him.

"Don't bother." She opened her car door and then leaned over to give him a kiss on his cheek. "No point in both of us getting out. You'll call me tomorrow?"

"You've got it," he replied.

He watched as she got out of the car and then headed to her front steps. Only when she was safely inside did he pull out of her circular driveway.

What was wrong with him? His sex drive had never taken any kind of a vacation before.

As he thought over the night he could think of two high points—the applause and hoots and hollers that had followed his speech and dancing with Debra.

Debra.

Why couldn't he get her out of his head? He'd hardly been able to take his eyes off her all night long. Surely it was just because it had been the first time he'd seen her in evening wear.

Dancing with Cecily was like dancing with a professional. She moved smoothly and gracefully, accustomed to partnering with him. Dancing with Cecily was effortless.

That hadn't been the case with Debra. She'd been stiff in his arms, difficult to guide in a natural rhythm and had stepped on his toes more than once, and yet he'd enjoyed that dance more than any one he'd had throughout the entire night.

His duty dictated that he chose a wife that would be best suited for his future plans and that woman was Cecily. But there was no question that Debra had somehow managed to crawl into his brain where she didn't belong.

But at the end of the dance they'd shared, she'd reminded him that their work together was over and it was time for both of them to get back to their separate lives.

Of course she was right. She was his mother's personal assistant and he hoped to become the next state senator. It was time to put her firmly out of his mind. He'd probably be far too busy in the next weeks and months to even think about her.

By the time he got home the adrenaline of the night had left him and he couldn't wait to get out of his tux and hit the hay. Tomorrow he would know how well he had been received tonight. Hoots and hollers were great, but donations to his campaign, endorsements from unions and fellow politicians would tell the true tale.

Included in the guest list had been several reporters to ensure that he got a little press time, all of them friends of Cecily's.

He knew Chad would already be busy filling his schedule with speaking engagements and burning up the phone lines to solicit support. Thankfully his right-hand man at Adair Enterprises was ready to step up when Trey wasn't there. He'd done everything humanly possible to prepare for what was ahead.

He'd just gotten his clothes off and was looking longingly at the king-size bed in his massive master suite when his cell phone rang.

Who would possibly be calling him so early in the morning? He grabbed his cell phone and saw his mother's number on the display.

"Are you calling to tell me how terrific I was tonight?" he asked teasingly upon answering.

"Actually, I'm calling to tell you there's been an accident," Kate's voice was brisk and filled with a concern that dropped Trey's stomach.

"Is it Grandma?" he asked.

"No, it's Debra. She had a car accident on the way home from the hotel and has been rushed by ambulance to Duke University Hospital."

Trey's heart hammered. "Is...is she badly hurt?" The words came out tortured by his tightening of the back of his throat.

"I don't have any details. Apparently Debra had me written down as her emergency contact. I got a call from the hospital but that's all they would tell me. I'm on my way there now."

"I'll meet you there," Trey replied. He hung up the phone and grabbed a pair of jeans and a shirt from his closet. His heart threatened to erupt from his chest with its frantic beating.

He was out the door and back in his car within ten minutes. An accident. She'd been in a car accident where an ambulance had carried her away. That meant it hadn't been a simple fender bender. It had been something far worse. How badly was she hurt? *Please, don't let her be hurt badly*, his heart pled.

At just a little after two o'clock in the morning he had little traffic to fight to get to the hospital. Had she fallen asleep at the wheel? He knew she'd appeared more tired than usual lately, but tonight she'd appeared well rested and glowing with good health.

He was relatively certain alcohol wasn't involved. He'd noticed that she'd only had club soda all night long and hadn't even drunk the wine that had been served with dinner.

So what could have happened and how badly was she hurt? By the time he entered the hospital parking area he had whipped himself into a near frenzy.

He followed the bright red signs that pointed him to the emergency area and found his mother already seated in one of the chairs. She rose at the sight of him, her features taut and radiating her own worry.

"I've let them know I'm here, but so far nobody has told me anything about her condition," Kate said. She had changed out of her evening gown and into a pair of black slacks and a blue-and-black-print blouse.

She looked tired and afraid, and seeing his mother's fear only increased Trey's. "How long have you been here?"

"Just a few minutes. They assured me that a doctor would be out as soon as possible to let me know what's going on and how she's doing."

Trey leaned back and released a deep sigh. Patience wasn't one of his strong suits. He wanted to rush through the double doors that separated him from wherever she was and demand immediate answers.

He needed to know that she wasn't clinging to life by a mere thread. But he also understood that he had to be patient and let the doctors perform whatever miracles needed to be accomplished to help Debra.

A police officer appeared just inside the door. He walked over to the receptionist station and then was allowed back through the doors to the emergency rooms.

Was he here about Debra? Had he been at the scene of the accident? Had anyone else been hurt? He felt as if he was going to explode with all the questions and frantic worry whirling around in his head.

It felt as if they'd been sitting there for hours when a

doctor finally came out to greet them. "Kate Winston?" he asked as Kate stood and nodded.

"I'm Dr. Abel Morsi and I've been tending to Debra."

"How is she?" Trey asked, unable to hide the worry in his voice.

"At the moment she's just starting to become conscious. From what I understand from the police who were at the scene, she blew through a red light, got hit on the rear end by another vehicle, spun out and hit a traffic pole head-on going at an excessive speed. Thankfully nobody else was hurt."

"And her injuries?" Kate asked, her voice trembling slightly.

Trey held his breath, his head pounding along with his heart in anxiety.

"She's a very lucky young woman," Dr. Morsi replied. "The worst of her injuries appears to be a concussion. She also has enough bumps and bruises that she isn't going to feel very well for the next few days. We're moving her to a regular room now. We'll keep her overnight for observation but she should be able to be released sometime tomorrow if all goes well and there are no complications."

Trey released the breath he'd been holding. "Can we see her?"

The doctor hesitated a moment and then nodded. "She's going to room two twenty-five. They should be getting her settled in there right now. My suggestion is that you peek in and let her know you're here and that she's in good hands, but don't stay too long."

Trey grabbed his mother's arm and pulled her toward the elevator bank, his mind tumbling inside out as he thought of what he'd just learned.

"She hit a pole at a high speed?" He looked at his mother with disbelief as they stepped into the elevator. "Debra isn't the type to speed or run a red light."

"Maybe she was so tired she didn't notice her speed," Kate replied. "Only she can tell us exactly what happened." They exited the elevator and followed the signs that would take them to her room.

They found it and entered, but stopped just inside as a tall nurse with long dark auburn hair was taking her vitals. She looked up at them, her eyes green like Debra's. She gave them a soft, caring smile. Her nametag identified her as Lucy Sinclair.

Debra lay on the bed with her eyes closed, a bruise already forming on her forehead and another on her cheek. She looked so pale, so lifeless. Trey could only imagine how many other bruises would appear over the next couple of days.

Lucy was just about to move away from her bedside when Debra's eyes snapped open and she gasped in obvious terror. Her hands rose out of the sheet and clawed the air.

Trey took a step forward, but his mother held him back as Lucy grabbed one of Debra's hands and leaned over her. "Debra, you need to relax. You're fine." Lucy's voice was soft and soothing.

"You're in the hospital," Lucy continued. "You've been in a car accident."

Debra's arms dropped and her hands covered her stomach. "A car accident? Oh, God, my baby," she whispered in what sounded like frantic desperation. "Is my baby okay?"

*Baby?* Trey felt as if all air had suddenly been sucked

out of the room, as if all the sound had completely disappeared. Debra was pregnant?

It was at that moment that Debra turned her head and saw him and his mother standing just inside the door. Her eyes widened and she began to weep.

## Chapter 9

Debra sat on the edge of the hospital bed, waiting to sign release forms and for one of Kate's staff members to come and pick her up. The midafternoon sun shone through the nearby window, but there was a chill inside her that had refused to go away since the moment she'd opened her eyes that morning.

A policeman had been her first visitor of the day, needing details from her of what had happened to file a report. She'd told him about her brakes not working, but when he heard where she had been right before the accident, she had a feeling he believed she might have been drunk. The blood work the doctors had arranged would clear her on alcohol being a contributing factor in the accident.

But what had happened? Why had her brakes failed? She got her car maintenance done regularly. In fact, it had only been about two months since she'd brought her car in to have the oil changed and hoses checked. So what had happened?

The chill intensified as she remembered the speeding of her car, the knowledge that she was going to crash and the frantic blare of her horn to warn anyone in her path.

The horn blare still resounded deep inside her brain, along with the terror that had accompanied the sound.

She'd been assured that the baby was fine, but there wasn't a single part of her body that didn't hurt. She felt as if somebody had taken the traffic pole she'd hit and beaten her with it over and over again.

Kate had called at ten that morning to tell her that arrangements had been made for Debra to spend the next couple of days in a guest room at the Winston Estate. There had been no arguing with Kate and Debra had to admit that the idea of being pampered and waited on for a day or two held more than a little appeal.

What she didn't want to think about was that moment the night before when she'd asked the nurse Lucy Sinclair about the welfare of her baby and then had realized that Trey and Kate had also been in the room.

They'd heard what she'd asked. They both now knew she was pregnant. The thought added to the echoing blare of the car horn from the night before, intensifying the headache that had been with her since she'd awakened.

Trey's face had radiated such a stunned expression and then Debra had burst into tears and the nurse had chased both Trey and his mother out of her room.

The cat was definitely out of the bag, Debra thought as she plucked a thread from the sweater that Haley had brought to her an hour before. Kate had sent Haley to Debra's townhouse to gather up not only clothing for her to wear while leaving the hospital, but also items for the next couple of days of recuperation.

Although Debra knew Kate and several of her staff had a spare key to her townhouse, she assumed Haley had used the key that had been in her purse since her purse was now missing and the morning nurse on duty had told her somebody from the Winston family had come to retrieve it.

"Here we are." RN Tracy Ferrell swept into the room with a handful of papers in her hands. "Dismissal papers for your John Hancock, and your driver has arrived to take you home."

She was somehow unsurprised to see Trey step into the room, followed by another nurse with a wheelchair. Debra's hand trembled slightly as she signed the dismissal papers, knowing that she had some lying to do in a very short time.

"How are you feeling?" Trey asked once the papers had been signed.

"Like I've been beaten up by the biggest thug on the streets," she replied. She winced as she transferred herself from the bed into the wheelchair.

They spoke no more as they got on the elevator and then she and the nurse waited at the hospital's front entrance while Trey went outside to bring the car to the curb.

Aside from the aches and pains that seemed to exist in every area of her body, she now had to face Trey and lie to him about the baby she carried.

As she slid into the passenger seat she saw the fatigue that lined his face; she could only guess the stress and concern that had probably kept him tossing and turning all night long.

"I was so worried about you," he said as he waited for her to pull the seat belt around her. "When we got the call that you'd been in an accident, I was scared to death."

"It isn't yours," she said, wanting to put him out of his misery as soon as possible. "I was already pregnant on the night we slept together."

His features showed nothing as he pulled away from the curb. "You're sure about that?"

"Positive," she replied with all the conviction of a woman telling the truth.

"So the baby is Barry's?"

"The baby is mine," she replied firmly.

He shot her a quick glance and then focused back on the road. "I'm assuming it wasn't an immaculate conception," he replied dryly.

"As far as I'm concerned that's exactly what it was," she replied. "Barry definitely isn't father material. I have no intention of telling him or ever talking to him again. The baby is mine and I'll... We'll be just fine."

He was silent for a long moment. "I'd want to know. If a woman was pregnant with my child I'd definitely want to know."

His words were like arrows through her heart, but she couldn't allow her own personal wants and desires to screw up his whole future, and that's exactly what this baby would do to him. She couldn't tell him the truth. She had to maintain her lie because despite what he'd just said to her the consequences to him were just too high.

He'd want to know, but he also wanted to be a senator and there was no way that she could see that the two could fit together.

"Barry wouldn't care," she finally replied. "A woman having his baby wouldn't change the kind of man he is, and he's not a good candidate for fatherhood. I'd rather raise my baby alone."

They drove for a few minutes in silence and she was sure that she'd convinced him the baby wasn't any of his concern. "So what happened last night?" He broke the slightly uncomfortable silence. "The report we got was that you were speeding and blew through a red light."

An arctic breeze blew through her as she thought of the night before and the certainty that she was going to die. "I was speeding and blew through a couple of red lights because my brakes didn't work."

"What do you mean?"

She shrugged and winced as every muscle in her back and shoulders protested the movement. "I braked and the pedal hit the floor, but nothing happened. I even pulled up the emergency brake, but the car still didn't slow."

A shudder went through her. "I was going down that big hill in front of the hotel and I picked up speed, but I couldn't stop. I couldn't even slow down. I kept thinking if I could just make it to the bottom and then start going uphill the car would slow enough that I could maneuver it off the road, but I never got the chance. I think the police officer who spoke to me this morning thought I left the party drunk last night and that's what caused the accident, but I didn't have a drop of alcohol last night."

"We'll get it all sorted out," he said. "Right now I'm just glad you survived. I was scared about your well-being, Debra." His voice was smooth as a caress and she wondered if he charmed all the women he came into contact with. It was possible he wasn't even aware of how deeply he affected her when he spoke to her, when he gazed at her with those beautiful blue eyes of his.

She settled deeper into the seat, exhausted both by her thoughts and the emotions that were far too close to the surface.

Thankfully the rest of the ride was accomplished in silence and by the time he pulled up at the front door of the Winston Estate, she was ready for a pain pill and bed.

Maddie met her at the front door and took her directly to the elevator that would carry her upstairs to the bedrooms. "You poor dear," Maddie said as she wrapped a gentle arm around Debra's shoulder. "We'll just get you into bed and take good care of you until you're feeling better."

Emotion rushed up inside her and tears burned at her eyes. Debra had never had anyone in her life who had taken care of her and right now she was more than grateful to Kate for insisting that she come here for a couple of days.

"Ms. Kate thought you might feel better with a nice new nightgown. It's hanging in the bathroom, if you'd like to change and go back to bed for a nap."

"That sounds perfect," Debra replied wearily. From a small sack she'd been sent home with she took out the bottle of pain pills she'd had filled at the hospital pharmacy and slowly walked to the adjoining bathroom. She'd been assured by the doctor that the pills were a low dosage that could cause no harm to her baby. Besides, she only intended to take one or two and then she'd be fine without them.

The nightgown was long white cotton with green trim and had a matching robe. Debra was grateful it wasn't silk. She was a cotton girl when it came to her favorite sleepwear.

A glance in the mirror showed her what her earlier reflection had shown her in the hospital bathroom. She had no idea how she'd gotten the bruise across her forehead, but since the accident it had turned a violent purple. *Lovely,* she thought and turned away.

The rest of her injuries were bruised knees, a friction burn on her shoulder from the seat belt and just the overall soreness of muscles. With a moan, she got out of the clothes she'd worn home and pulled on the nightgown that Kate had provided for her. The soft cotton fell around her like a comforting cloud.

She used a crystal glass next to the sink to wash down two pain pills and then carried the glass and the pills back into the bedroom where Maddie awaited her.

"You need to rest now," Maddie said as she took both the pill bottle and the glass from her and set them on the nightstand. She then tucked the sheets around Debra like a mother hen securing her chick for the night. "Myra is making her famous chicken soup for you to have later."

"She shouldn't go to any trouble," Debra replied, already feeling a deep drowsiness sweeping through her. The trip home from the hospital and the conversation with Trey had exhausted her.

"Don't you worry about it. Don't you worry about anything. You just relax and if you need anything, Birdie is working up here today and she'll be checking in on you regularly. You call for her and she'll come running." With a final sympathetic smile, Maddie left the room.

"Birdie" was actually Roberta Vitter, a fifty-year-old woman who worked as one of the maids in the house. Her domain was the upstairs, dusting and cleaning the bedrooms and baths so they were always ready for any guest who might arrive.

Debra had been placed in the bedroom they all referred to as the blue room. The walls were a faint blue and the bedspread was a rich royal-blue. The lamp next to the bed had a blue-and-white flower pattern and the furniture was all dark cherry.

It was a beautiful room, but as Debra waited for sleep to take her all she could think about was that the blue of the room reflected the blue of Trey's eyes and the blueness of her emotions.

She'd done it. She'd managed to make Trey believe the baby wasn't his. She should be feeling enormous relief, as if a big weight had been lifted from her heart.

Instead her heart felt as if somehow in the past half an hour it had irrevocably broken.

Trey had left the Winston Estate the moment he'd delivered Debra there, knowing she would be in good hands between his mother and the staff. He'd driven to Adair Enterprises and holed up in his office.

A deep weariness made the sofa look inviting, but he knew a quick power nap wouldn't solve the problems. At the moment he wasn't even sure what the problems were, he only knew he was troubled on a number of levels.

He should be feeling triumphant. The morning paper

had carried a photo of him and Cecily with the headline of North Carolina's New Power Couple, and had gone on to quote part of his speech from the night before and his aspirations to serve as senator for the beautiful state that was his home.

However, the trauma of Debra's accident and then the bombshell news that she was pregnant had kept him awake most of the night. He'd alternated between praying that she would be okay and wondering if the baby she carried was his, and if it was, what he intended to do about it.

He hadn't come to any concrete conclusions other than he would support Debra and be an active participant in his baby's life. He wanted children and while he hadn't thought about a pregnancy being the consequence of the night he'd shared with Debra, he realized he wasn't so upset to believe that he might be the father of her baby.

He'd been oddly disappointed this morning when she'd told him the baby wasn't his and that small twinge of disappointment had only managed to confuse him. He wasn't sure he absolutely believed that the baby was Barry's and not his. Unfortunately there was nothing he could do about it as she'd told him so.

She'd created a confusion in his life since the night they'd spent together. Since that night he had desired her to the point of distraction, but he had to be stronger than his desire for her.

Duty. It had been pounded into his head by Walt and his mother since he was a child, duty to the family business and to a place in politics. As the eldest of the Winston children, his mother had encouraged him to be a good example to his younger brothers and Walt had told Trey his destiny was to do great things both for Adair Enterprises and for the country.

And duty required difficult decisions, personal choices that were smart. And Debra definitely wasn't a smart decision, especially now if she was in fact carrying another man's child.

What concerned him the most at the moment was her telling him that the car accident had been caused because her brakes had failed. It took him a single phone call to find out that her car had been towed to an impound lot.

The next call he made was to his brother Thad. Thad answered his cell phone on the second ring. "Winston."

"Thad, it's Trey."

"Ah, half of the new power couple in town," Thad said dryly. "I saw your photo in the paper. Calling to try to get my vote?"

"Actually, I'm calling you because I need a crime-scene investigator. Would you have some time this afternoon to stop by my office so we can have a discussion about something that has come up?"

"You've definitely captured my attention, brother," Thad replied. "Anything else you can tell me?"

"I'd rather we talk in person," Trey said.

"How about four o'clock?"

"Whatever works for you."

"Then let's make it four o'clock at your office. And if I'm not out of there by five you buy dinner from that bistro or whatever it is where you normally order those killer sandwiches."

Trey smiled. "It's a deal."

The two men hung up and Trey's smile fell. He leaned

back in his chair and steepled his fingers in thoughtful contemplation.

There was no way he believed that the car accident had happened in any way other than what Debra had told him. She had no reason to lie about the brakes not working and it was something that could easily be checked.

He didn't have the resources to fully investigate what had happened in Debra's car, but Thad did. And what good was it to have a law-enforcement official in the family if you didn't occasionally take advantage of the fact?

With the meeting set for four, Trey got to work on Adair Enterprises business. Saturdays were always the time he checked in with their satellite operations and with the end of the month approaching he had the usual financial busywork to do.

The afternoon flew by both with work and thoughts of Debra. He had been so frightened last night when he'd heard she'd been in a car accident and rushed to the hospital. She had appeared so fragile, so vulnerable this morning when he'd arrived to pick her up.

The bruise on her forehead told only part of the story of her injuries. He could tell with each movement of her feet, with every small action of her body that she ached from the near-death ordeal.

It could have ended in such tragedy. She could have been killed. She could have killed other innocent people. It was only by sheer luck she'd survived with only a concussion and various bumps and bruises.

He knew she was in good hands and was grateful that his mother had insisted Debra spend a few days recuperating at the estate. The thought of her all alone and hurting at her townhouse swelled a pain inside him.

He had a feeling from what little she'd shared of her past that she'd been alone for most of her life, that she'd never had anyone to depend on but herself.

Thank goodness she hadn't lost her baby. He could tell by the way she'd talked of her pregnancy that she was already invested in the baby she carried, was probably already making plans for the birth and life after.

It had been a little over two months since they'd slept together and if she already knew she was pregnant on that night, then she had to be approaching or already be in her second trimester.

It hadn't shown. As he thought of the vision she'd been the night before in that amazing spill of emerald green, there had been no hint of a baby bump or maybe he just hadn't noticed.

He kept busy until four when Rhonda announced the arrival of his brother. Thaddeus Winston was thirty-one years old and wore his light brown hair slightly shaggy. He was dressed in a pair of black slacks, a white shirt and a jacket that Trey knew hid his shoulder holster and gun. He was not just a crime-scene investigator, but had all the full capabilities and powers of a member of the Raleigh Police Department.

"How are you doing, brother?" Trey got up from behind his desk and shook Thad's hand. He then motioned him to the sitting area of the room. "On duty or would you like a drink?"

Thad sank down on the sofa. "Off duty and Scotch neat would be perfect," he said.

Trey went to the minibar at the back of the room and poured two glasses of Scotch. He handed one to

Thad and then sat in the chair opposite him. Thad took a sip of the drink, placed it on the coffee table in front of him and then leaned back, his hazel eyes filled with curiosity.

"What am I doing here? We don't exactly hang out on a regular basis."

"That was your choice," Trey replied. Thad had long ago turned his back on the family business and definitely didn't like anything that had to do with politics.

Thad nodded, accepting the fact. "You mentioned something on the phone about needing my skills as a crime-scene investigator. What's happened?"

Trey explained to his brother about the event the night before and Debra's car accident on the way home. As he spoke Thad listened attentively.

Trey knew his brother had a reputation for being an intelligent, valued asset to the police department. If anyone could get to the bottom of Debra's brake issue, it would be Thad and the strings he could pull with his police buddies.

"Alcohol not an issue?" Thad asked.

"Definitely not, and when her toxicology results come back they will prove that she wasn't drinking. She's pregnant, so she didn't even have wine with dinner."

"You know traffic issues and accidents really aren't my field," Thad said.

"But you know the people on the force that could launch an investigation into this. I just want to know if it was some sort of mechanical failure or something else."

Thad raised an eyebrow. "Something else? As in something nefarious?"

Trey shrugged. "It just seems odd that something like

that happened on the night I pretty much told everyone that I intend to run for senator."

Thad's frown deepened. "And what has Mom decided to do? Has she said anything about her own political future?"

"It's my personal opinion that she's going to run," Trey said truthfully. "Although officially she hasn't said anything yet, it's just a feeling I have."

Thad took another drink of his Scotch and then leaned back against the sofa. "To be honest with you, I hope she doesn't run. Politics has never done our family much good."

Trey knew his brother was thinking about their father. "Dad was a cheater first, a senator second," he said softly.

"It's not just that," Thad said, although Buck's cheating had taken a toll on their entire family. "It's also the idea of a national spotlight being on all of us again. It's bad enough that you've gone to the dark side," he said wryly.

"You know that Mom is going to do what she decides to do and she'll make her decision based on many factors, including the price we'll all have to pay if she decides to run for president."

"I know, but I also know that I intend to maintain some distance from all of it. You know I love you all, but I love my job and I don't want everyone else's ambition to screw around with my nice, quiet life."

"I understand that," Trey replied. "But as far as I'm concerned, running for public office isn't just a job for me, it's a calling."

"I get it, but I don't have to particularly like it. You

know you'll win the election. You always get what you go after."

Trey smiled. "I hope to win, but who knows what could happen between now and the day that people actually cast their votes." His smile faded as he thought of another subject. "Have you visited with Grandma Eunice lately?" he asked.

"Not lately enough," Thad admitted. "It's been a couple of weeks. Why? Is she sick?"

"I'm not sure what's going on with her," Trey replied and explained what had happened the last time he'd visited their grandmother. "Secrets and lies, that's all she kept saying before Sassy finally gave her a sedative. Do you know any deep dark secrets about our family that might come to the surface during a campaign?"

Thad shrugged. "Beats me. We all weathered the biggest secret in the family, that our father was a womanizer who didn't give a crap about his wife and kids. When Mom became vice president I'm sure there were people looking for secrets and lies to bring her down, but nothing ever came out."

Trey knew their father's betrayal was responsible for Thad deciding to remain a bachelor. He maintained he had no taste for family life given what they'd seen in their parents' marriage. Thad finished his drink and then stood. "I'll have to call in some markers but I'll get Debra's car from the impound lot to the police-station garage where a mechanic can take a close look at it."

"I really appreciate it, Thad."

His brother flashed him a smile. "You just appreciate the fact that I'm leaving here before five o'clock and you don't have to buy me dinner."

Trey laughed and walked his brother to the door. "If you want to hang around, I'll be glad to buy you dinner."

"Thanks, but I want to get right on this thing with Debra's car. Hopefully I'll have an answer for you by the end of the evening."

"That would be terrific," Trey replied.

Once Thad had left, Trey returned to his desk, his thoughts scattered like the seeds of a dandelion in a breeze. At least he'd set into motion obtaining some answers about what had happened to cause Debra's accident last night.

She might have blown a hose and the brake fluid had all drained out. Or the brakes might have failed for some other mechanical reason.

Trey admitted he knew a lot about business and politics, but he was fairly ignorant of the workings of a car. A trained mechanic at the police garage would know what to look for and in the meantime all Trey could do about that particular issue was wait.

He'd already spoken to Cecily first thing this morning, but he found himself wanting, needing to check in on the woman who was in the forefront of his mind.

He called the house and Maddie answered the phone. "Hi, Maddie. I just thought I'd call and check in on our patient."

"Do you want me to transfer the call to her room?"

"No, that's not necessary. I was just wondering how she's doing." He didn't want to bother her if she was sleeping, nor did he feel like it was a good idea to speak to her until he had something concrete to say. It wasn't enough that he just wanted to hear the sound of her voice.

"She's been sleeping most of the afternoon, poor

thing. Myra is getting ready to take her up some of her chicken soup and she'll probably go back to sleep after she eats. It's the best thing for her. Sleep heals, you know."

"I know," Trey said with a smile. "You've spent most of my early life telling me that."

"And that's because of you three boys you were always the most difficult to get to sleep each night," Maddie replied. "You always had a hard time winding down."

"I still do," he admitted. "Well, I just wanted to do a quick check in to see that Debra was resting comfortably," he replied.

"You know we're all taking good care of her."

Once he was finished with the conversation, he decided to call it a day and head home. Thad would contact him by cell phone and his work in the office was done for now.

It took him only twenty minutes on a Saturday late afternoon to get from the Adair Enterprises offices to his home just outside the Raleigh beltline.

The six-bedroom, eight-bathroom mansion wasn't as impressive as the Winston Estate, but it was more house than Trey had ever imagined for himself.

It had been his mother who had encouraged him to buy it when it had come on the market a year before. It still didn't feel like home and he knew what he was missing were the skills of a decorator and the company of a spouse.

Sooner or later he'd need to rectify that situation. There was no question that he would be a more appealing candidate with a wife by his side, especially given his father's reputation for being a cheating ladies' man.

As a single man, Trey knew the public might be more apt to tar him with the same brush. A wife was as important as a good campaign manager.

He frowned as he walked through the front door and threw his car keys on the nearby marble table in the foyer. When had he become the coldhearted soul who would make a decision as important as marriage simply because it was politically appealing?

The silence of the house thundered around him as he walked through the great room with its high ceilings and modern furnishings. There was just the minimum of furnishings, nothing decorative to add any warmth or personality.

He had a cleaning service who came in once a week, but other than that he had no house staff. Most days he ate all of his meals out so he didn't require a cook and he figured once the time was right his wife would staff the house with the help she thought was important and do the decorating that would make the house feel like a home.

He went into the kitchen and put on a pot of coffee and as he waited for it to percolate, he stood at the windows that overlooked a lush backyard and a large patio surrounding a swimming pool.

His head filled with a vision of a hot summer day, of the large brick barbecue pit spewing the smoky scent of cooking meat, of colorful umbrellas open against the shimmer of the sun and the taste of tart lemonade in his mouth.

He closed his eyes and allowed the vision to play out. There should be children in the pool, laughing and shouting as they splashed and swam from one end to the other... *His* children.

A sense of pride, of joy buoyed up in his chest as he thought of the children he would have, children who would carry on the Adair Winston legacy.

And in his vision he turned his head to smile at the woman who'd given him those children, the woman who was his wife. His eyes jerked open and he realized the woman he'd seen standing beside him in the vision wasn't Cecily at all, instead it was Debra.

Irritated with the capriciousness of his own mind, he poured himself a cup of coffee and went back into the great room where he sank into the accommodating comfort of his favorite chair.

Lust. That's all that it was, a lust that he felt for Debra that refused to go away. But he certainly wasn't willing to throw away all his hard work, all his aspirations, by following through on that particular emotion. That would make him like his father and that was completely unacceptable.

No matter what he felt toward Debra, she was the wrong woman for him. He had to follow his goals, his duty to pick the best woman possible to see him to his dreams, to the dreams his grandfather Walt had encouraged him to pursue.

Besides, it wasn't like he was in love with Debra. He liked her, he admired her, and he definitely desired her, but that wasn't love.

Debra inspired his lust, but Cecily inspired confidence and success and encouraged his ambition. If he used his brain there was really no choice. The lust would die a natural death, but his relationship with Cecily would only strengthen as they worked together for his success. At least that's what he needed to believe.

It was almost eight when his cell phone rang and he saw that it was Thad.

"Hey, bro," he said.

"Trey, Debra was telling the truth," Thad said. His voice held such a serious tone that Trey's heartbeat reacted, racing just a little bit faster.

"A malfunction of the brakes?" he asked.

"I'd say more like a case of attempted murder. The brake line was sliced clean through."

## Chapter 10

Debra stared at Trey in stunned disbelief. He and his brother Thad had come into the bedroom just after breakfast to tell her the news that somebody had cut her brake lines. Somebody had obviously tried to kill her.

"But who? And why?" She was seated in a chair next to the bed, clad in her nightgown and robe. She raised a trembling hand to her head, where a pounding had begun. None of this made any sense. How could this be happening to her?

"That's what I want to talk about with you," Thad said. He remained standing with a small pad and pen in his hand as Trey eased down onto the foot of the bed. "We were hoping you might have some ideas for us."

She looked from Thad to Trey and then back again. "Ideas? Ideas about who would want to hurt me? Who might want to kill me? There's nothing for me to tell you. I can't imagine anyone doing something like this to me."

"You were lucky you weren't killed," Thad said, his hazel eyes hard and intent. "At the very least you could have been hurt badly."

"It has to be some sort of a mistake," Debra protested, her heart taking up the pounding rhythm of her head.

She felt as if she'd once again taken a plunge into the sea of insanity, like her items disappearing and then reappearing, like the guest list found in the freezer.

Somehow, someway, this was all part of her craziness because it felt impossible that Trey and Thad were here to tell her that somebody had intentionally tried to kill her by cutting her brake lines.

Maybe she should mention those other things to Thad? Perhaps she should tell him that she felt like somebody was trying to gaslight her, that she couldn't possibly be as absentminded as she'd been over the past couple of weeks.

She immediately dismissed the idea, certain that one thing had nothing to do with the other. Her absentmindedness didn't cut her brake lines and telling him about the other things might only manage to muddle the case.

"Have you had problems with anyone? Old boyfriends you've ticked off?" Thad asked. "People maybe you worked with on the event that you might have rubbed the wrong way?"

"No, nothing like that," she replied.

"There is an old boyfriend," Trey said and Thad looked at him and then gazed back at her expectantly.

"Barry. Barry Chambers. He owns Chambers Realty, but he wouldn't want to hurt me. We broke up weeks ago. He's old history and in any case he's not the type of man to do something like this."

"Who broke up with whom?" Thad asked.

"It was a mutual thing, but he broke up with me before I got a chance to kick him to the curb." Once again she raised a hand to her forehead, where she knew her bruise had already begun to take on the colors of green and yellow. "The breakup was quite civilized, done in a public place over dinner."

She steadfastly kept her gaze away from Trey, who had ended that night with her in a hotel bed where they'd had wild, passionate sex. "Trust me, Barry doesn't care enough about me to try to kill me or hurt me in any way," she added.

Thad frowned. "That brake line didn't just cut itself. Somebody had to have intentionally crawled under your car while you all were inside the hotel dining and dancing. That somebody had something sharp enough to cut the brake line." He looked at his brother. "Could this have anything to do with Mom or you?"

"I don't see how," Trey said slowly. "But I have no clue what to think."

"I'm just a glorified secretary, for God's sake," she exclaimed as horror washed over her. She dropped her hand from her forehead to her lap. "Maybe somebody got the wrong car?"

Trey's frown deepened. "What do you mean?"

"I drive a common type of car, nothing fancy or unusual. Probably half the staff at the hotel drives something similar to my car. This has to be about somebody else. It can't be about me. I can't imagine anyone wanting to hurt me for any reason." She swallowed hard against a rising hysteria.

Thad drew a hand through his hair. "If you think of somebody, no matter how crazy it sounds, you need to contact me." He reached into his coat pocket and withdrew a card. "Meanwhile, I'll check out the hotel and see if the answer lies with somebody there. In any case, it's possible somebody saw something that night that might help us find out who is responsible for this."

"Thank you, Thad," Debra said. He nodded and left the room. Trey remained seated at the foot of the bed, his gaze focused intently on her.

"How are you feeling?" he asked.

"A little shaken up, especially now that I've been told that somebody tried to kill me," she replied, her voice trembling slightly. "Honestly, Trey, I can't imagine anyone hating enough to do something like this. I can't imagine anyone hating me at all."

"I can't either," he admitted with a soft tenderness that soothed every exposed nerve of her emotional chaos.

"Maybe it really was just a case of mistaken car identity and Thad will figure it all out. Maybe it has something to do with somebody who works at the hotel."

She shifted positions in the chair. "You know, there is one person who kind of creeps me out and keeps asking me out on dates. I turn him down all the time, but, I can't imagine him having anything to do with this."

Trey's eyes narrowed to blue slits. "And who is this person?"

She hesitated a moment and then replied. "Jerry Cahill."

One of Trey's eyebrows lifted in obvious surprise. "You mean Secret Service Jerry Cahill?"

She nodded and released an uncomfortable laugh.

"I'm sure it's nothing, that I'm just overreacting. It's just whenever he's on duty at the side entrance he always stops my car and wants to know why I don't want to go out with him."

"And what do you tell him?"

"That I don't have time to date and obviously I'll be having less time for personal relationships in the future." It was a backhanded reference to the fact that it wouldn't be too terribly long before she'd be juggling both her job and single parenthood.

"I'll check it out," Trey said, his voice filled with a simmering anger. "His job is to guard the house and my mother, not to make any of the staff feel uncomfortable."

"I don't want to get him into any trouble," Debra replied hurriedly. "He's never done anything to me except flirt, and one day I thought I saw him just standing outside my townhouse."

"Why didn't you mention this before?" Trey asked.

"Because I thought he was harmless. I mean, he's a Secret Service man. They go through all kinds of security and background tests to get their jobs. They can't be the bad guys."

Trey's jaw clenched. "Anyone can be a bad guy, Debra. Men have been known to do terrible things to women they feel have rejected them."

Wearied both physically and mentally, Debra sagged back in the chair. It all felt like too much… The accident that wasn't an accident, the crazy incidents of forgetfulness or whatever they were. She felt as if her brain was stuffed with too many strange things and she had somehow entered an alternate universe like the Twilight Zone.

Trey stood up and walked over to her. He held out his hand. "Come on, I think it's time for you to be back in bed. It's not even noon yet and you look exhausted."

"Attempted murder does that to a woman," she replied. She eyed his hand and hesitated a moment, almost afraid to touch him, afraid that a simple touch would force out all her emotions that she'd tried to keep in check.

She finally slipped her hand into his and he pulled her not just out of her chair, but into his arms. A sob caught in her throat as he held her against him, his hands lightly caressing up and down her back.

"It's going to be okay," he murmured, his breath a warm promise against her hair. "We aren't going to let anything happen to you."

She couldn't help it, she began to cry. All of the uncertainty of the past few weeks coupled with the accident and now the knowledge that somebody had deliberately tampered with her car mingled together in a roar of emotions she could no longer contain.

She hadn't realized until this moment how badly she'd needed to be held, how much she'd wanted strong arms wrapped around her, assuring her that she was okay.

She leaned into him, drawing in the comforting heat of his body, breathing in the familiar scent of his cologne. His heart beat against her own, a steady rhythm that slowly calmed the racing of her own heartbeat.

Her tears finally ebbed, leaving her spent and clinging with her arms around his neck, her face turned into the hollow of his throat. She wanted to kiss him, to tip her head up and feel his lips pressed against hers.

She felt loved. In his arms she felt loved as she'd

never felt in her entire life. She wanted to stay in this room, in this moment forever.

And for just a crazy instant she wanted to tell him that she was madly in love with him, she wanted to confess that the baby she carried was his.

Thankfully at that moment he released her and she got back into bed, her love for him shoved down and buried deep inside her as she pulled the sheet up to cover herself.

It was unusually warm for the last few days of January as Trey drove to his mother's mansion to take Debra home to her townhouse Wednesday morning.

He didn't want her to leave the safety of his mother's place, but Debra had insisted that she'd overstayed her time at the estate and needed to go home and get settled back into her usual routine.

She'd told him she was also ready to get back to work. Haley had stepped in to take her place while she'd been recuperating, but now it was time for Haley to step aside and let Debra resume her position.

So far nothing had come out of the investigation Thad was conducting in regard to the cut brake line. Nobody at the hotel had seen anything unusual the night of the dinner and Barry had an alibi for the evening.

Thad and Trey had spoken to Jerry Cahill together the day before. Trey had found the Secret Service man slightly arrogant and completely indignant that anyone would believe he would do anything to harm a member of the family or the staff.

He confessed that he liked to tease Debra, but Trey told him in no uncertain terms that his "teasing" wasn't welcomed and he should not bother Debra or anyone else on staff again. It was not only unbecoming, but it was unprofessional, as well.

Jerry had agreed, but Trey had seen a flash of anger in the man's eyes that he didn't like. Jerry didn't know it, but he was under investigation by his bosses to make sure he wasn't some loon who had managed to slide into the system where he didn't belong.

Trey pulled up to the front door of the mansion and got out, enjoying the fact that no coat was needed and the forecast for the next week mentioned highs in the upper sixties.

Thankfully the long-term forecast was for Raleigh to enjoy an unusually mild week or two. That was fine with Trey, he'd prefer not to battle the cold and ice or snow, although he doubted that winter was finished with them yet.

Spring was his favorite season, the time for rebirth and green grass and lush flower gardens. He reminded himself that he needed to hire a gardener so that he would have some flower beds when spring arrived.

Maddie let him into the house and told him that Debra was waiting for him in the sitting room. He walked in and couldn't help the way his heart lifted at the sight of her.

Her forehead bruise was still visible, although fading with each day that passed. She was seated on the sofa, clad in a pair of jeans and a pink sweater.

A medium-size pink duffel bag and her purse sat on the floor next to her. Her eyes lit up as she saw him and he didn't know if she was happy to see him or just happy to see her ride home.

"I still think you going home right now is a bad idea,"

he said as he sank down in the chair next to the sofa. "I'd prefer you stay here for a while longer."

"I'm feeling fine and I need to go home."

"If I were your boss, I'd insist that you stay here," he countered.

"Thankfully you aren't the boss of me," she replied, "and I've taken advantage of your mother and the staff's kindness long enough. It's time for me to get back to my own home and my own routine. Tomorrow I intend to be back at my desk here as usual."

She lifted her chin in a show of defiance, as if she expected Trey to give her more of a hard time. He knew that look of steely strength that arrowed from her eyes. He'd seen it when she'd been negotiating with the hotel. Sweet little Debra had a will of iron when necessary.

"Besides," she continued, "if I don't get back to work, Kate will hire Haley to take over my position permanently."

Trey laughed at the very idea. "Yeah, like that's ever going to happen. You know my mother is totally devoted to you. You don't have to worry about your job."

"All the more reason that I need to get back to work for her. I'm feeling much better, my bruises are going away and it's time to get back to my own life."

"That's what scares me," he replied. "We still don't know who was responsible for your accident."

"And we may never know, but that doesn't mean I have to suddenly stop my life." She stood and grabbed both the duffel and her purse. "My car was targeted, not me, and I still believe that somehow it was a crazy mistake and some creep cut the lines on the wrong car. Besides, why not target my house, smother me in my sleep or shoot me when I'm driving to work?"

She shook her head. "This was done in a public place. For all we know it was done by a couple of whacked-out teenagers looking to cause trouble."

Trey stood and took the duffel bag from her. He knew she was right in that she couldn't just stop living because of what had happened, but he still didn't like the idea of her being all alone in her townhouse when they couldn't be sure that she wasn't the target of the brake failure. He definitely didn't believe that it was the work of teenagers looking for a thrill.

"Do you really think Haley wants your job?" Trey asked when they were in his car and headed to her townhouse.

"Of course she would," Debra replied without hesitation. "She's bright and ambitious, but there's no way I think her desire to have my job led to her trying to kill me, if that's where you're going with this conversation. I still refuse to believe that anyone tried to kill me."

Trey hoped she was right, but just to be on the safe side he made a mental note to tell Thad to check out Haley and any of the other interns that worked for his mother.

"What are you going to do about a car?" Trey asked as he pulled up to the curb in front of her home. He knew her vehicle would be in police impound for quite some time.

"The insurance company has totaled mine out, so I'll be getting a check in a week or two. I'm going to call for a rental later this afternoon and then maybe when the insurance pays out I'll go car hunting. It was time for a new car anyway."

They got out of the car and as he grabbed the luggage, she dug her keys out of her purse. When they reached the front door she unlocked it and pushed it open, then turned to him and took the duffel bag from him.

"Thanks for the ride home, Trey. I really appreciate it."

"Not so fast," he said and slid inside the foyer. "I want to do a check of the locks on your doors to make sure you're secure when you're home."

While he did want to check her doors and windows, the honest truth was he wasn't ready to leave her company yet. He walked through her living room and into the kitchen where he knew she had a back door.

He was intensely aware of her trailing behind him, having dropped the duffel bag and her purse in the living room. "I'm sure my locks on my doors are more than adequate and, besides, nobody has ever tried to break into my house," she said.

He checked the dead bolt and lock on her back door and then turned to look at her. "While I'm here I wouldn't mind a cup of tea or maybe some of that special mint hot cocoa of yours."

Her beautiful eyes narrowed. "Why didn't you just ask me to invite you in for something to drink instead of making up some stupid pretense of looking at my locks?"

"I did want to look at your locks," he protested and then laughed as she gazed at him in disbelief. "Okay, you busted me. I just wanted to sit with you for a little while."

"Why?"

He looked at her in surprise. The simple question wasn't easily answered, at least not completely honestly. He wanted to tell her that he loved watching her, that she was charmingly uncomplicated and he found her lack of artifice refreshing. He wanted to tell her that he'd much rather spend time with her than the woman he intended to marry, but he didn't.

"I enjoy your company," he finally replied. "And I'm formally declaring my intentions to run at a press conference next week and I have a feeling the next couple of days are the last I'm going to see of any real peace and quiet."

She pointed to a chair at the table. "I'll make the hot cocoa."

She worked with a graceful efficiency that hadn't been present on the night he'd danced with her. He smiled to himself as he thought of how often her feet had knocked into his in the short period he'd held her in his arms. Okay, so she wasn't going to win a dance contest anytime soon, but he didn't intend to enter one anytime soon, either.

To be as far along in her pregnancy as she claimed she was, she didn't show at all. "Are you eating enough?" he asked.

She turned from the counter to look at him in surprise. "I'm eating fine…. Why?"

His gaze drifted down to her abdomen. "You don't have any baby bump."

A blush colored her cheeks and one hand fell to her stomach. "The baby is just fine. I'm eating fine and if you saw me without my clothes you'd be able to see the baby bump." She turned back to the cabinets to get some cups.

It was the worst thing she could have said to him, because a vision of her naked took hold of his brain and refused to shake loose. Even with a huge pregnant belly, she'd still be beautiful naked. He clenched his fists, his short nails digging into his palms. He couldn't think about her like that. He had no right to entertain such thoughts.

By the time she carried two cups of cocoa to the table and sat down across from him, he'd managed to banish the evocative vision from his brain.

"How are you going to manage it all?" he asked. "I mean being a single working mother?"

She took a sip of her drink and then lowered her cup. "The way hundreds of other women do it every day of their lives. I'm blessed that I make enough money that I'll be able to hire a good nanny to take care of the baby while I'm at work. I'm equally blessed that I work for your mother, who for all intents and purposes was a single mother herself while your father was a senator."

Trey had a difficult time arguing with her about that. When he was young, weeks would go by when his father wasn't in the house. Of course none of them knew about the mistresses that were a part of his life.

"Do you know whether you're having a boy or a girl? Isn't this about the time they can tell the sex of the baby?" It was ridiculous, the little rivulet of jealousy that tingled through him as he thought of her carrying another man's child.

"I don't want to know the sex ahead of time," she replied. She took another sip and then stared down into her cup, as if the topic of conversation was making her uncomfortable. But, when she looked back at him it was with a soft smile. "All I care about is having a healthy baby."

"If you don't know the sex of the baby then how will you know what color to paint a nursery?"

"There are more colors than pink and blue," she replied. "I'm planning to paint the guest bedroom a bright yellow with lots of bold primary color accents. I've heard using bright colors stimulates a baby and helps them learn."

Emotions rose up inside him as he gazed into her eyes, where the love for her unborn child radiated. "You're going to make a fantastic mother."

"I know I will," she replied with an easy confidence. "I know what it's like to grow up feeling unloved and unwanted. I know all the things I didn't have as a child and this baby is going to be the most important, beloved thing in my world. I intend to spend each and every moment of the day and night letting him or her know that."

He remembered the vision he'd had of children laughing in a swimming pool, the joy that had filled him as he'd experienced the love of his imaginary family.

He wanted to be part of Debra's family. He wanted to be as important to her as the child she carried. It was the very last thing in the world he should want. He took another drink, finding it suddenly bitter.

Pushing back from the table, he stood, needing to get out of there, needing to get away from her. "I should go and let you get settled back in here," he said.

An oppressive force pushed against his chest and he knew it was the ever-present desire he felt whenever she was near him. It wasn't just a desire to hold her in his arms. He wanted to hear the ring of her laughter, watch her as she cooked. He wanted to know her opinions about everything from the weather to religion, from baby diapers to politics.

She was dangerous to him. He knew it in his heart,

in his very soul. She was dangerous to everything he'd dreamed about, everything he wanted in his future.

He left the kitchen and didn't realize she'd followed him to the front door until she called his name. He turned back to face her.

"Did I say something wrong?" she asked, obviously confused by his abruptness.

"No...nothing like that."

"Then what? I can tell something is wrong," she said, her green eyes so soft, so inviting.

Something snapped inside him. He pushed her up against the foyer wall as his mouth captured hers. He'd lost his mind, given in to the raw driving need inside him. There was no right or wrong, just his desire for her.

She gasped in surprise and he plunged his tongue into her mouth as she wrapped her arms around his neck and pulled him close...closer.

His hands slid up under the back of her sweater, reveling in the feel of her silky bare skin. She moaned in pleasure as his fingers worked to unclasp her bra.

Wild. He was wild with the taste, the scent of her. Reason had left his mind as he moved his hands around to cup her bare breasts.

Trapped between the wall and him, Debra made no attempt to escape, but rather turned her face to break their kiss and then pulled her sweater over her head. It dropped to the floor, along with her bra and once again their lips met in a fiery kiss that filled the void in his soul, that stoked the flames of his passion for her even higher.

He wanted her naked and gasping beneath him. He wanted a repeat of the night they'd shared. He'd wanted it since he'd put her in the cab the morning after.

"I want you, Debra," he finally managed to gasp. "I've wanted you again ever since we spent that night together."

It was as if the sound of his voice shattered her, splintered the moment and harsh reality intruded. She shoved against his chest and quickly leaned down to grab her sweater to cover her nakedness.

"This is madness," she whispered, her eyes glowing an overbright green. "I won't lie, Trey. I want you, too. But we both know we can't do this. It would be a mistake for both of us."

He suddenly felt small and selfish. He backed away from her. "Of course you're right." He released a deep sigh, but he wasn't sure if it was a sigh of regret because she'd stopped him or one of relief because she had.

"I know your hopes and dreams and I want those for you, Trey. I also know that I'm a complication you don't need in your life." She remained leaning against the wall. "You will do great things, Trey, and you need the right woman by your side. We both know I'm not that woman."

She straightened and took a step back from him. "This…energy or chemistry or whatever you want to call it between us can't be allowed to flourish. I think it would be best if we see as little of each other as possible in the future. I understand that we'll run into each other at the estate, but there's no reason for you to come here anymore."

"You're right," he said. "Of course you're right. And now I'll just say goodbye."

He turned and lunged through the door. He didn't look back as he strode to his car. Once inside he stared at the front door, which was now closed.

Closed. Debra had to be a closed book in his life. Making love to Debra wasn't fair to her and it certainly wouldn't be fair to Cecily.

*Duty versus passion,* he thought as he drove away from her townhouse. Passion waned, but duty and dreams lived on and ultimately Trey knew that Debra was right. He would do the right thing and choose his duty over any crazy desire that was probably fleeting.

# Chapter 11

It had been two days since Debra had almost lost her mind in Trey's arms, two days ago that they'd nearly made a terrible mistake.

She was back at her desk, although her thoughts weren't on her work and she forcefully kept them off Trey. Instead she wondered how much longer she could keep up the pretense that everything was just peachy in her personal life.

This morning when she'd driven through the side entrance to come to work, Jerry Cahill had been on duty. He'd motioned her on through and it was only when she parked and glanced in her rearview mirror that she'd seen him glaring at her.

Obviously he'd been questioned about her car accident and wasn't too happy about being called on the carpet. Still, he wasn't uppermost in her mind as she contemplated the past two days.

Things had begun disappearing again. Her favorite pink mug had been missing this morning when she'd gone to the cabinet to retrieve it for a morning cup of tea. Yesterday she'd been half-crazed when a throw pillow she normally placed in the center of her bed was found in the bottom of the clothes hamper.

She was obviously suffering some sort of a mental breakdown and it not only frightened her for herself, but also for her baby. Her hand fell to her lap and she rubbed her belly in a circular motion. Her slacks had felt tighter this morning. The baby was growing and she was losing her mind.

What if she cracked up altogether? What if she wound up in some mental institute? Then what would happen to her baby? If she gave birth would somebody hand the baby to Barry to raise because everyone thought the baby was his?

She shuddered at the very thought.

Despite her desire to keep Trey out of her thoughts, he kept intruding. She wasn't sure what caused her more stress: the thoughts of losing her mind or her overwhelming feelings for Trey.

He'd held an unexpected press conference the day before and had officially announced his decision to run for the office of state senator. Cecily had been at his side, as she should have been, as it was supposed to be. They had looked perfect together, poised and at ease in front of the cameras.

But, for the first time in her life, Debra understood why some women chose to be mistresses. It wasn't always about money or the thrill of forbidden fruit, sometimes it was just about love.

She loved Trey enough to want any piece of himself

that he could give to her. Fortunately she loved herself enough not to compromise her true wants and needs, her very soul, by becoming his mistress. And in any case, she knew the core of him, she knew who he was as a man and knew he would never take a mistress. It wasn't in his moral fiber to do such a thing.

Debra was an all-or-nothing kind of woman when it came to love and commitment. Besides, Trey hadn't spoken to her about love, he'd told her he wanted her, that he desired her, and that would never be enough for her.

The Friday morning flew by as she focused on the usual work that kept Kate's schedule running smoothly. At noon she stopped and went into the kitchen where Myra fixed her a sandwich and some coleslaw. She ate quickly, grateful that she didn't encounter any other members of the family, and then returned to her office.

She wasn't in the right frame of mind to put up with Sam's moodiness and although she'd spoken to Thad a couple of times over the past few days, he'd had no new information to give her as to who might have been responsible for her car accident, an accident she still refused to believe was a specific attack on her personally.

She'd just settled back at her desk when a knock fell on her door. Kate poked her head in. "How about we have a chat in my office?" she asked.

"Sure," Debra agreed. She picked up a memo pad.

"You don't need to bother with that. We won't be talking about anything that requires note-taking."

"Okay." Debra got up from her desk and followed Kate into her office. As Kate sat behind her desk Debra sank down into one of the chairs in front of her.

"I just wanted to check in with you and see how

you're doing. How you're feeling." Kate leaned back in her chair, obviously relaxed.

"To be honest, I think my pregnancy hormones are making me a little crazy," Debra replied. "I've been misplacing things and finding them in strange places. I'm having a little trouble concentrating, although it isn't affecting any of my work for you," she hurriedly added.

Kate smiled. "I wasn't concerned about that. I remember when I was pregnant with Sam I had the same kind of issues."

"Really?" Debra asked.

"Really. Of course, Trey was two at the time and he didn't help my sanity any. I remember one day I took him to the park to play and then an hour or so later I got into my car and realized I was about to drive off without him." She laughed and shook her head. "Thank goodness I had Maddie here to keep me at least partially sane."

Debra's relief was enormous. Maybe all of the strange things that had been happening to her really were due to hormones gone wild.

"One of the things I wanted to talk to you about was next Sunday I'd like to have a family continental breakfast on the patio. The weather has been so unusually lovely I thought it would be nice to get everyone together and discuss the ramifications of my running for president."

"Is there something you need me to do? Pastries to be ordered or anything like that?"

"No, Myra will take care of everything. I'm just telling you because Sunday is your day off and I'd really like for you to be there."

"I'd love to come," Debra replied, pleased to be included.

"My decision will affect you as well as the family," Kate continued, "so I want you to have a voice in the process. Are you planning on taking off time when the baby is born?"

"Maybe just a couple of weeks," Debra replied, although the idea of leaving the baby at all with anyone for anything was painful.

"You know, there's no reason for you to leave the baby while you work here. We can set up one of the bedrooms as a nursery and Maddie would love to take care of a little one again."

"Really? So I could bring the baby to work with me?" Debra's heart expanded with happiness.

"I don't see a problem at all." Kate grinned. "My goodness, we've been together so long, Debra, I feel like you're giving birth to my grandbaby. It will be nice to have a little one in the house once again."

Debra prayed the expression on her face didn't change, although the weight of her lies about the father of her baby slammed into the bottom of her heart. "Your family has always been like my own. You know I think of you as a surrogate mother."

A wash of pain flickered across Kate's face, gone so quickly Debra wondered if she'd imagined it. She stared at a family photo on her desk. "I always did want a little girl." She looked back at Debra. "But fate gave me three strapping boys who have been the joys of my life."

"And this baby will be the joy of my life," Debra replied, feeling terrible that Kate would never know that the child she carried *was* her first grandbaby. "But, you can count on me to juggle motherhood and work with no problem."

Kate gave her an affectionate smile. "It never occurred to me otherwise."

Minutes later back at her desk, Debra thought of the Sunday morning breakfast. She would have to see Trey again. It would be the first time she'd seen him since they'd practically attacked each other in her foyer.

He'd started it, but she'd desperately wanted him to finish it. She'd wanted him to drag her up the stairs to her bedroom and make love to her. It had only been a surprising flash of sanity that had saved them both from making another mistake. Whatever it was between them was strong and just a little bit frightening in that Debra had almost no control in her desire for him.

At least Kate had managed to put her at ease a bit as far as her forgetfulness was concerned. She smiled as she envisioned Kate getting into her car to leave a park and suddenly realizing the car seat where Trey should be was empty. Now that was the height of absentmindedness.

By the time six o'clock came she was ready to call it a day. She knew the unusual fatigue she suffered was from her pregnancy, a fatigue that hopefully would pass when she went into her second trimester in the next few weeks.

On her way home she thought about stopping in at some department store to pick up a few pairs of maternity pants and skirts. It wasn't going to be long before the clothes she owned would no longer fit her belly bump.

It was a fleeting thought. She was too tired to shop. She'd make plans tomorrow to take off an hour early and shop then. It would be nice to have something comfortable to wear to the breakfast on Sunday.

At the moment she just wanted to get home, eat some dinner and curl up on the sofa in front of the television where hopefully a good sitcom or crime drama would chase away thoughts of the man she loved, the man she was certain would be the next North Carolina senator… as long as she stayed out of his life.

Trey felt as if he were living some sort of weird double life. During the days he worked at Adair Enterprises and then in the past three evenings he'd had two business dinners to attend and had dined with Cecily the other night.

He hadn't slept with Cecily since the night he'd slept with Debra. He'd made a million excuses to Cecily about their lack of intimacy. Too busy, too tired, not good for his public image to be seen coming and going from her house before they were married, the excuses had fallen from his lips with a surprising ease.

He knew that Cecily was frustrated with him, but she took each of his excuses in stride, telling him coyly that they'd catch up on lost time once they were married.

The truth of the matter was that Trey couldn't imagine making love to Cecily when his passion and his emotions were still tied to Debra.

And it was emotion and fear for her that had him doing something crazy each night. When darkness fell he found himself parked across the street from Debra's townhouse where he'd remain until the wee hours of the morning.

He knew it was crazy, but he couldn't help himself. Even though there was no concrete evidence that somebody specific had targeted Debra by cutting her brake line, Trey believed danger had touched her and wasn't finished with her yet.

He was afraid for her, and so he had taken it upon himself to be her secret nighttime bodyguard. Anyone who got too close to her house while she slept peacefully inside would have him to deal with.

He had a conceal-and-carry permit and a 9 mm with him on these nightly surveillance details. He was dead serious about seeing that no harm came to Debra or the baby she carried.

The only downfall of these nightly visits was that each morning when he got to his office he directed Rhonda to hold all his calls for a couple of hours so he could catch up on his sleep.

Tonight was like the past two nights. It was just after midnight and although it was Saturday the neighborhood was quiet. Debra had turned off the light in the house around nine or so, letting him know she was having an early night.

He yawned and slumped down a bit in the seat, trying to find a more comfortable position to sustain for the next couple of hours.

Was he being foolish? Maybe, he conceded. But he'd rather be foolish than take a chance and have any harm come to Debra. Did he intend to do this nightly vigil every night for the rest of his life?

Definitely not, but he would be here until something or someone managed to make him believe that the cut brake lines had been as Debra had believed, an accident of the wrong car being targeted and not something personal against her. Only then would he stop this madness and get on with his life.

His life.

He stared unseeingly at the center of his steering wheel. He should be thrilled with the direction his life was traveling. Since the dinner party and the press conference the donation dollars had begun to pour in, Chad had put together a machine made of devoted people to work campaign headquarters, which was being set up in a downtown storefront.

Banners and signs had been made to hang on the outside of the building and it always jarred him just a bit to pull up and see his own face smiling from one of those signs.

Cecily was more than ready to step in as a supportive wife and partner and there was no question that she would be an asset to his career. She had money, connections and the personality that would serve him well.

Yes, everything was falling nicely into place. So, where was his happiness? He'd assumed he'd be euphoric at this point in the process, but his happiness seemed to be sadly absent.

He glanced back at Debra's house and frowned as he saw a faint red glow coming from someplace inside, a glow that hadn't been there minutes before.

Was Debra awake? Had she turned on some kind of light? If so, it was a strange red light. A lick of flame danced before the front window.

*Fire!* It was fire.

His mind screamed the word as he fumbled with his cell phone and called 911. As he gave Debra's address to the dispatcher he got out of the car and raced for the front door.

With the call made, he tossed his cell phone in the

grass and pounded on the door with his fists, calling her name at the top of his lungs.

The odor of smoke drifted through the door, making his blood freeze. Was she unconscious? Already overcome by smoke that had risen to her upstairs bedroom?

Panic seared through him as he rang the doorbell and then pounded once again, screaming her name as the flames at the window grew bigger and more intense.

Vaguely aware of lights going on in the houses around hers, conscious of the distant sound of sirens, he picked up a flowerpot that was on her stoop and raced around to the back of the townhouse.

His heart thumped painfully fast with every step. He finally made it to the kitchen windows where just inside he'd sat at the table and had coffee with her. He raised the heavy pot and threw it through one of the windows, shattering the glass and allowing him entry.

The air in the kitchen wasn't bad, but when he entered the living room the smoke tickled the back of his throat and obscured his vision.

The curtains at the windows blazed and dropped malicious imps of flames onto the carpet below. Although his first impulse was to race up the stairs to Debra's room, instead he ran to the front door, unlocked it and pulled it open so that the arriving firemen could easily access the house.

Swirling cherry-red lights announced the arrival of the emergency vehicles as Trey raced up the stairs, the smoke thicker now, causing him to pause as he was overcome with a spasm of coughing.

He clung to the banister until the spasm had passed and then continued upward. There were three doors upstairs and thankfully all of them were closed, hopefully keeping most of the smoke in the narrow hallway.

A night-light shone in a wall socket, guiding him forward despite the thickening smoke. The first door proved to be the guest room.

Across the hall was a bathroom where he quickly wet a hand towel with cold water. He entered the door at the end of the hallway and saw Debra unmoving in the bed.

His heart stopped beating for a second. Was she dead? Overcome by smoke? But the smoke was only now just drifting faintly into the room.

"Debra?" He ran to the side of her bed, but she didn't move at the sound of her name. "Debra!" He shook her and gasped in relief as she roused.

"Trey?" She sat up in obvious confusion and shoved a tangle of hair off her face. "Trey, what's happening? Why are you in my bedroom?"

"Fire. There's a fire downstairs. We've got to get you out of here." He didn't wait for her to get out of the bed. He handed her the wet cloth. "Put this over your nose and mouth," he said and then he scooped her up in his arms and rushed down the hallway toward the stairs.

On the lower level he could hear the sound of firemen at work and when he reached the living room the fire was out and only the smoke and soot remained.

Trey carried Debra directly out the front door, where emergency vehicles had been joined by news vans. It wasn't until he tried to lay her down in the grass that he realized she was crying.

"It's okay," he said, shouting to be heard above the din. He was aware of a familiar reporter standing nearby, but his focus was solely on Debra. "You're safe now," he said in an effort to comfort her.

She shook her head and clung to him, her sobs of fear breaking his heart. "You saved my life," she said, the words coming out in deep gasps. "You saved our baby's life."

In the glow of the headlights around them he saw the horror on her face as the words left her lips. Everything else faded away...the lights, the people and the sound. The entire world shrunk to just him and her and the words that had just fallen from her lips.

She released her hold on him and instead wrapped her arms around herself as she shivered, refusing to meet his gaze.

"*Our* baby?"

She looked up at him. Her tear-filled gaze held his as she slowly nodded her head and then began to weep once again. He stood, his head reeling with the information that the baby she carried was his. Not Barry's, but *his* baby.

He helped her to her bare feet as the fire chief approached them. "There's not a lot of damage," he said. "It looks worse than it is, mostly smoke. We didn't even have to use our hoses. We got it out with fire extinguishers. It was intentionally set, an accelerant used. I'm guessing gasoline by the smell of things," he said to Trey and then turned his attention to Debra. "We'll do a full investigation but I'm afraid you'll need to find someplace else to sleep tonight."

"I'll take you to Mom's," Trey said. He took Debra's arm and looked at the fire chief. "You'll see to it that a guard is posted for the duration? I broke a window in the back to get inside."

"A police officer is already standing by. We'll make sure everything is secure before we leave here."

"And you'll let us know what your investigation discovers?"

"Absolutely, Mr. Winston." He smiled sympathetically at Debra. "We should be finished with our documenting the crime scene by midday tomorrow. If you get a good cleaning crew in here you should be able to return home either tomorrow night or by Monday."

"Thank you," she replied, her voice barely audible among the other noise.

"Let's get out of here," Trey said. He found his cell phone where he'd tossed it in the grass and then they started for his car.

Before they could get there a bright beam of a camera light flashed in Trey's face and a microphone was thrust in his direction.

The reporter he'd seen earlier smiled like the cat that had swallowed the canary. "Mr. Winston, would you like to make a statement about Ms. Prentice's pregnancy?"

"No comment," Trey growled and grabbing Debra closer to his side, he hurried her to his car.

Once she was in the passenger seat, he slid behind the wheel and started the engine with a roar. He pulled away from the curb, a myriad of emotions racing through him and he was afraid to say anything to her until he'd sorted them all out.

She shivered and he didn't know if it was because she was clad only in a copper-colored short nightgown or if it was because she didn't know what to expect next.

Hell, he didn't know what to expect next. There was a part of him that was filled with great joy at the idea of her carrying his child and there was also a part of him that battled anger that she'd intended to keep the baby a secret from him, to pretend that the baby belonged to her old boyfriend.

He couldn't begin to think about the fact that somebody had gotten into her house without him seeing them. That person or persons had set her living room on fire. He hoped the initial assessment was wrong and that it had been faulty wiring or something other than a man-made flame.

For several long minutes they rode in silence and it was finally he who broke it. "You were never going to tell me the truth about the baby?"

"The last thing I wanted to do was screw things up for you," she replied. "I figured it would just be easier to pretend the baby was Barry's and then you get to have your shining future with Cecily and everyone would be happy."

The fact that she'd lied for him to keep his dream alive stole away any anger he might harbor against her. She was willing to sacrifice the Winston power and influence for his happiness, to assure that he reached his dreams.

She'd been willing to go through all the struggles and sacrifices as a single mother to allow him to reach his own goals.

Once again silence fell between them. His brain felt half-contused from bouncing around in his skull. Too many things had occurred in too short a time.

"I'll arrange a cleaning crew to come to your place as soon as the fire department releases it," he said. "I'll also see to it that a security system is installed." He didn't even want to acknowledge at this point that somebody had apparently entered her house and set fire to the curtains.

He pulled up to the side entrance of the estate but didn't turn off the car, nor did she make a move to leave. "That reporter, he heard what I said." Her voice was a whisper. "It will be all over the news tomorrow." She stared straight ahead, her face pale in the illumination from the dashboard. She finally turned to him, her eyes wide and holding a soft vulnerability. "What do you want me to do?"

"What do you mean?" He eyed her curiously.

"I could lie. I could say that the reporter misunderstood what I said, that I was confused by the fire and everything that was going on."

"That's definitely not going to happen," he replied. And it was at that moment he knew he wasn't going to marry Cecily. Even if he got to be where he wanted to be in the political arena, he didn't want the cool, absolutely perfect Cecily next to him.

"Marry me," he said.

Her eyes widened. "Don't talk crazy."

"It's not crazy," he responded. "You're the mother of my child. We'd make a family and you'd never have to worry about anything."

"That's a ridiculous idea and I won't marry you." She opened the car door and in the dome light she looked ghostly pale and exhausted. "Right now I'm going inside to sleep and in the morning I have to figure out who got into my house and tried to burn it down with me still inside. You deal with the press however you want to. I'll follow your lead. I just can't deal with anything else tonight."

She got out of the car and slammed the door. He remained sitting in the car long after she'd disappeared inside the house.

A baby…a fire… His head ached with the night's events. Cecily was going to be angry when he broke it off with her, but that was the least of his problems at the moment.

What concerned him more than anything was the fact that he believed twice now somebody had tried to kill not just Debra, but the child she carried, as well… His child.

Tomorrow he'd deal with Cecily. Tomorrow he'd also discuss his intention to be a huge part of the baby's life. He'd have to deal with whatever the news reports contained and he needed to speak to Thad about this newest threat against Debra.

The one thing he didn't care about at the moment was any ramifications this might have on his career. And the odd thing was that he wasn't sure he cared.

# Chapter 12

*"Marry me."*

Debra awoke with the ring of Trey's words echoing in her head. She was in the same bedroom where she'd stayed following her car accident and as she thought of everything that had happened the night before she wanted to pull the blankets up over her head and never get up again.

A glance at the clock on the nightstand let her know it was after ten. Obscenely late for her to still be in bed. She should be at her desk, she thought and then realized it was Sunday. She should at least be at her house finding out what the fire marshal had learned. She should be anywhere but under the covers thinking about how often she'd fantasized Trey saying those two words to her.

*"Marry me."*

In her fantasies he'd spoken the words because he

loved her, because he couldn't imagine a life without her. In her dreams he'd held her in his arms and kissed her with love and commitment as they planned a future together.

In reality she knew he'd said the words in an effort to begin damage control and perhaps because he wanted to be a part of his baby's life. He'd proposed to the baby inside of her, but not to her.

There had been no love offered from him. If she'd agreed it would have been like a business deal to him, a merger to get accomplished for the best results possible.

She was worth more than that. The off-the-cuff proposal had stabbed through her loving heart like an arrow. She wouldn't be his lover and she refused to be an inconvenient wife to him.

Hopefully, despite her pregnancy, he could make things right with Cecily and continue on his way. Surely he could figure out a way to make Cecily forgive him for a single night's indiscretion. Of course eventually there would be custody issues to deal with, weekends and holidays when the child would be with him… With them, instead of with her.

She turned over on her back and stared up at the ceiling, reluctant to face any part of the day. Somebody had tried to kill her last night. Somebody had come into her home and started a fire in the wee hours of the morning. If Trey hadn't been there she probably would have died of smoke inhalation long before the flames reached her bedroom.

She frowned thoughtfully. What had Trey been doing at her house at that time of night? How had he managed to be at exactly the right place at exactly the right time when it should have been the last place he'd be? It didn't make sense, but then nothing about her life lately had made any sense at all.

Somebody had gotten into her house. Who? Who had crept in and started a fire that would have certainly been the death of her if Trey hadn't rescued her?

A knock fell on her door and Kate came in carrying a cup of hot tea. Debra wanted to hide her face in shame. Instead she pulled herself up to a sitting position and took the cup of tea that Kate offered her.

Kate sat on a tufted chair next to the bed. "Well, my dear, you've created quite a stir."

"Kate, I'm so sorry," she said miserably.

"Sorry about what?" Kate smiled at her kindly. "I should be angry with you for not telling me that you're carrying my first grandbaby, but I'm not. I understand why you lied about the father of the baby."

"I didn't want to mess things up for Trey and now I've ruined everything," she said, fighting back a wave of tears that threatened with every word. She set the tea on the nightstand, afraid of spilling it and making even more of a mess of everything.

"Nonsense," Kate said briskly. "Oh, there's no denying that some adjustments will need to be made, but Trey is intelligent and flexible. This won't stop him from getting where he wants to go."

She pursed her lips and held Debra's gaze. "You know, somehow I'm not surprised by the news. There is an energy between you and my son that I've noticed every time the two of you are in the same room."

"It was just one night. One crazy, stupid night," Debra replied. "Only I would be stupid enough not to think about birth control."

"Debra, darling, you aren't the first woman in the world to make a mistake where that's concerned."

"But…the press," Debra protested.

Kate gave her a look of distaste. "The news is out everywhere with such salacious headlines that one would think the two of you committed some heinous murder rather than slept together. Trey has a press conference this afternoon at four to address the issue."

Kate motioned to the cup on the nightstand. "Drink that before it gets cold." Debra grabbed the cup and raised it to her lips as Kate continued. "Trey spoke to Cecily this morning. He told her that under the circumstances he was breaking off their relationship for the time being. He told her he needed some time to figure out all the ways this will impact him."

Debra swallowed hard. "How did she take it?"

Kate leaned back in the chair. "According to Trey she was a bit upset, but in the end quite gracious about the whole thing. She said she still intended on being involved in his campaign and wished him well in his personal life if they didn't manage to reconnect. Cecily is a survivor, Kate. She's a barracuda who will find a mate based on criteria that will make her the most successful in the endgame."

"But surely she's terribly hurt and Trey has to make her understand that I don't mean anything to him, that it was all just a terrible mistake. Surely they can work through it. She is in love with him," Debra replied.

Kate smiled. "I seriously doubt that Cecily is in love with Trey. She is in love with who he will become and where that would take her. If they don't get back together she'll move on and will be quite fine, I'm sure."

She stood. "I'm not sure how you and Trey intend to

work things out between you, but I'll have you know
that I intend to embrace that baby with all the love I
have to give. And now, speaking of Trey, he and Thad
are in the sitting room and want to talk to you."

She moved toward the doorway. "Haley happened to
have a pair of sweats and a T-shirt that you can put on.
Anything I own would be too short on you. The clothes
are laid out in the bathroom. Once you're showered and
dressed, we'll see you downstairs."

The minute she left the room Debra set her cup down
and flopped her head back on the pillow. She didn't
want to face Trey. She didn't want to talk to Thad. She
just wanted to hide for the rest of her life.

But she couldn't hide. Reluctantly she got out of bed
and carried her teacup with her into the bathroom and
set it on the counter while she got into the shower.

She hadn't noticed the odor of smoke that had clung
to her until it was washing away down the drain. She'd
spent her morning thinking about Trey and all the ramifications of her secret unexpectedly being spilled. Now
it was time to think about who had been in her house
and who wanted her dead.

Haley's gray sweatpants fit comfortably and the navy
T-shirt hid the fact that Debra didn't have on a bra. Trey
had carried her out the night before in her nightgown
and so she hadn't been wearing one. Kate had even provided a pair of flip-flops for her to wear.

She slid on the shoes and then walked down the stairs
with dread weighing down each footstep. She dreaded
seeing Trey again and she knew that Thad was here to
talk about the fact that somebody had tried to kill her.
The fire made the cut brake lines very personal and
this thought chilled her to the bone. Two attempts on

her life… Who could be behind them? And why would anyone go to such trouble to kill her?

Trey was seated on the sofa and Thad in a chair opposite him. Both of them stood as she entered the room. She motioned them back down and then sat on the opposite end of the sofa from Trey, carefully keeping her gaze away from him.

He probably hated her for spilling her secret at a place and a time where a reporter would overhear. He probably hated her for making him scramble to deflect any negativity that might come in his direction at this important time in his life. She was also the reason he'd had to break it off with Cecily. Such a mess she'd made of everything.

"How are you feeling?" he asked.

"I'm okay," she replied and finally forced herself to look at him. There was no anger shining from his eyes, there was nothing but a gentle caring. *For the baby,* she thought. He would put aside any anger he might feel toward her for the sake of the baby she carried.

"We need to talk about what happened last night," Thad said.

She nodded and then looked at Trey again. "Why were you there last night? How did you happen to be there at just the right time?"

She was surprised to see a faint color creep up his neck. "I'd been parked outside your house every night since you quit staying here. I just had a bad feeling after the car accident and so I was spending my nights parked outside your place, watching to make sure nobody bothered you."

She stared at him in stunned surprise. He'd been doing that for her and he hadn't even known yet that the baby was his. He'd been there each night, keeping vigil over her. Maybe he did care about her just a little bit.

"Thank goodness he was there," Thad said. "I touched base with the fire marshal this morning and the fire was definitely set at the foot of the curtains in the living room, probably with a pile of papers and gasoline."

"I just don't understand this," she replied. "I mean, if somebody wanted to kill me, then why set the fire? Why not just creep up the stairs and stab me while I slept? Why not shoot me with a gun and be done with it?"

"I'm guessing that whoever is behind all of this wants your death to look like an accident. The point of ignition in the living room was just beneath an outlet. If the fire department hadn't gotten there as quickly as they did because of Trey's phone call, then the fire chief might not have smelled the gasoline and it might have been written up as a tragic electrical fire."

Debra rubbed her hand across her forehead, where a small headache was forming. "I don't understand any of this."

"My team checked the house. Other than the window Trey broke to get inside and him unlocking the front door to enable the firemen to enter, there appeared to be no point of entry that wasn't a normal one, which leads me to believe somebody got in using a key. So, my question to you now is who has keys to your house?"

She stared at Thad. A key? Somebody had used a key to get into her home? The misplaced items, the guest list in the freezer… Was it possible somebody had been accessing her house all along? Was it possible she wasn't losing her mind after all, but rather was being made to believe she was going mad?

"Strange things have been happening for the last several weeks," she said. "Cups disappear and reappear in the cabinets, a paperweight on my desk vanished and then two days later was back where it belonged. I thought I was losing my mind. I believed I was going insane."

"Why didn't you say anything before now?" Trey asked in surprise.

"Because I thought it was me. I thought I was doing those things to myself." She slumped back on the sofa, horrified and yet relieved. "Keys, your mom has a key and Haley has one. I imagine several people on staff have a key to my house because occasionally they're sent to pick something up from there."

"What about Barry?" Trey asked.

She looked at him and slowly nodded. "Yes, Barry has a key. He never gave it back to me after we broke up." Her head reeled. Was it possible Barry had known she intended to break up with him and had pulled an end run by breaking up with her before she got a chance? Was it possible he was so angry with her that he could be behind these deadly assaults on her?

At this point she didn't know what to think. "Can I get into the house?"

"You won't want to stay there until some cleanup work is done," Trey replied. "I've got a crew in there now. They should be finished by sometime late this afternoon. I suggest you stay here for tonight and tomorrow you should be able to go back home."

"You'll have a new security system that Trey is having installed. It will alert you if anyone tries to get into a door or window in the house. He's also made sure that all the locks on the doors are being changed. Whoever has a key now will find that it doesn't work if they try to get in again." Thad looked down at the notes he'd taken and then back at her.

"Right now I'm going to see how many house keys I can retrieve from the people you've said have one and each person better hope they have good alibis for the night of the dinner and last night." He rose from the chair. "And on that note I'm out of here and will check in with both of you later."

Debra turned to look at Trey, unsure what to say to make anything better. "I'm sorry about you and Cecily. Hopefully you two can work things out despite everything that's happened. I never meant for any of this to get between the two of you. I hope you told her that I don't expect anything from you."

Trey held up a hand to halt her ramble. "Cecily is fine," he replied. "I told her I needed a break to figure things out, but right now I'm more worried about you than any other relationship. I think you need to take the day and rest. Later tonight if everything is ready and I know that the security is up and working, then, if you want, I can take you home."

"How bad is the damage?"

"Actually less than what I initially thought. The only area that was damaged was around the front windows. Your living room will need a new paint job, but the firemen got enough windows open quickly after putting out the flames that the smoke damage was minimal."

She nodded and stared at the coffee table. "I'm sure we'll have lots of things to discuss and work out in the future, but right now everything just seems too overwhelming."

"Which is why I would encourage you to eat a good

breakfast and then maybe go back to bed for some extra sleep." His voice was tender and filled with a caring that both soothed and somehow hurt at the same time.

He cared about her because of the baby, she reminded herself. As she thought about the car accident and the fire, she only hoped she managed to stay alive long enough to give birth to a healthy full-term baby.

Trey stood in Debra's living room, checking to make sure everything had been done that could be done to clean up the mess and secure her safety. The doorknobs had already been changed out and the security company was finishing up its work.

He'd even had a painting crew come in to Sheetrock and paint the wall that had been damaged. At least the house now smelled of new paint instead of smoke.

His press conference had gone as smoothly as he'd expected it to go. He'd made an announcement that Debra Prentice was carrying his child and while the two had no plans to marry he intended to be a loving, supportive father to his baby and a friend and support to Debra.

Surprisingly, in the world of political news it had made only a small splash. Both he and Debra were single, consenting adults and that fact took any salacious elements out of the situation.

Cecily had even made a statement of support for him, showing her to be a classy lady as she lauded the many good qualities he possessed and the fact that she and Trey had agreed to take their personal relationship one day at a time.

Trey knew she was giving a signal that she would stand by her man. But as much as Trey appreciated her loyalty, after speaking with her and telling her they needed to take a break from each other, he'd felt more relief than he'd expected.

He hadn't realized how much pressure everyone had been subtly putting on him to pop the question, make a formal announcement of an engagement. Now with that pressure off him, he realized whether good or bad for his campaign he wasn't ready to marry Cecily.

All in all, politically he'd weathered the storm, but that didn't mean all was well. There was no question he was frightened for Debra and he'd spent much of the day working names of people around in his mind, as if the guilty person would suddenly appear in his head like a magical vision.

At the moment his suspicions were on Haley, who had jokingly told Debra time and time again that she was after Debra's job.

As he thought of the sequence of events as he knew them it made a strange kind of sick sense. How better to undermine Debra's confidence in her ability to do her job than by gas-lighting her into thinking she was losing her mind?

Maybe the results of that hadn't worked as quickly as she'd hoped. Haley had known that Debra would be at the dinner party and Haley also knew Debra's car.

He didn't believe that Haley had actually crawled under the car herself, but she was young and pretty and probably had a male friend who could do it.

What he'd like to do was grab Haley by the scruff of her neck and force her to tell the truth one way or the other. But Thad had made it clear to Trey that he was to stay away from the investigation because it was now in the hands of the Raleigh Police Department.

Just when Trey had convinced himself that Haley was responsible, he'd change his mind and think about Jerry Cahill. The Secret Service agent had made it clear that he wanted to date Debra, and Debra had made it equally clear to him that she wasn't interested. Cahill would know how to cut brake lines. He probably even had the ability to break into a house and leave no trace behind.

And then there was the possibility of it being somebody not even on Trey's radar. The only thing he knew for certain was that Debra was in danger and he was doing everything he could to assure that her home was secure.

Although as a crime-scene investigator Thad wouldn't specifically be driving any investigation, Trey also knew his brother would make sure that things were being done right and that the people who needed to be interviewed and checked out would be.

Thad might not spend a lot of time with the family, but when anyone was threatened, he was definitely a Winston at heart, ready to jump in and protect them at any moment.

"Hey, thought you might be here."

Trey looked at Sam in surprise as he walked through Debra's front door where a technician from the security company was at work. "What are you doing here?"

Sam shrugged. "I got bored at home, so I figured I'd take a ride and I wound up here. I brought you a present."

He tossed a plastic bag to Trey, who looked inside and laughed as he saw a package of tiny diapers. "Thanks, I think we're going to need a lot of these."

Sam and Trey walked outside into the front yard

and away from the men working in the house. "Do you have any ideas about who was responsible for this?" Sam asked.

"Lots of ideas, but not a real clue," Trey replied.

"What about that guy Debra was dating before?"

"Barry Chambers. Debra insists he wouldn't be involved in anything like this."

"What about Cecily?"

Trey laughed. "Definitely not her style, besides what would be her motive?"

Sam raised an eyebrow. "Uh…you're having a baby with another woman?"

"The things happening to Debra started long before anyone knew that Debra was pregnant. In any case, Thad and the police are involved, so hopefully they'll figure things out."

Sam pointed to the cameras located on each corner of the house and above the front door. "It's going to be easier to break into Fort Knox than this house when you get finished with it."

"That's the idea," Trey told him.

"Why don't you just marry her and put her in that secured mansion you bought?" Sam asked.

"I asked her and she said no."

Sam's eyebrows rose. "That's a surprise. I didn't think anyone had ever told you no," Sam said with a touch of dry humor.

Trey smiled with affection at his brother. Sam's calm moods came so rarely and when they did he remembered how much he loved Sam, how much he wished for better things for the brother who had served his country with honor and come home damaged. "I can't believe I'm going to be a father."

"You'll be good at it," Sam assured him. "I'll tell you one thing, I like Debra a hell of a lot better than I ever liked Cecily."

Trey looked at Sam in surprise. "Why don't you like Cecily?" He'd thought the entire family was happy when he'd started dating the beautiful, wealthy socialite.

Sam scowled. "Cecily has eyes like a shark… Cold and dead. She smiles prettily, but the smiles never quite reach her eyes. She reminds me of…" His voice trailed off and he shook his head. "Never mind," he said, tension in his voice.

"What, Sam? She reminds you of what?"

"Nothing. I've got to get out of here. I just wanted to deliver the baby's first gift to you."

"Sam?" Trey called after his brother as he turned on his heels and headed for his car. Sam didn't look back or acknowledge Trey again. He got into his car and drove off.

Trey couldn't begin to imagine what demons chased his brother since his imprisonment and torture at enemy hands. Apparently he saw something in Cecily's dark eyes that brought back those terrible demons to his head.

He wondered if Sam would feel the same way about Cecily if she had blue or green eyes. He just wished that somehow, someway, his little brother could find some help and ultimately peace in his heart.

He checked his watch. He had a seven-o'clock meeting with Chad to discuss any further ramifications of Debra's pregnancy and Trey's impending fatherhood and how it might affect the campaign going forward.

As far as Trey was concerned, his press conference had addressed the issue and now it would be a nonissue.

He still wanted his dreams of becoming a state senator, but he also wanted to be the best father in the world.

When he'd asked Debra to marry him and she'd turned him down, there was no question that he'd been hurt and that had made him realize he cared about her more than he wanted to admit to himself.

But it was obvious she didn't feel the same way about him. There had been no hesitation when she'd told him no. Her firm reply had left no room to even discuss the matter.

She didn't love him. It was as simple as that. They'd had a night of passion and it was a passion that still simmered inside him, still boiled between them, but ultimately she didn't love him.

And he wasn't sure why that fact ached in his heart. While he cared about Debra deeply, surely he wasn't in love with her?

He thought of how she'd looked the night of the dinner dance, with that spill of emerald-green silk clinging to her curves. Despite her lack of dancing skills, she'd felt so right in his arms.

He remembered how much he enjoyed sitting in her cozy kitchen, talking about anything and everything except politics. He'd felt relaxed and at home. Was it the surroundings or was it the woman herself?

Cecily had seen him as a candidate, as a means to an end—her end. And he'd accepted that as being enough because he knew that ultimately they would make a good team.

But was being a good team enough for him? Why had he so easily accepted a relationship without love? He was fairly certain the answer was in his own childhood, where it was clear his mother and father didn't love one another but had stayed together because of an understanding between them.

He stared back at Debra's house and remembered that hot, sexy moment when they'd almost made love in her foyer. She'd said they couldn't do that anymore, that they couldn't allow themselves to lose control, but that was before he and Cecily had called it quits.

Debra might not love him, but she definitely felt passion for him. Why couldn't they follow through on that again? Every muscle in his body tensed and his blood flowed hot through his veins as he thought of making love to her once more.

He'd like that. He'd like the pleasure of stroking her smooth skin once again, hearing her soft moans of pleasure as he took possession of her.

Now all he had to do was somehow convince her that she wanted him again, too.

# *Chapter 13*

It was Sunday night and Trey was on his way to the estate to take Debra back home. It was almost nine o'clock and while she knew she should be growing tired, she'd already spent most of the day in bed resting.

From what Trey had told her on the phone, he'd spent most of his day making sure her townhouse was ready for her return. She didn't know how she would ever repay him for everything he'd accomplished in such a short amount of time.

She knew he'd probably pulled all kinds of strings to get the place clean and secure in a single day so that she could get back where she belonged.

Maybe she should be afraid to go home since it had only been the night before that somebody had crept into her house and tried to kill her. But Thad was hunting down anyone who might have had a key to her place, new doorknobs and locks had been installed and according to Trey if a squirrel managed to so much as brush against a door or window the police would arrive within minutes.

Besides, she knew that Trey would never allow her to return to a place that wasn't safe, not as long as she carried his baby.

She absently caressed her stomach as she sat in the family sitting room waiting for Trey's arrival. Kate had left earlier for a charity event and Sam had gone to his room. Maddie had retired for the night and the house held an uncharacteristic silence.

It wouldn't be quiet for long. She had a feeling in the weeks and months to come the estate would be a buzz of activity as both Trey and Kate began campaigning in earnest.

Although Kate had yet to make an announcement that she intended to run for president, Debra had a feeling next Sunday's morning breakfast would be her time to hear any concerns that the family might have to say and then she'd let them know that she'd decided to run.

Kate was as much a political animal as her husband before her and now her son. Debra knew she had a steely will and was not just ambitious but truly believed she would be the best choice for the country. Ultimately, Kate would be driven by a sense of duty.

She jumped as Trey suddenly appeared in the doorway.

"You startled me. I didn't hear you come in." She tried not to notice how handsome, how sexy he looked in his jeans and a blue button-up shirt.

"Sorry, I didn't mean to startle you." His gaze was dark and unreadable. "Are you ready to go?"

"I'm definitely ready." She rose from the sofa, feeling strange not to have a suitcase or a purse. But she'd arrived here with nothing but the nightgown she'd been wearing when Trey had pulled her out of the townhouse. She'd thrown the nightgown away, not wanting any memories of the night somebody had gotten inside her home and set a fire in an attempt to kill her.

"I can't believe everything you got accomplished today," she said when they were in her car.

He flashed a smile. "It helps to be a Winston when you want to get things done. People tend to jump through hoops in an effort to please."

"Even on a Sunday?"

"Even on a Sunday," he replied.

She imagined he'd paid extra dollars to get the work done on a Sunday. She wasn't sure she would ever be able to pay him back, but she was determined to do so even if it took years.

"Sam got me a present for the baby," she said. "It's a cute bib that says I Love Mommy." Her heart expanded as she thought of the unexpectedness of the gift.

"He brought me a present for the baby, too. Diapers." Trey laughed. "I guess he figures you get feeding duty and I'm going to get diaper duty."

"It works for me," Debra joked. But of course she knew that separation of baby duties would never work. They'd be living in different homes, leading separate lives. He would be a busy state senator while the child was growing up, but no matter how busy his life would become, Debra knew he'd be a fabulous father.

She knew that if you stripped away the political aspirations, the trappings of the shrewd businessman, what would be left was a caring, giving man. He was a loving grandson to his grandmother, a role model for his younger brothers, and a help and support to his mother.

He had a good sense of humor and a large streak of kindness. That was who Trey Winston was at his very core. And those qualities were what would make him a loving, caring father and what made her love him.

"You know I'd never let you return home if I didn't think it was safe," he said, interrupting her contemplations.

"I know that," she affirmed. "Have you spoken to Thad today about the investigation?"

"Officially the investigation is being headed by Lieutenant Al Chase, but unofficially Thad is working on it as much as he can. He called me about an hour ago and said they had interviewed Barry, who indicated that on the nights of both incidents he was working late with his secretary. Apparently his secretary confirmed his alibis."

Debra released a dry, humorless laugh. "Well, of course she would. They've been sleeping together for years. That's why I wanted out of the relationship with him. He's had a relationship with his secretary, who is married and has kids, since he opened the real estate office."

"From what Thad said, Lieutenant Chase wasn't impressed with the alibi so Barry isn't home free."

Debra frowned thoughtfully. "Barry is a slimeball, but I just can't see him being behind any of this. He has no motive to hurt me."

"He has no motive that you know about," Trey countered. "If there's one thing I've learned in big business and politics, it's that there are some crazy-ass people out there."

"And it's so comforting to think that one of them is after me," she replied.

Trey reached out and placed his palm on her thigh. It wasn't a sexual touch, but rather meant to soothe her. "We're not going to let anyone hurt you, Debra. Thad and the police will be able to figure this out and put the guilty party behind bars." He removed his hand from her leg and returned it to the steering wheel in time to park by the curb in front of her house.

She knew he'd be coming inside. He needed to show her the new security system and how to work it. She gasped in surprise as she walked into the living room. It smelled of new paint and carpet cleaning, of washed walls, and showed no sign of the life-threatening event of the fire.

She shuddered to think of what might have happened if Trey hadn't been parked outside, if he hadn't seen the first flames and jumped into action. Consciously she shoved those thoughts away and continued to look around. The curtains that had hung in the window were gone, but wood-slatted blinds were in their place.

"I didn't want to buy new curtains for you. My mother has always told me all my decorating taste is in my mouth, but I thought the blinds would be fine until you can shop for something else," he said.

"They're perfect," she replied. "Everything looks perfect. I don't know how to thank you. We'll set up some sort of payment plan so that I can pay you back for everything this has cost you."

He waved a hand to dismiss her offer. "I'm not worried about that now. Let me show you how to work the new security system."

As he showed her the monitor next to the front door

and how to switch it to views of different areas from the cameras mounted outside, she tried not to smell his cologne, not to revel in the warmth of his nearness.

"If the alarm goes off, you'll immediately be contacted by the security company. If there is no danger, then you're to answer that everything is fine. If there's somebody with you and you're in danger, then you're supposed to say that everything is okay. Fine is safe. Okay is danger."

Debra nodded, taking in the information that might save her life. "When you enter the house you'll have two minutes to punch in a code that will reset the security behind you. I set up the code and I've got it right here." His gaze held hers intently as he handed her a small piece of paper he pulled from his pocket. "You and I are the only ones who know the code. Don't share it with anyone on staff at the estate or friends or neighbors," he said.

"Trust me, I intend to memorize the number and then I should probably eat this piece of paper to assure nobody finds it," she kidded.

He grinned. "I'm not sure that's necessary."

"After everything I've been through I think it is." She wrapped her arms around herself, suddenly chilled as she thought of everything she'd endured. "Would you like something to drink?" she asked, not sure if she wanted to be alone just yet. "I think I might have some orange juice in the fridge."

"I'll tell you what, why don't you get the juice and I'll build you a nice fire."

"That sounds perfect." He started work on the fire and she went into the kitchen. By the time he had the fire crackling in the fireplace, she had two tall glasses of juice waiting.

"We can take it into the living room," she said.

"Sounds perfect," he agreed. Together they went back into the living room with their glasses and sank down on the sofa.

"What a difference a day makes," she said, and released a pent-up sigh. "I feel like I've ruined things for you."

"You haven't ruined anything, Debra. You've given me a great gift. Your pregnancy will be old news within a couple of days, but for me it's the beginning of a wonderful event that will last the rest of my life."

Debra took a sip of her drink. "I was so afraid, I mean it wasn't exactly like we planned this. I was so worried that if you found out, if anyone found out that the baby was yours, then it would ruin all of the dreams you had for yourself and I didn't want to do that to you."

"As far as I'm concerned nothing has changed my dreams. The only thing you have done is added to the dreams I have for myself."

"But, I totally messed things up between you and Cecily," she replied.

He shrugged. "Cecily and I made a great political team. But I wasn't in love with her and I'm sure she wasn't in love with me. You probably did me a favor, because had we gotten married based on mutual ambition alone, we may have ended up two bitter, unhappy people and in the end that's what I experienced with my own parents. I don't want that for myself."

Debra shook her head in amazement. "You Winstons have always managed to turn any negative into a positive."

"That's because we don't see negatives, we only see opportunities. You're giving me the opportunity to be a dad." His eyes darkened with emotion. "And I didn't realize how badly I wanted that until you told me you were pregnant with my baby."

He turned his head and stared at the fire. "I don't know what the future holds, but I can tell you what I want at this very minute." He turned back to look at her. "I want you to know that I haven't had sex with Cecily since the night you and I spent together and what I want right now is to make love to the mother of my child on that red rug in front of the fire."

Debra paused with her glass halfway to her mouth, stunned by his words and by the heat of desire that pulsed in his eyes, desire that instantly pulsed through her.

Part of the reason she'd stopped their near lovemaking in her foyer was because she knew he was going to marry Cecily, because she didn't want to be that woman who cheated with a man who was already taken.

She'd made that mistake on the night they'd been together, and had refused to make it yet again when they'd almost lost it in her entryway.

She set her glass down, her hand trembling slightly. "I won't be your mistress, Trey. I won't be your baby mama who you occasionally stop by to have sex with. I want better than that. I deserve more than that." She drew a tremulous breath. "But I won't lie. I want you again. I want you tonight and then we're never going to be together intimately again."

One last night with him to remember, she told herself. One final time to be held in his arms, to feel his body against hers. A final chance to love him without inhibition, without restraint, surely after all she'd been through she deserved that.

"Are you sure? I don't want to talk you into doing something you aren't comfortable with."

"The only thing that is making me uncomfortable is how long it's taking you to kiss me," she replied.

He shot across the small space between them on the sofa and wrapped her in his arms as his mouth covered hers in a fiery kiss that stole her breath away. Her heartbeat responded by rapidly fluttering in her chest.

It was almost frightening how easily he could take her from zero to a hundred on the desire scale. Although she would never speak of her love for him aloud, she could show him in her kiss, in the intimacy that was about to follow.

The last time they'd had sex, it had been hot and wild and completely spontaneous. Now she wasn't having sex with him, she was making love with him…for the first and the very last time.

They kissed for some time before he broke the contact and stood. He held out his hand and she took it as he led her to the soft throw rug in front of the fireplace.

He lowered her to the floor as if she were a fine piece of china and then he stretched out next to her and took her in his arms once again.

As their lips met, Debra fought against the wild emotion that rose up in her heart. Love. She felt as if she'd loved Trey Winston forever.

Despite the fact that she knew he loved her because she carried his baby, at the moment it didn't matter what he felt for her. She just wanted to give to him everything her heart had to give. It didn't matter if he couldn't give her back what she wanted from him.

The fire warmed her, but not as much as Trey's mouth plying hers with heat, not as much as the love that burned hot in her soul.

As they continued to kiss, she began to unfasten the buttons of his shirt, wanting, needing to feel his bare, muscled chest, the strength of his naked shoulders.

Once she had his shirt unbuttoned, he threw it off and reached for the bottom of her T-shirt. He pulled it over her head and tossed it across the room and then he drew her against him, their nakedness melded together as her breasts rubbed his naked chest.

His lips once again captured hers and she tried not to think about the fact that after tonight they would both be going cold turkey in their addiction to each other.

It didn't take long before kissing and hugging wasn't enough. He kicked off his shoes and tore off his socks, then shucked his jeans and navy briefs in a hot minute. At the same time she shimmied out of the sweatpants and her panties.

For several sweet moments he hovered just above her, his gaze sweeping the length of her. "You are so beautiful," he whispered.

He was beautiful as well, with the light of the fire illuminating his muscles and emphasizing his handsome features. "Don't talk…. Kiss," she said breathlessly.

He complied, once again slanting his mouth down to hers where their tongues swirled as their bodies fell together like two pieces of a puzzle.

His hands were everywhere, cupping her sensitive breasts, sliding down her stomach, running across her back. It was as if his fingers, his palms hungered for the feel of her skin and she couldn't halt the small moan of pleasure that escaped her.

She, too, loved the feel of his skin and ran her fingers down the length his back and then up to grip his shoulders and then the biceps that were like rocks.

He tore his mouth from hers and trailed kisses down her jawline, into the soft hollow of her throat and then licked one of her nipples, creating an electric current that raced through her from head to toe.

He toyed with first one nipple and then the other and she could feel his turgid manhood against her thigh, letting her know he was fully aroused.

His mouth left her breasts and dragged down to her lower stomach, lingering there as if he were kissing the baby she carried inside. She squeezed her eyes tightly closed as once again emotion welled up from deep inside her.

*Love my baby, love me,* a little voice whispered in the back of her head. The voice was silenced as his hands slid down her stomach, lightly touched her inner thigh and then caressed the center of her that throbbed with need.

Rational thought left her as she raised her hips to meet the intimate touch, as the build-up of sexual tension climbed higher and higher.

He moved his fingers faster and then slowed as he teased and tormented her. She dug her fingers into the rug on either side of her as his fingers once again worked faster and she gave in to the waves of pleasure that washed over her, leaving her gasping, crying and laughing all at the same time.

"Again," he whispered, his eyes filled with the joy of her pleasure. Once again his fingers found the same spot and began to move…slowly, sensually rubbing and caressing as she struggled to catch her breath.

He seemed to know exactly what she needed, what she wanted and then she was there again, crying out his name as her body shuddered with a second release.

She grabbed his hand to stop him from touching her again. She needed to catch her breath, she wanted to give back to him a little of the sheer pleasure that he'd just given to her.

She sat up and pushed him onto his back, determined that if this was the last time they were going to be together, she would make sure he had as much trouble forgetting it as she would.

He lay perfectly still as she leaned over him and kissed him on the lips. Her kiss was soft and light, just a promise and then she began to trail kisses down the length of his chest and stomach.

Light and teasing, she kissed and licked his skin, loving the taste of him on her tongue, loving the way he groaned her name as she made her way down his lower abdomen.

His body held a tension that she reveled in as his hands tangled in her hair and he once again moaned her name. She licked first one inner thigh and then the other as she took him in her hand. Hard and throbbing, his arousal was magnificent and she loved the fact that it was her he wanted.

"Debra." Her name escaped him in a husky, strangled protest. "I need to be in you now. If you touch me anymore I'll lose it."

"We wouldn't want that," she replied, surprised by the husky want in her own voice.

He sat up and laid her down and she opened herself to receive him as he moved into position on top of her. As he eased into her, his mouth sought hers. The kiss was achingly tender and brought tears to her eyes once again.

*Love my baby. Love me.*

The words reverberated around in her head as he moved his hips against her in a slow, long stroke and she gasped at the sheer pleasure that soared through her. He broke the kiss and cradled her against his chest as his hips moved faster against her, into her.

She was vaguely aware of the crackling fire nearby, but the real fire was inside her, burning a forever impression onto her heart and into her soul as he took her to the heights of pleasure once again.

He tensed and whispered her name as he found his own release and then collapsed, holding the bulk of his weight off her and onto his elbows on either side of her.

He stared down at her, his features relaxed, yet his eyes dark and fathomless. She had no idea what he was thinking. She wasn't even sure he was thinking.

She only knew that this was a kind of goodbye for her, that she would never compromise herself again with him, no matter how much she loved him, because she loved him.

He finally rolled over to his back beside her. "It was even more amazing than I'd remembered."

She sat up, feeling too naked, too vulnerable as he gazed at her. "It's just sex, Trey, and it's never going to happen between us again."

She got up and pulled a red-and-yellow-striped blanket from the back of her sofa and wrapped it around herself. He sat up and reached for his briefs, as if he, too, suddenly felt too naked.

"We'll be great at co-parenting," she continued.

He finished dressing without saying a word. Had she

made him mad? Had he really thought he could maybe convince her to continue a sexual relationship with him?

She'd be an easy sex fix throughout the stresses of a campaign, a quick drive-by physical relief whenever he stopped by to see the baby.

*No way, no how,* she thought firmly. She'd compromised herself enough tonight. She'd sworn she'd never settle for a piece of a man's heart instead of the entire thing. She'd determined long ago that when it came to love, for her it was all or nothing.

When he was fully dressed he stepped over to her and pulled her into his arms. She allowed the embrace, even leaned into him, knowing that if nothing else she could always trust him to have her safety and her welfare in his heart.

"I won't let you down, Debra," he said, his voice a whisper against her ear. "Anything you need, at any time, I'm just a phone call away. We're tied for life now through our baby and all I want for you is happiness." He released her and stepped back.

She followed him to the front door, emotion a tight knot in the center of her chest. "I'll see you next Sunday at your mother's place," she said as he reached the door.

He turned back to face her. "I can't say that I'm not sorry we aren't going to be intimate again. I love making love to you, but I have to respect your wishes. Everything is going to work out fine. If nothing else, we'll parent our child and be good friends."

"I'd like that," she replied, but of course it was a lie. At the moment she couldn't imagine loving Trey the way she did and settling for a friendship. Hopefully, eventually she would be able to do just that.

"Then I'll see you Sunday morning."

Her tears began the minute she punched in the code to reset the security after he'd left. Hot and burning, they trekked down her cheeks as her chest grew more and more tight.

She should just go to bed and forget about tonight, forget about Trey Winston. Instead she curled up back on the hearth and wrapped the blanket more firmly around her, chilled despite the warmth of the fire.

She stared into the flickering flames and remembered the gentleness of his kiss on her belly, a kiss she'd believed was meant for the baby growing inside her.

Her child would always have a place in the Winston family. Trey would make sure that his son or daughter was loved and accepted without question.

A sob escaped her, followed by another and another. She curled up on her side on the rug where she could still smell the scent of his cologne and she wept.

She cried because somebody was trying to kill her and she had no idea who or why. Finally she cried because despite what Trey had just said to her, she'd never felt so alone. Everything had changed and she no longer knew where she belonged.

## Chapter 14

Trey slept little the night after making love with Debra again. He'd tossed and turned with thoughts rioting in his head, creating a chaos of visions that had made sleep next to impossible.

The week had flown by since then. He'd kept himself busy at work and had given a couple of speeches to local businessmen and at a lunch for the fire department. He'd spoken to Debra on the phone each day, but hadn't gone by the townhouse to see her.

The investigation into both the cutting of her brake lines and the fire in her house had stalled out despite Thad's working hard to find the guilty party in any spare time he had. But there was always another crime scene for him to investigate, always a new mystery to be solved.

Trey had also stayed away from the estate for the

past week. He had no reason to go by there and didn't want to make Debra feel uncomfortable.

It had been a long week for him. He felt as if he was in withdrawal… Debra withdrawal. The idea of never making love with her again was downright depressing. But, he knew it was time to think of her only as the mother of his child, a woman who intended to go on living her life without him in it other than as the father of her firstborn child.

She would probably eventually marry somebody and perhaps have other children. Trey would make sure that whatever man she chose would be a stellar stepfather to his child. This thought also depressed him.

He was ridiculously glad when Sunday morning came and he knew at least he'd see Debra at the breakfast his mother had arranged.

It was a perfect Sunday morning as he left his home to head to the estate. The sun shone brightly and although it was only just before ten the temperature had risen to the mid-sixties as the area enjoyed an unusual streak of mild temperatures that, unfortunately, wasn't going to last. Still, right now it was perfect for breakfast outside by the pool.

He'd chosen a lightweight black-and-gray-patterned sweater with a pair of black jeans for the casual family breakfast that morning.

Hopefully the weather would stay decent through the next weekend, when his mother was the keynote speaker for the chamber of commerce Valentine's Day celebration.

During the past week he'd spoken to his mother several times and knew how she was looking forward to the Valentine Ball, but more importantly to the speech she would be giving at the event.

He had a list of things he wanted to accomplish in the next week that had nothing to do with either Adair Enterprises or his campaign. He wanted to visit his grandmother again. It had already been too long since his last troubling visit with her.

Secrets and lies. He hadn't been able to forget how upset his grandmother had become during his last visit, and he hadn't been completely satisfied by his mother's explanation. Secrets and lies. Hopefully it was just the meaningless ramblings of an old woman whose mind was starting to slip.

He knew things were going to start to go crazy with his schedule in the next weeks and it was important that he get out to the nursing home to see how she was doing. His last visit had been so unsettling, but he hoped his next one would be better, that she'd be better.

He also wanted to find a contractor who could paint one of his bedrooms in yellow with primary colors as trim to sort of match what Debra would be doing in her guest room for a nursery.

He'd use the guest room closest to his master suite and turn it into a baby wonderland. He planned on being a hands-on father in a way his own dad had never been. He loved that baby already and, like Debra, he intended to let the child know that he or she was both wanted and loved.

Buck had been too busy being an important senator and sleeping with other women to be much of a parent to his three sons. Trey wanted to be a better kind of father even though he and Debra wouldn't be together.

And it had been that which had kept him tossing and

turning all night. He was so confused about his feelings toward Debra. He'd somehow hoped that in making love with her one last time his constant, overwhelming desire for her would wane or disappear altogether.

But that hadn't happened. Even now, driving to his mother's home for breakfast as he thought of Debra a fresh wave of physical desire punched him in the gut.

His feelings for her didn't stop with the simple, uncomplicated emotion of physical lust. He wanted her safe from harm, he wanted to say things that caused her eyes to twinkle and laughter to spill from her lips.

He not only wanted to talk to her about his campaign, but he also wanted to share with her his worry about his grandmother. He wanted to confess the fact that he loved to watch old John Wayne movies and he liked his popcorn with extra butter, that some country songs could bring tears to his eyes.

He wanted to tell her that he and his brothers had once played cowboys and he and Sam had tied Thad to a tree so tightly they hadn't been able to untie him. Thankfully a gardener had been working nearby and had used a pair of gardening shears to cut the ropes.

For an hour afterward, Thad had chased them with a big stick, threatening to whip them if he managed to catch them. He tightened his hands on the steering wheel as the happy memory played out in his head.

He had so many memories of home and his brothers. Growing up they had been almost inseparable. But adulthood had brought so many changes. Sam had closed himself off mentally after coming home from overseas and Thad had removed himself both emotionally and physically from the core of the family.

For the first time in his life Trey realized he was

lonely. He was thirty-five years old and had nobody in his life who saw the essence of the man he was at his very core. Everyone only saw the top layer, the successful businessman, the new candidate for senator.

He could be something different with Debra. He thought of the peace of just sitting with her in her kitchen, of how relaxed he felt when it was just the two of them together and he didn't have to put on any kind of a public facade.

Was it possible he was in love with Debra? The thought shot through his head so forcefully, it momentarily took his breath away.

Was this what love felt like? This need to see her face, to make her happy? This desire to keep her safe and see no harm ever came to her? This passion to hold her in his arms, not just while making love but through the night while she slept?

Even if he did love her, it didn't matter. He'd asked her to marry him and she'd told him no. It was obvious she wanted him in a physical sense, but she wasn't in love with him.

Funny that the first thing he would fail at in his life was love. Although he wasn't laughing. He pulled through the side entrance of the estate and as he parked his car it was with an aching heart that felt somehow bruised.

He glanced at his watch as he got out of his car. He was early and from the lack of cars in the side parking area none of his siblings had arrived yet.

He knew that Debra had been invited to attend his mother's breakfast also. With the realization of the depths of his feelings for her, he felt unusually vulnerable.

Somehow, someway, he had to get over it. They had a lifetime of working together as partners to raise their child. He couldn't let unwanted emotions get in the way.

He walked into the kitchen where it was obvious Myra had been busy since early this morning as the fragrances of a variety of foods mingled together to make a heavenly scent.

"Don't you go touching anything in here, Trey Winston," Myra said sternly as she hurried into the kitchen from another area of the house. At her heels was Tiffany Burgess, one of the kitchen helpers.

Trey held his hands up in innocence. "I was just thinking about maybe pouring myself a cup of coffee, that's all."

"Everything is already set up out back by the pool. We just have a few more things to finish up to get the food out there. Now go on with you, coffee is there and your mother should be downstairs anytime now."

He left the kitchen, walking past Debra's and then his mother's office. Just off the foyer was a large ballroom that his mother used when giving charity balls or other such events. It had been a while since she'd used it.

He passed it, as well, and went on to the family sitting room where double doors led out to the pool area. The staff had been busy.

A long glass-top table had been set up with bright turquoise placemats and white plates. Turquoise-and-white-patterned cloth napkins were neatly folded by each place and the silverware gleamed in the sunshine. It looked both inviting and like a signal of the summer to come.

A second table held the beginnings of a buffet. A silver coffeepot and cups took up one end along with a pitcher of orange juice and a tiered serving platter that held a variety of sweet rolls and plump muffins. On the other side of the table hot electric servers awaited food to be placed into their bins.

Trey served himself a cup of coffee and then carried it to a chair away from the table and closer to the pool. In the springtime the beauty of his mother's backyard was breathtaking, with flowerbeds splashing color and a waterfall that spilled over rocks and then disappeared into a large decorative urn.

In the distance a tree line stood outside the black wrought-iron fence. The trees were far enough away that they couldn't be used to help anyone scale the fence, but in the springtime when in full leaf, provided a beautiful green backdrop to the large yard.

Looking around the yard and pool area, Trey made a mental note that it was past time for him to do something about his own property. He'd talk to his mother about her landscaping services and see if he could borrow somebody to tell him what would be best to plant.

It was impossible to miss the men who were stationed at the four corners of the yard. The Secret Service would never allow Kate to sit in her own backyard without them present. He doubted that his mother even thought about their presence anymore. They had been a constant in her life since she'd served as vice president.

He sat up straighter in his chair as Thad walked outside. Clad in a pair of black slacks and a white shirt and jacket, he looked more like a businessman than a cop. But Trey knew the slight bulge beneath his sport coat indicated a shoulder holster and gun.

The two brothers had been on the phone to each other several times a day throughout the week as Trey checked in to see if there had been any new information about the attacks on Debra.

He raised a hand in greeting to Trey and then poured himself a cup of coffee and walked over to where Trey sat. "Don't ask," he said in greeting. "Because if you ask I'll have to tell you we have nothing new."

"You still haven't been able to identify any real person of interest?" Trey asked.

"We have a couple persons of interest, but no evidence to tie them to any of the crimes. Everyone we've spoken to has an alibi that so far we've been unable to break."

"What about Haley?" Trey asked in a low voice, even though he knew the intern wasn't at the house on Sundays.

"We spoke to her. Her alibi for the nights in question was that she was at her place alone." Thad shrugged. "We haven't been able to absolutely place her at home, but we also haven't been able to disprove that she was there. The motive that you've come up with, that somehow she wants to get rid of Debra so that she can have Debra's job is a bit weak."

"It's the only motive I could come up with given that Debra isn't the type of woman who makes enemies."

"I know you've got her all locked down in that townhouse of hers, but she still needs to watch her back when she's out of the house," Thad said. "Since we have no real motive and no real suspects, we can't warn her in advance should something else happen."

Trey nodded, a new little hole ripping in his heart as he thought of something bad happening to Debra. "I'm thinking about talking to Mom about maybe getting her some full-time security. Maybe one of the Secret Service men knows somebody who wants to moonlight and shadow Debra to make sure she stays safe when she's away from home."

"Might not be a bad idea," Thad agreed. "At least until we can get a break on the case." He took a sip of his coffee and eyed Trey with open speculation. "Why do you want to run for the Senate?" he asked.

Trey looked at him in surprise. "Because I think I can make a real difference for the state of North Carolina, because I see problems and issues that I believe I can help to fix. Why?"

Thad raked a hand through his hair and released a deep sigh. "I just feel like politics is what screwed up our whole family life and I can't imagine why you'd want to put yourself out there like that."

"Thad, I know you love what you do. I know you feel a true calling in your work. That's the way I feel about politics. That's the way mom feels about politics. It's not just a job—it's a true calling, a real passion and a need and desire to make things better in the world."

At that moment Debra stepped outside. Clad in a pair of leg-hugging jeans and a blue-and-green-patterned sweater, she looked more beautiful than ever.

She paused just outside the door and offered a smile to the two brothers. It was at that moment, with her hair gleaming in the sunshine and her smile warming him from head to toe that Trey knew without a doubt that he was madly in love with Debra Prentice.

That crazy anxious jangle of nerves accompanied an acceleration of her heartbeat at the sight of Trey. She turned and poured herself a glass of orange juice, grateful that at least her hands remained steady.

She had to get used to seeing him and not loving him. She had to transform her love to a friendship for the sake of their baby. She had to figure out how to stop being in love with him and just love him as the father of her child.

"Good morning," she said as she carried her cup to where the two men were located near the pool.

"Back at you," Thad said with a smile.

At least he was here to serve as buffer, she thought as Trey murmured a greeting, his blue eyes far too intense as his gaze remained on her.

Was he thinking about their last moments together, a flickering fire, a red throw rug and desire spiraled out of control? Certainly she'd been thinking about it since then, every single day for the last week.

But, she refused to think about it now. It was done. They were finished, and this morning's breakfast was all about Kate. "Where is the lady of the hour?" she asked.

"She hasn't made an appearance yet," Thad replied.

"Neither has Sam," Trey added.

They all turned to look as Myra and Tiffany came back outside, each carrying metal baking pans that they placed in the awaiting electric warmer.

"Your mother and Sam should be out here any minute," Myra said as she and Tiffany disappeared back into the house.

"I have a fairly good idea that I'm not going to like what I hear here this morning," Thad said.

"I'm sure you're probably right," Trey agreed.

Debra sipped her orange juice, wishing Sam and Kate would come outside so things could get underway and she could get back home.

She wasn't even sure why Kate had included her in this family gathering. It wasn't like Debra was really a part of the family.

Sam was the next one outside and once he'd joined them with a cup of coffee in hand, he pointed to the glass of juice Debra held.

"I'm glad my niece or nephew is getting a dose of vitamin C this morning instead of a cup of caffeine," he said.

The shadows that always darkened his blue eyes were gone for now and Debra was grateful that he appeared to be in a fairly good mood. Hopefully nothing that occurred during the breakfast would bring the terrible darkness back into his eyes.

"What are you all doing over there when I have this lovely table set beautifully for everyone?" Kate's voice pulled everyone's attention toward her as she stepped out of the back doors and onto the patio.

"We were making plans to overthrow the monarchy," Thad said with a wicked grin.

Kate laughed. "I know Debra isn't a part of such a plan and it would take far more than three big men to get the job done right."

She looked stunning in a pair of tailored black slacks and a red blouse with a black cardigan sweater flung over her shoulders. "Come on, come on. Let's fill our plates and get this party started."

It took some time for all of them to serve themselves and then get seated. Debra was grateful to find herself across the table from Trey rather than seated next to him. Instead she sat next to Thad with Sam across the table next to Trey, and Kate at the head of the table.

The conversation remained light and easy as they ate.

Debra was pleased to discover that it was late enough in the day that the food tasted delicious and she suffered no nausea or belly rolling.

As the conversation turned to the brothers' childhood, stories began to roll out that had Debra both relaxing and laughing. The stories of brotherly antics and love also made her realize how much she'd missed out on by being the only child of an alcoholic mother.

She also realized that she didn't want her baby to be an only child. Siblings weren't just brothers and sisters; they were also friends and support systems for lifetimes.

But she couldn't be sure what the future held. Right now she just wanted to have a healthy pregnancy and baby, deal with the co-parenting issues with Trey and figure out what the next step in her personal life might be.

The breakfast talk went from old memories to the mildness of the weather and finally to Kate's upcoming speech for the chamber of commerce event the following Saturday night on Valentine's Day.

It seemed ironic to Debra that she was pregnant and yet had nobody to send her flowers or chocolates for the special lovers' day. But she'd never gotten flowers or anything from a man on Valentine's Day.

Barry had been one of few men she had dated in her lifetime and they hadn't even known each other last Valentine's Day.

Throughout the meal she was acutely conscious of Trey's gaze lingering on her. Dark and unreadable, something about his unwavering attention made her uncomfortable.

What was he thinking? Was it possible that he might fight her for full custody when the baby was born? Certainly with the Winston power, influence and money, it would be a battle she'd lose.

Her hand fell to her stomach, as if to somehow protect her baby from such a confrontation. Surely that couldn't be what he was thinking. They'd spoken about co-parenting. But what might happen when he married? Once he had a wife, might not he want his child to live with them full-time?

*Stop borrowing trouble,* she reprimanded herself. Without a magical crystal ball there was no way to see what the future might hold, and she'd just have to deal with everything one day at a time from here on out.

She definitely didn't want to think about the fact that the investigations into the attacks on her had yielded nothing. At least with her new security in the townhouse she felt completely safe when she was there.

It wasn't until they had all finished eating, their plates had been removed and their coffee and juice refilled that Kate raised a hand to get everyone's attention.

"I'm sure you're all wondering why I asked you to come here for breakfast this morning," she began.

"Not really," Thad muttered under his breath.

"Before I make my final decision about what my future is going to hold, I wanted to give you all a chance to talk about your concerns," she said.

Debra stared over Trey's shoulder to the distant tree line, knowing that she didn't have a pony in this show. Kate needed to hear from her sons, not from one of her son's baby mama. Besides, Kate already knew that Debra was up for whatever she decided.

"I'm considering announcing formally my decision to run for president of the United States next Saturday night at the chamber of commerce event." She looked at her sons expectantly.

Debra focused her attention back to the table. "You know I'll support that decision," Trey said.

"You're going to do what you want to do anyway," Sam added, his voice holding resignation.

Thad frowned. "I just don't understand why you'd want to do this given what politics has done to our family in the past."

"If you're talking about when you were young and your father was a senator, the only thing I can tell you is that our family fell apart because of your father's bad choices, not because he was in the Senate," Kate replied.

"You should have left the bastard," Sam said, his eyes taking on the darkness that they held far too often.

"I did what I needed to do to keep the family together," Kate replied with a steely note. "Things weren't so terrible for all of you when I served as vice president and as an ambassador."

"That's because nobody ever cares that much about the vice president," Thad said. "But as President of the United States every move you make will be in the spotlight and a lot of that spotlight is going to bleed over onto us." He raked a hand through his shaggy brown hair. "But I guess we can all handle that if this is what you really want."

"Sam?" Kate looked at her middle child with affection.

He shrugged. "I know you want to do this and I'm not going to be the one who stops you from pursuing what you want."

"So I have tentative blessings from everyone?" Kate asked.

"I think you can say that you have complete blessings from everyone," Trey replied.

Kate turned and motioned to Myra, who stood just inside the door and held a silver tray with flutes of champagne. "Then this calls for a celebratory toast."

Thad laughed dryly. "You've already got the champagne poured. You weren't worried a bit about getting our blessings."

Kate beamed a smile around the table as Myra stepped outside. "I knew my boys would only want my happiness and this is something I feel destined to do."

Myra went around the table, handing each of them a glass of champagne. "No bubbly for you," she said when she got to Debra. "You have a flute of nice white grape juice."

"Thank you, Myra," Debra said as she accepted the delicate, thin glass.

Kate stood and held up her glass. "Bear with me, I have a rather long toast to make."

Debra smiled inwardly as she saw all three of her sons roll their eyes, as if they were accustomed to "bearing with" their strong, assertive mother.

The rest of them remained seated, giving Kate her moment to shine even at a family breakfast.

"First of all to Debra, who will forever be a part of this family and hopefully continue to play an important role in my professional life as well as my personal one." Kate smiled at Debra and then looked at Sam.

"To my middle son, Sam. You awe me with your bravery, with your honor and duty you showed by serving your country. I only pray that your heart and soul eventually heal as your body does. I love you, Sam."

Debra felt herself getting a bit teary as Kate honored each of her children.

"Thaddeus," Kate continued. "I'm so proud of the life you've made for yourself as a part of law enforcement. You honor the family name with your work as a public servant. I love you, Thad."

She turned her attention to Trey. "And to my first-born, who has not only driven the family business to new heights, but is also about to discover the insane world of politics and parenthood. I love you, Trey, and wish only good things for my boys in the future."

She raised her glass. "Cheers."

*"Gun!"* Thad suddenly screamed and pointed to the trees in the distance.

And then the world exploded.

# Chapter 15

A thousand things occurred almost simultaneously, creating wild chaos. A shot sounded. The glass table shattered, cups and glasses crashing to the ground. Trey dove across the broken table to reach Debra who sat in her chair stunned.

He scrambled to her, yanked her from the chair and pulled her to the ground. Sam grabbed his mother's hand and pulled her down also as Thad and half a dozen Secret Service men raced in all directions. Thad and a couple of men ran to the side entrance gate and out of the backyard.

Two other agents rushed to stand next to the shattered table, their backs to each other and their weapons drawn as they protected everyone on the ground. Several more agents raced to the back of the yard, their guns pointed up at the tree where the shooter was no longer visible.

"Are you okay?" Trey asked as he covered Debra's body with his on the hard concrete near the pool.

Around them chaos continued to reign as men yelled to each other and another gunshot split the air. Trey could feel the frantic beat of Debra's heart against his own.

Her breath came in gasps of terror against his collarbone and his brain worked to try to make sense of what had just happened, what was still happening. "Yes," she replied, her voice small and scared.

There was no question that somebody had been in those trees, that Thad had spied what apparently had been a man with a gun. The gun had been fired, shattering the table, but had the bullet been meant for his mother or for Debra?

His body shuddered at the thought of either woman being shot. He looked over at Sam, who had their mother down against the concrete, a look of anguish on his face.

Trey knew his brother was probably wishing he had his weapon on him, but Sam had been deemed unfit for duty and all of his weapons had been taken from him by the army brass who had released him.

Trey's body jerked as another gunshot exploded and then Thad's voice rose in the distance. It had a triumphant tone and Trey felt the muscles in his body begin to relax a bit.

One of the Secret Service men standing near them talked into his radio, listened a moment and then turned to face everyone on the ground. "They've got the shooter in custody."

The two agents remained on guard as both Trey and Sam rose and helped Debra and Kate to their feet. It was only as he saw Debra's terror-filled eyes that he recognized the bottomless depth of his love for her.

He pulled her to him and she willingly huddled in the secure embrace of his arms. Love. It flowed through him, unmistakable and undeniable. But he didn't know what to do about it, knew there was nothing to be done about it.

"Well, that's the way to end a toast with a bang," Kate said in a slightly shaky voice as Sam helped her to her feet.

"We'd like all of you to move as quickly as possible into the house," Secret Service Agent Daniel Henderson said as he took Kate by the arm. "It's for your own safety. We don't know who else might be out here somewhere."

As Daniel ushered Kate back into the house, Trey did the same with Debra, still unsure who the ultimate target had been. They all took seats in the sitting room and waited, the silence in the room growing more and more tense with each minute that passed.

Had there been more than one shooter? Had this been some sort of an organized attack? Trey's mind raced to make sense of what had just occurred.

Thad, Jerry Cahill and Robert D'Angelis appeared at the back door. Between Thad and Robert was a thin man in scruffy jeans and a black jacket. His hands were cuffed behind him and Robert held a high-powered rifle with a scope in his hand.

"Ms. Winston, do you know this person?"

Trey stared at the man. He was small and slender and wore a black sweatshirt and jeans. His eyes were dark and a smirk formed on his thin lips as if everyone else was in handcuffs and he was free.

Sam lunged toward him. "Who are you and why were you shooting at my mother?" he yelled. Kate stopped him from advancing by grabbing his arm.

"I don't have to talk to you," the man said with a scowl. "I don't have to talk to any of you. I know my rights. Besides, if I don't talk then I get some time in prison. If I do talk then I get a bullet to the back of my head. It's a no-brainer. I don't have nothing to say to nobody."

"I've never seen him before in my life," Kate finally said.

"Get him out of here," Sam growled. "Get him the hell out of here."

Thad and Cahill took the man back out the door where Trey assumed he'd be handed over to Secret Service agents and other authorities to deal with.

Sam turned his wrath on Daniel Henderson and Robert D'Angelis. "How in the hell did this happen? How did that little creep manage to get up in a tree with a rifle without any of the agents noticing? I want to know who didn't do their job."

"I don't know how this happened, but I promise you by the end of the day we'll have some answers," Robert replied, his gray eyes cold and narrowed. "Now if you'll excuse me, I'll go find out as much information as I can right now."

He headed through the house, toward the kitchen and the side door that would bring him out by the guesthouse where the security operations and agents worked from.

Trey turned to look at Debra, who stood beside him, frozen like a deer in headlights. It was only then that he saw a trickle of blood seeping from her hairline down the side of her face.

His heartbeat spiked as he grabbed her by the arm. Had one of the bullets grazed her? "Debra, you're hurt," he said. Had a piece of shattered glass from the table ricocheted to her?

"What?" She looked at him with blank eyes.

"Your head… You're bleeding." He dropped his hand from her arm.

She raised a hand up and touched the area and then stared at the blood on her hand and then back at him. "It must be glass from the table."

"We need to get you cleaned up," Kate said briskly, back in control despite the horror of what had just happened.

Somewhere in the back of his mind Trey knew it was this very trait, the ability to function with a cool head in a crisis, that would benefit the country if Kate was elected.

"Maddie," Kate turned to the housekeeper who hovered in the doorway. "Take Debra into one of the bathrooms and clean up her face and check to make sure she doesn't have any glass in her hair or on her clothes. I'm going upstairs where Birdie can help me do the same thing. Sam and Trey, you both need to make sure there isn't any glass in your clothing or hair."

"Come on, honey," Maddie said to Debra as she walked across the room and gently took Debra's hand in hers. "Let's go get you all cleaned up."

The two women left the sitting room and Kate turned to Daniel Henderson, the last agent left in the room. "You can go, Daniel. We're good now. Just please keep me informed of anything you hear about the investigation into what just happened."

Daniel gave Kate a stiff half bow. "You know I'll do whatever I can to get to the bottom of this, but I imagine by now all kinds of agencies will be moving in to take over the investigation. Of course the Secret Service will be doing most of the work."

"Just keep me informed." Kate headed out of the sitting room while Daniel left by the back doors.

Sam remained in place, his hands in fists at his sides and angry frustration evident in every muscle in his body. "I should have seen that guy in the tree. I should have been paying more attention. I was trained to watch out for snipers."

"Cut yourself a break, Sam," Trey replied. "You weren't trained to look for snipers in our backyard at a breakfast. But I'd like to know who hired that guy. From what he said he was definitely a hired gun."

Sam's hands relaxed. "Either that or he was just a thug trying to make a name for himself and he just added in that bit about a bullet to the head business to make us believe he was nothing more than a hired gun."

Sam threw himself into one of the nearby chairs. "Hell, she hasn't even formally declared yet and already somebody is trying to kill her."

"At this point we can't be sure exactly who the target was," Trey replied, also sitting down in a chair near Sam.

"Who else would the target be?" Sam asked, looking at Trey as if he'd lost his mind.

"Maybe rumor had gotten out that you've been a real cranky ass to live with and Mom actually hired that man to put you out of your own misery," Trey said with a teasing tone.

"Ha ha, very funny," Sam replied.

"Okay, then Thad could have been the target because of his police work, or me because I've declared my intentions to run for senator." He paused a moment, his chest burning with anxiety. "Or the target could have been Debra. She's already been targeted by somebody twice. Maybe this was a final attempt to get rid of her."

Sam drew a deep breath and fell back into the chair. "What a mess."

"I suggest we both do what Mom said and head into bathrooms to check ourselves for glass," Trey replied.

Definitely a mess, Trey thought as he went in one direction and Sam disappeared in another. Somebody had just missed being shot and even though they had the shooter in custody Trey wasn't feeling optimistic that any agency would be able to get any real information out of the creep.

Was it possible that this would make his mother change her mind about running for president? Somehow Trey believed that if anything this would make her more resolute to follow through on her plans.

Trey knew that beneath Kate's pleasant exterior beat the heart of a warrior and a will of steel. She knew the dangers the office held and he had a feeling she would still be just as determined to make a run for the White House.

What he needed to do was talk to Thad and bring up the fact that it was possible the target wasn't Kate at all, but rather Debra.

Debra.

His heart filled with the newly realized love he felt

for her. Yes, everything was a mess. A man had just shot to kill somebody seated at the table and he was in love with a woman who apparently didn't love him back, a woman who might have been the intended victim of the shooting.

Debra sat on the toilet lid as Maddie used tweezers to pick pieces of glass from her hair and off her sweater. Maddie had already cleaned the blood off her face and Debra had sat like a child being ministered to by a loving mother.

She knew that she was in a little bit of shock because everything felt surreal. Her heart had finally found a normal rhythm after having beat nearly right out of her chest.

Everything that had happened to her—the mad drive in the middle of the night with no brakes, the fire that had occurred in her house—both seemed like mere nuisances when compared to what had just happened.

Somebody had shot a gun with the intent to kill. It was only by chance that Thad had seen the man in the tree and his warning shout had apparently made the gunman lose his aim.

Who had he been aiming at?

Who had been his target?

The logical answer would be Kate, but Debra couldn't stop the idea that kept coming back into her head, the idea that the target had been her. A shiver worked through her.

"Are you cold?" Maddie asked with concern. "Would you like a blanket or something around your shoulders while I finish up?"

"No, I'm fine. I'm just suffering from a little bit of

post-traumatic stress. I don't think I've ever been quite so frightened."

"You just need to relax now. You're safe and at least they caught the man. Besides, it's not good for your baby for you to be so stressed out."

Debra nearly laughed. Her baby wouldn't know how to exist without stress. Debra had been mentally frazzled since the moment she'd taken those three pregnancy tests. God, that felt like years ago. So much had happened in the past four weeks.

The thought that she was losing her mind, the crash of her car, the fire in her house... The only good thing that had happened was that since the new security system had been installed nothing in her home had disappeared only to reappear later.

Still, the idea that somebody had enjoyed free access to her home to try to drive her crazy and then had moved to more deadly means of getting rid of her would haunt her until somebody had been caught and jailed for the offenses.

"There, I think we got them all," Maddie said as she stepped back from Debra. On the vanity counter on a paper towel were about a dozen slivers of glass in various sizes.

Maddie took Debra's chin and raised her face so that she could look into Debra's eyes. "Are you sure you're okay, honey? Maybe a nice hot cup of tea would help calm you down a bit."

"That sounds wonderful," Debra agreed as she got up from her sitting position. "And thank you, Maddie, for taking such good care of me."

Maddie smiled. "That's what I do. I take care of

Winstons." She swept up the paper with the glass in her hands and then left the bathroom.

*But I'm not a Winston,* Debra thought as she stared at her reflection in the mirror over the sink. She looked shell-shocked, her hair a mess, her eyes too big and still filled with the terror that had momentarily made it impossible to move away from the shattered table.

Trey had virtually thrown himself across what was left of the table to get to her and pulled her to the ground where he'd covered her body with his, protecting her from harm.

No, not her, but their baby. He'd been protecting his baby from harm. She just happened to be carrying that baby. She left the bathroom, unsure if she wanted the cup of tea or not.

What she really wanted was to be at the townhouse, safe within the walls of her highly secured home. What she wanted was to know who was behind the attacks on her, who was responsible for wanting her to believe that she was going crazy.

Trey met her in the hall, his eyes dark and his expression radiating concern. "Are you sure you're okay?" he asked.

She nodded. "It was just a small cut. Maddie got it to stop bleeding and I'm perfectly fine." She raised a hand to tuck her hair behind her ear and knew the tremble of her hand belied her words.

"Okay, so I'm not so fine," she admitted. "I'm definitely shaken up and Maddie is making me a cup of tea to calm my nerves."

"Then let's go to the kitchen and have a cup of tea." He took her by the elbow, his touch gentle and warm.

They entered the huge kitchen and went directly to

the small table where Sam often sat to have his morning coffee.

"Just in time. Maddie told me you would be in for a nice cup of tea," Myra said, and set a cup in front of Debra. "Do you want sugar? Lemon? And do you want a cup, too, Trey?"

"No, thanks, I'm good."

"And this is fine for me. Thanks, Myra." Debra wrapped her hands around the heat of the cup in an attempt to warm the cold places that had found a home inside her during the past thirty minutes.

For a few moments she and Trey sat in silence. Debra sipped her tea and looked out the window where a number of security agents were gathered in front of the guesthouse.

Somebody's head would roll for the breach in security, she thought. "I wouldn't want to be the agent in charge of security for that quadrant of the yard."

Trey followed her gaze and then looked back at her. "Somebody will figure it out. I just thank God that Thad saw the guy before he managed to hurt somebody."

Debra took a sip of her tea and then returned the cup to the saucer. "You know it's possible it wasn't about your mother."

He held her gaze and in the depths of his troubled eyes she realized the thought had already crossed his mind. "We can't jump the gun. We don't know who the target was supposed to be right now."

"But you understand that given everything that has happened to this point in time, it's very possible I was the target." Just saying the words out loud leeched any warmth she might have gained back out of her body.

She shoved the cup of tea aside. "What I'd really like

to do right now is go home." Tears burned at her eyes and blurred her vision as she stared down at the table. "I just want to go home," she repeated softly.

"Then I'll take you home." Trey stood and touched her shoulder.

"But my car is here."

"Debra, I'd feel better under the circumstances if I drive you home. You're still upset and I can always bring you back here for work in the morning and you'll have your car here to drive home tomorrow night."

She nodded and stood. She was grateful that he was taking charge, that she didn't have to drive herself. Sometimes it was better to allow somebody else to take care of things and this was definitely one of those times. She'd been taking care of herself for her entire life and just for a little while she wanted to abdicate control.

They were escorted to Trey's car by two agents with guns drawn and gazes narrowed and focused on their surroundings. Debra felt as if she had entered an action film set. Surreal. How had her life gotten so dramatic, so intense?

She breathed a sigh of relief as Trey pulled out of the driveway and away from the estate. "I have to say, Kate sure knows how to put on an exciting breakfast."

"Let's hope we never have one as exciting as this one again," Trey replied. "The shooter, you didn't recognize him, did you?"

"No, I'm fairly sure I've never seen him before in my life, but that doesn't mean he wasn't hired by somebody to kill me." The words created an almost physical pain inside her. The idea that somebody hated her so much was unbelievable.

"Keep in mind that we don't know that this attack was about you," Trey said.

"I understand that. I get that your mother might have political enemies, but we both know I have an enemy, too, and maybe that person has given up trying to kill me and make it look like an accident."

"Thad will be checking it out along with the Secret Service," he replied. "I intend to talk to Thad about the fact that this might have been an attempt on you and not on Mom."

Debra stared out the side window. "It just all feels so horrible, to know that there's somebody out there who wants me dead. I've never done anything to anyone. I've never harmed anyone. Who could have such hatred for me?"

"I wish I knew, Debra."

They were silent for the remainder of the ride and she was grateful for the quiet. She still was trying to process what had happened, how quickly a lovely family toast could have turned into a complete and utter tragedy.

When Trey pulled up to the curb in front of her townhouse, he shut off the engine and then turned to look at her. "Stay put," he said.

She watched as he got out of the driver side and then came around to her side of the car and opened her door. He instantly pulled her out of the seat and surrounded her with his own body.

Awkwardly they made their way to the front door, him like a shield wrapped around her back. She was tense, expecting a gunshot at any moment or a knife-wielding maniac to jump out of the bushes nearby.

She didn't relax until they were safely inside the house with the security on. She collapsed onto the sofa and Trey sank down next to her. It only took a simple touch from him and she was in his arms, crying out the stress and fear as he held her tight and murmured words of comfort.

Her crying jag lasted only a couple of minutes and then she sat up and wiped the tears from her face. "I'm okay now. I just needed to get that out."

He smiled at her. "My mother always said that a good cry never hurt anyone." He leaned back against the sofa cushion. "So I guess there's no Sunday specialty cooking planned for today."

"I'm thinking dinner is going to be something nice and easy," she replied.

"Maybe you should put something in your stomach now," he suggested. "I noticed you didn't eat much earlier."

It was obvious he was in no hurry to leave and she wasn't sure she wanted him to go just yet. Nerves still jangled through her and the horror of the morning lingered.

"A bowl of soup might be good," she replied. She pulled herself up from the sofa and he followed suit.

"Why don't you just go into the kitchen and sit at the table and I can handle the soup," he said.

She thought about protesting, but instead merely nodded. "Thank you, I appreciate it. I'm still feeling just a little bit shaky."

Together they went into the kitchen where Debra took a seat at the table and Trey moved to the pantry where she stored her canned goods.

"I see chicken noodle, tomato and split pea." He looked back at her and made a face. "You don't really eat that split-pea stuff, do you?"

She laughed, unable to help herself at his look of utter disgust. "Actually I do and I love it. But I think a bowl of chicken noodle will be just fine, and open two cans if you'd like some, too."

"Maybe I'll just do that," he replied as he grabbed a saucepan from the baker's rack.

"Wouldn't you rather be back at the estate checking on the investigation instead of here babysitting me?" she asked, suddenly feeling guilty for taking up his time.

"The Secret Service will take over any investigation so there's really nothing I can do there. Thad will have his nose in things and will let me know of any breaking news."

He paused to use the can opener and poured the contents of the two soup cans into the saucepan. "Besides, I can't think of anyplace else I'd rather be right now than here with you eating canned soup."

He placed the saucepan on a stove burner and turned it on and then dug into her silverware drawer for a big spoon. She stared out the window and wished he wouldn't say things like that to her. He shouldn't be so nice to her. He made her want more than what he'd ever be able to offer to her.

She shouldn't have even let him come inside. This whole scene was a little too domestic for her taste. It brought up the yearning for it to be real, for them to be together as a true couple.

As he stirred the soup, Debra found her gaze wandering around the room, looking everywhere but at him. It was bad enough that she could smell his familiar cologne, a scent she thought she'd never get out of her mind.

She frowned as she spied something under the edge

of one of her lower cabinets. Had she dropped something that had rolled there? She couldn't imagine what it was, but it appeared to hold a touch of sparkle.

"What are you doing?" he asked as she got up from her chair.

"There's something here on the floor under the cabinet." She bent down and grabbed it, then stood and opened her hand. It was an earring. A diamond and ruby earring that she'd never seen before in her life.

"What is it?"

"It's an earring, but it isn't mine." She looked at him in confusion.

Trey stepped away from the stove to see what she held. His face paled and he stumbled backward a step.

"Trey? What's wrong?" Debra's heart began to pound as she saw the odd look on his face as he stared at the piece of jewelry.

"I know that earring. I bought a pair of them for Cecily."

Debra frowned. "How would one of Cecily's earrings get into my kitchen?" She gasped in stunned surprise as the realization of who was behind the attacks on her became apparent by the piece of expensive jewelry she held in her hand.

## Chapter 16

Trey stared at Debra for a long moment, trying to make sense of the earring she held in her hand. They were an unusual design and unmistakable. He specifically remembered purchasing them five months before and surprising Cecily with them over dinner at La Palace. Since that time she had worn them often.

Had she worn them when she'd set the fire in this house? Had they adorned her ears when she'd been moving cups and shifting around items to make Debra doubt her own sanity?

Cecily?

His mind boggled with the irrefutable evidence that she'd been inside Debra's home. Cecily had been behind everything. He couldn't seem to wrap his mind around it.

"I understand if she was angry when she found out

I was pregnant with your child, but most of the terrible things that happened occurred before anyone knew I was pregnant by you," Debra said thoughtfully. "Why would she try to hurt me when she didn't know anything about us?"

"I need to call Thad," Trey said as he fumbled his phone out of his pocket. "If she's responsible for everything that's happened to you then she needs to be arrested and charged."

As he punched in the number to connect him with his brother, Debra moved the saucepan and turned off the stove. "Thad." He was surprised that his voice shook with tension as he heard his brother answer the phone. "Can you get over to Debra's townhouse? I think we've found the source of the attacks on her."

With Thad's assurance that he'd be right over, Trey sank down at the table, still stunned by this new development. Debra sat down next to him, the earring on the table between them.

"I'm sorry, Trey," she said softly.

He looked at her incredulously. "Why are you sorry?"

"Because I know you cared about her, that you had intended to make her your wife. I'm sorry because I know that if what we believe is true you have to be hurting."

"Hurting?" He stood and slammed his hands down on the table. "I'm so angry right now she's lucky she isn't here in front of me. I knew she had a cold streak inside her, but I had no idea the evil that she has to possess to do what she's apparently done."

"She must have known about that night we spent together," Debra said.

Trey drew a deep breath and once again sat down

at the table. "I don't see how she could have known. I certainly never said anything about it to anyone and I'm sure you didn't, either. It was spontaneous, neither of us planned for it to happen. How could she have known about it?"

He closed his eyes, trying to recreate that night in his mind. He'd called Cecily and had invited her to join him in his celebration, but she'd been at a charity event and had told him she really couldn't get away.

Was it possible she had decided to show up at the restaurant anyway? Had she seen him and Debra and watched them as they left together to get the room in the nearby hotel?

Why hadn't she confronted him at the time? Why hadn't she told him that she knew about his tryst with Debra?

The doorbell rang and Trey got up, indicating that Debra should stay seated while he let his brother in. "I figured you'd be tied up with the shooting at the house," he said as Thad stepped inside.

"Right now the Secret Service is in charge of the crime scene and investigation, but if they think I'm going to leave it to them, then they don't know me," Thad said grimly. "So what's this about you believing you know who is behind the attacks on Debra?"

"Come on into the kitchen," Trey said. As Thad followed him Trey realized the stunned surprise he'd initially felt had transformed into a cold hard knot of anger in his chest.

Cecily had tried to kill the woman he loved, the woman who carried his baby. He'd sat across the table from her a hundred times at special events and in restaurants. He'd held her in his arms and gazed into her eyes and considered a future with her and yet he'd never seen the evil that had to dwell inside her.

As he and his brother entered the kitchen, the sight of Debra seated at the table made him realize just how superficial his feelings had been for Cecily.

The woman he truly loved sat in the chair with big green eyes and a touch of worry on her face. Debra might not love him, but he knew without a doubt she cared about the man he was, not the man he might some-day become.

It took only minutes for Trey to explain about the earring that Debra had found beneath the lower cabinet. Thad immediately called Lieutenant Al Chase, who agreed to meet them at Debra's house and then Thad placed the earring inside a small plastic bag and joined them at the table as they waited for Al to arrive.

"I have no idea how she might have gotten a key to my house," Debra said.

Thad gave her a rueful smile. "I've got news for you, Debra. There are key rings all over the estate that some-body could have plucked up and brought to your house, found the appropriate key, had a copy of it made and then returned the original to the key ring."

"And she could have hired some thug to crawl be-neath my car on the night of the dinner and cut my brake lines." Debra shook her head as she stared at the earring encased in plastic on her table. "She smiled at me that night, thanked me for everything I'd done for Trey. She was so nice and all the while she'd plotted my death."

Trey reached across and covered one of Debra's hands with his. "It will be over soon," he said. If Thad hadn't been present he would have told Debra what was in his heart, that obviously Cecily had seen her as a threat because somehow Cecily had known Trey was deeply in love with Debra.

"It's definitely possible that sniper in the tree this morning had nothing to do with Mom, but was somebody Cecily hired to kill Debra," he said instead.

Thad frowned thoughtfully. "That would definitely be nice for the Secret Service who are not only investigating but pointing fingers at each other as to who was responsible for that area."

At that moment the doorbell rang again and Lieutenant Chase arrived. Once again Trey told the story of the earring and everything he now suspected Cecily of being responsible for, including the possibility of her being behind the shooting that morning at the estate.

"Sounds to me like we need to speak to Cecily," Al said. "Do you know if she's home?"

Trey pulled his cell phone from his pocket. "I can find out." He punched the number he'd dialed a hundred times before and when she answered he was pleased that his voice betrayed none of the rage that had built up inside him with each moment that passed.

"Cecily, it's me," he said when she answered.

"Trey!" She was obviously surprised.

"I was wondering if you were going to be around for a little while this morning. There's something I'd like to talk to you about."

"Yes, certainly I'll be here. What time do you want to come by?"

"Right now."

"Oh, okay. I'll be waiting for you."

He could tell by the slight purr in her voice that she was expecting a reconciliation.

He was looking for reconciliation, too. He hoped that

by the time they finished talking to her they would finally have the answers as to who had been behind the attacks on Debra.

And once he knew she was safe, despite the intense love he felt for her, it would be time for him to give her the space to go on with her life, a life that would include him only as the father of their child, not as the husband, the lover, the life mate he wished he could be.

Debra knew that neither Al nor Thad were particularly happy that she had insisted she go with them to Cecily's house, but she wanted to be there, she wanted to look into Cecily's eyes as she attempted to deny what Debra knew in her heart she had tried to do.

Trey and Debra were in his car, followed by Thad and Al in a police car behind them. They drove in silence and Debra absently rubbed her lower abdomen as she stared out the passenger window and thought about the coming confrontation.

Even if Cecily lied about having done anything, the evidence of her earring in Debra's kitchen at least indicated that she'd been in Debra's house without an invitation.

She wasn't sure why a little bit of anxiety dwelled within her, but it was there, along with a huge hope that this truly was the end of all the madness for her.

She just wanted to get back to her work, back to a normal life. She wanted to focus on the baby, on transforming her guest room into a nursery and interviewing potential nannies.

She just wanted her life back—a normal, sane life that made sense. Was that too much to ask?

Her anxiety mounted as Trey drove up the long driveway to Cecily's large home.

Cecily had been born wealthy and it showed in the house she lived in. Although not as grand as the Winston Estate or Trey's home, it was a two-story colonial with massive columns and a sweeping veranda.

It was a perfect backdrop for a beautiful Southern socialite who spent most of her time attending charity events and getting her photo in the society pages.

It had already been agreed that Trey would greet Cecily at the front door and then the others would follow him inside. It would be a surprise attack that would hopefully catch the woman off guard and allow her to make a mistake.

When Trey knocked on the front door, Thad, Al and Debra stood out of sight on one side. Debra's heart thudded rapidly in her chest. Was she about to come face-to-face with the woman who had tried more than once to orchestrate her death?

The door opened and Cecily's voice drifted out on the cool air. "Trey, darling. Come in."

Thad and Al stepped up behind Trey. "Oh, I didn't realize you'd brought company with you." Her voice remained pleasant until Debra showed herself. "What's she doing here? Trey, what on earth is going on?"

"We need to talk to you, Cecily. May we all come inside?" Trey asked.

Cecily was dressed in a chocolate-brown dressing gown with jeweled buttons running from her breasts to the floor. Her hair and makeup were perfect and Debra would guess that she'd expected something far more intimate to happen when Trey had called to visit her.

"Of course," she replied with a new coolness in her

voice. She ushered them all into a formal living room that was a mix of white furniture and mirrored coffee tables.

Debra's discomfort level immediately increased. The room was cold, almost sterile, the only color coming from a large painting of a younger Cecily that hung on the wall.

Introductions were made between Al and Cecily, who had never met, and then Debra and Trey sat on the sofa while Cecily sank down in a nearby chair. Al and Thad remained standing. "So what's this all about?" Cecily asked. "I don't believe I've ever had one of Raleigh's finest in my home before, although I contribute heavily to the Wives of Fallen Officers charity."

"And we appreciate that," Al replied. "But I have some questions to ask you that have nothing to do with your charitable contributions," Al said.

"Questions about what?" Cecily's gaze met Trey's, Thad's and then Al's, but she refused to acknowledge Debra by even glancing at her.

"We'd like to know where you were on the night that Debra's living room was set on fire," Thad said.

Cecily released a tinkling laugh. "I have no idea. I'm not even sure what night she had the fire." Al told her the date. "I'd have to check my social calendar," she answered. "I stay so busy, off the top of my head I can't remember that specific night."

"We'll wait for you to get your calendar," Al replied, his deep voice filled with a firm resolve.

The pleasant smile that had curved Cecily's lips fell as she rose from her chair. "My secretary usually takes care of this, but I have a copy of my calendar on my notebook. I'll just go get it."

She left the room and as she did Trey reached over and lightly touched Debra's hand, as if to offer silent support, a hint of protection against the woman everyone had thought he would one day marry.

Cecily returned with her electronic notepad in hand. She sat back down and touched the screen to flip pages until she came to the one that held her calendar. "Ah, that night I was at a birthday party for a girlfriend."

"And what time did this birthday party end?" Al asked.

She frowned. "I think it broke up around ten."

"And then what did you do?" Al asked.

"I came home and went to bed…alone." She shot a quick glance at Trey and her brown eyes darkened to black. "Just tell me what this is all about. I'm an important woman and I have things to do. I have no idea why you're asking me such silly questions." There was a definite edge to her voice. "And I still don't understand what Debra is doing here. She's nothing but Kate's assistant and if you're here on some sort of official police business, then she has no place here."

Debra opened her mouth to respond, but Trey once again placed a hand on hers to halt anything she might be going to say. "Debra wanted to be here because she doesn't understand what you were doing in her home when she didn't know you were there," Trey said.

"I don't know what you're talking about. I've never been in Debra's house before. I don't even know exactly where she lives," Cecily protested.

"Then maybe you could explain how this got beneath her kitchen cabinet." Al pulled the earring in the clear plastic bag out of his pocket.

Cecily stared at it and then looked at Al. "I've never seen that earring before in my life."

"I have," Trey replied and got up from the sofa. "I bought them for you. I still have the sales receipt for them and I distinctly remember you wearing them when we went to the Christmas ball. I'm sure we can dig up a photo from that night."

When Cecily looked at Trey her lips twisted into an ugly sneer. "I came to the restaurant that night. I was late and saw the two of you together... You and that slut leaving the restaurant and going to the hotel. I sat in my car all night at the hotel and then I saw you put her in a taxi the next morning."

Debra gasped. "It was just a stupid mistake, Cecily. It would have never happened again, and you and Trey could have stayed together."

"You're having his baby!" Cecily's voice was a near screech of outrage.

"And I didn't intend for him to ever know about the baby," Debra replied.

"He's in love with you, you stupid cow." Cecily jumped up from her chair, the notepad falling to the floor and she glared at Trey.

"You think I didn't know? You think I didn't see the way you looked at her? The way you look at her now? You were supposed to love me. I was the woman who was going to help you achieve greatness. She's nothing, and yet you even stopped sleeping with me after you had her that night in the hotel room."

"So you tried to kill her," Trey said flatly as he stood to face her.

Cecily appeared to have lost all consciousness of the presence of anyone else in the room except herself and Trey. She took a step closer to him. "I did what was best for you…for us, Trey. At first, I just wanted her to think she was going crazy, believe that she was no longer capable of doing her job with Kate. I thought it would protect you if she decided to go public. Who would believe a crazy woman who couldn't even keep track of things in her own house?"

"But that didn't work." Trey's voice was emotionless.

"I had to do something. I couldn't just let all of your dreams and all of mine slip away." Cecily gazed at him as if she didn't understand why he would be upset with her.

"And so you hired somebody to tamper with her brakes."

Cecily stepped closer to him, her gaze softening as she toyed with one of the jewel buttons on her gown. "Don't you understand, Trey? She had to go." Her eyes took on a pleading look. "You might think you love her, but she isn't right for you. I'm what you need to get you where you want to go. She was nothing more than an obstacle that had to be removed so that we could build your future together, the way it is supposed to be."

*She's insane,* Debra thought. She's crazy as a loon, first in believing that Trey was in love with Debra and secondly in believing that by killing Debra she was assuring him the bright future Cecily saw herself in with him.

Debra held her breath as Cecily placed a hand over Trey's heart. "Don't you understand?" Cecily said. "The brakes…the fire… Everything I did was for you, for us. We want the same things; we are the same kind of people."

Trey grabbed her hand by the wrist and threw it off

him. "We aren't the same, Cecily. We aren't the same at all. At the very least the difference between us is that I have a conscience."

Cecily stared at him and then threw back her head and laughed. "A conscience? You stupid fool, you'll never make it in the world of politics if you have a conscience."

"Cecily McKenna, you are under arrest for the attempted murder of Debra Prentice," Al said, ending the confrontation.

Cecily gasped as he pulled her hands behind her and cuffed them. "I was only doing what had to be done," she replied and then laughed again. "You have no real proof that I've done anything wrong. I have a reputation as a charitable, law-abiding citizen. I'll hire the best defense attorney in the United States!" She screamed the words as Al led her out of the house.

"You haven't seen the last of me, Trey. We were destined for greatness. We're the power couple and you belong to me."

"Shut up." Al's voice could be heard just before the slam of his squad car silenced Cecily's voice.

"Is that earring enough to build a solid case against her?" Debra asked worriedly as she got up from the sofa.

Thad smiled at her. "Don't worry, Debra. They'll build a rock-solid case against her, and you and Trey will never have to worry about her again. Can I catch a ride back to your place with you guys? It appears Al forgot that I rode with him. He's already gone."

They locked Cecily's front door and minutes later were on the road back to Debra's place. As Thad and Trey talked about the case they would build against Cecily, Debra stared out the window and thought about what Cecily had said about Trey loving her.

How ironic was it that she'd nearly been killed by a woman who was under the mistaken impression that Trey loved her when nothing could be further from the truth. Trey cared about her as the mother of his child and he certainly loved the baby she carried, but Cecily had been twisted by knowing about the night Trey and Debra had shared together, a night that had just been a terrible mistake.

*Then how do you explain the second night?* The question whirled around in Debra's head, but she dismissed it as they pulled to the curb in front of her house.

It was over now. Cecily was arrested, the threat was finally gone and it was time for her to get back to living a new kind of normal life and planning for a baby and shared custody.

Her momentary worry that Trey would want to fight her for full custody seemed silly now. She knew Trey's heart and she knew there was no way he would do anything like that to hurt her.

They would co-parent well together because despite the fact that he didn't love her, they respected and genuinely liked each other and that's what was important.

Trey parked in front of her house and they all got out of the car. If felt like it had been a lifetime ago that they'd all been seated at the table in the Winston backyard about to celebrate with a toast when the gunfire had erupted.

"She never said anything about hiring somebody to shoot me," Debra said as they all got out of the car.

"We'll figure it all out, Debra," Thad assured her. "As it stands right now we can't be sure if she was responsible for the shooter or if somebody else was, but we won't stop digging until we have all of the answers. We know for sure she was in your house and she admitted to being responsible for the cut brake lines and the fire. That's enough to hold her on attempted murder charges even without what happened this morning at the breakfast. I'm out of here." With a lift of his hand in a wave, he hurried toward his car.

Trey walked with her to her front door. "Can I come in?" he asked. "As I remember, there's soup meant for the two of us waiting."

She smiled at him, her heart filled with both love and relief. "I think I could even rustle up a couple of grilled cheese sandwiches to go with that soup."

"Sounds good to me."

It felt far too comfortable, him following her into the kitchen. "I still can't believe she did everything she did because she thought you loved me," Debra said as she opened the refrigerator door to get out slices of cheese.

"I do love you."

She ignored the slightly faster beat of her heart as she closed the fridge door. "You love me because I'm the mother of your baby."

"No, I'm in love with you, Debra." His blue eyes held her gaze. "I would be in love with you whether you were carrying my baby or not, but I know you don't love me. When I proposed to you, you made it clear you weren't interested in me in that way."

The slices of cheese slipped from Debra's fingers and fell to the floor. "I thought you were proposing to the baby... I mean, I thought you were proposing to me because you thought it was the right thing to do and you always do the right thing."

"Then let me make it perfectly clear to you," he said as he took a step closer to her, his eyes lit up with a warmth, with a promise as he reached out and placed his hands on her shoulders. "I'm in love with you, Debra Prentice, and I can't imagine living the rest of my life without you by my side."

"But I'm not good material to be a politician's wife," she protested, finding it hard to think, to concentrate as she stared up into the bottomless depths of his eyes. "I don't know how to help you make your dreams come true. I don't know how to dance and sometimes I can be quite clumsy…"

His hands squeezed her shoulders with gentle pressure. "Just love me, Debra. I don't need you to work my campaign for me. I have Chad to do that. I don't need you to be the perfect political asset. I just need you to be my wife, to cook me special meals on Sundays and listen to everything that's in my heart. I just need you to love me and no matter what else happens in my future, my dreams will come true."

Debra's heart swelled so big in her chest she couldn't speak. She could only nod like a bobblehead doll. He seemed to understand as he pulled her tight against his chest and captured her lips with his in a kiss that stole her breath and lifted her heart to a place it had never been before.

*Love my baby. Love me.*

"I love you, Trey," she finally said as his lips left hers. "I've loved you since the moment I first met you. I don't care if you're a senator or you empty the garbage pails at the Senate. I just want to be your wife, to be a soft place for you to fall after a long day. I want to sit in front of a fire snuggled in your arms and watch our baby play."

"Babies," he replied and took her mouth once again in a kiss that banished loneliness, healed wounds and promised a lifetime of passion and love.

# Chapter 17

The ballroom at the Capital Hotel was magnificent, with five-story, floor to ceiling windows on three sides, and chandeliers that appeared to be sparkling stars against the deep blue high ceiling; it would have been impressive empty.

But tonight it wasn't empty. White-clothed tables surrounded the large polished dance floor, each table decorated with a red-and-pink floral arrangement in the center. Tiny red glittering hearts had been scattered around the arrangements, an instant reminder that it was Valentine's Day.

Debra felt as if it had been Valentine's Day for the past week, ever since she had accepted Trey's proposal. That morning she'd awakened to him serving her breakfast in bed and along with the bacon and eggs and orange juice had been a blue velvet ring box. As the server took their plates away from one of the front tables where they all sat, she admired the sparkle of the two-carat solitaire.

"Wishing it were bigger?" Trey asked her as he leaned closer to her.

She smiled at him, as always her heart expanding at the very sight of his handsome face. "Not at all. As it is now I have trouble lifting my hand."

He laughed and settled back in his chair and looked around the table with the expression of a contented man. For the past week they'd shared many long talks about their future, deciding on two children but keeping the possibility of a third open.

He'd taken her to his house where she'd declared that she absolutely hated it and that she'd need a big budget to transform the cold, beautiful house into a warm, inviting home. He'd taken her into his arms and assured her that it would be warm and inviting as long as she was there with him.

The plan was for her to put her townhouse on the market and within the coming weeks move into Trey's home. She wanted to be settled and married before the birth of the baby and she knew Trey felt the same way.

Every night of the past week he'd slept at the townhouse, snuggled with her in her bed. They'd made love each night and she wondered if she'd ever tire of the feel of his arms holding her tight, the taste of his lips against her own. He rubbed her belly each night and told the baby a ridiculous made-up bedtime story that always ended in her laughing.

No, she would never tire of Trey Winston. They would be together through good times and bad, through

thick and thin, with their mutual love for each other to
shelter them from each and every storm.

It had definitely been a magical week. Cecily was
still in jail. Surprisingly, the wealthy socialite hadn't
been so wealthy after all. She'd been living on credit
and had been on the verge of bankruptcy. She had been
unable to make the huge bail the judge had set.

It was obvious that Trey had not only been her dream
man because he wanted to be a senator, but also because he was wealthy enough to save her from her own
financial ruin.

Debra released a sigh of happiness. They shared the
table with Kate, Sam, Thad and the president of the
chamber of commerce, Bob Duke, and his wife, Sherri.

Dinner had been a pleasant affair, with everyone in
the festive mood of the evening. All of the men wore
tuxes and the ladies were visions in ball gowns, the pre-
vailing colors red and white and pink.

Debra and Trey had gone shopping for her dress,
a bright pink with a fitted bodice with tiers of white
and vivid pink that went from her waist to the floor.
The tiers effectively hid the baby bump that was now
clearly visible.

The guest of honor for the night, Kate, was a vision
in white with ruby bling in a gorgeous necklace and
matching earrings to add color to the sophisticated,
simple white gown.

Dinner had been entertaining, a bit of political chat-
ter at first, but then the conversation had changed to the
weather forecasting cold and snow possibilities in the
next week. Bob had shared disastrous Valentine's Days
he'd spent with his wife, Sherri, in the thirty years they
had been married.

"Men just don't always get it right." Sherri had laughed after Bob had tried to justify that a new garden tractor was a perfectly acceptable Valentine's Day gift to his wife.

There had been plenty of laughter, but Debra would have been perfectly happy if it had just been her and Trey alone in front of her fireplace.

Trey leaned closer to her once again. "It won't be long now and I'll have you in my arms on the dance floor."

"Be afraid…be very afraid," she replied in mock soberness.

She got the expected result she'd wanted. He laughed, that low, rich laughter that she desired to hear every day and every night for the rest of her life.

When the last table had been cleared, Bob turned and whispered something to Kate. She nodded and smiled around the table at all of her family as Bob got up from his seat and approached the podium at the front of the room.

He tapped the end of the microphone, testing to make sure it was turned on and then began to speak. "I'd like to welcome you all to the Chamber of Commerce Valentine's Day Charity Ball. I hope you've enjoyed your dinner and I also hope you've all had an opportunity to check out the room next door where we have a silent auction taking place. Pull out your checkbooks, men, there's plenty of jewelry and goodies over there that the ladies will want."

Everyone laughed and Trey's hand found Debra's beneath the table, radiating his love, his happiness through their physical contact.

"And don't forget to stick around for the dancing,"

Bob continued. "We have a terrific band standing by for your dancing pleasure. But now, it's my great pleasure to introduce our speaker for the night, although she scarcely needs an introduction. Kate Adair Winston is one of our own who has served not only the city of Raleigh with her charitable work, but also has served the United States as former vice president and former ambassador to France. Her family business, Adair Enterprises, has brought jobs and revenue to our fair city. Kate, we welcome you."

Applause filled the room as Kate rose from the table and took her place behind the podium. She had no notes. Debra had helped her work on the speech over the past couple of days and she'd heard it a dozen times as Kate had practiced it over and over again so that she would have it fully memorized.

Trey released her hand and relaxed back in his chair as Debra rubbed her lower stomach, caressing the baby who would be born into love, a child who would grow up in an intact family.

The room was utterly silent as Kate reached the podium, an indication of the respect she commanded. She turned to thank Bob and there was a distinctive ping sound.

"No!" Sam erupted and lunged from the table in an attempt to reach his mother.

Everything happened at the same time. The center of Kate's white dress exploded in red as Secret Service agent Dan Henderson reached her before Sam, took her down to the floor and covered her body with his. Two more pings resounded, followed by the crackling of glass at one of the huge windows.

Screaming filled the ballroom, along with the sound

of running feet and Secret Service swarming the area. Thad was on his phone, and then raced for the exit as Trey tugged Debra under the table.

*Gunshots,* Debra thought in horror. Kate had been shot. She squeezed her eyes tightly closed as she thought of the red stain that had suddenly appeared on Kate's stomach. Was Kate dead? Debra's heart pounded with dreadful intensity.

As Trey huddled next to her, his arm tightly around her shoulders, she was able to pick out familiar voices among the din. Sam sobbing and screaming in agony, somebody else shouting about a lockdown and finally the scream of sirens as emergency vehicles and local law-enforcement officials began to arrive.

Jerry Cahill leaned down beneath the table, his eyes cold and hard. "We need to get the family out of here right now," he said. "We're clearing the ballroom. All the guests are being moved to other areas of the hotel, but we have a car waiting for you two and Sam to head to the hospital where your mother is being taken."

Trey nodded and as he pulled Debra from beneath the table, he motioned to the distraught Sam to come with them. Two ambulance stretchers had already arrived in the room and it looked like both Kate and Dan Henderson were being loaded.

"I should have seen this coming," Sam sobbed as Trey threw an arm around his shaking shoulders and they all followed Jerry out of the ballroom. "I should have been able to save her. There were so many I couldn't save, but I should have saved her." Sam appeared to be shattering, his words indicating some sort of post-traumatic stress in addition to his fear for his mother.

Jerry led them to a back entrance of the hotel, all the while talking and listening on his radio. He stopped them at the door, appeared to get some sort of confirmation, and then with his gun in his hand, opened the door.

Directly ahead of them was a black sedan that Debra knew probably had bulletproof windows. Sam got into the front seat and she and Trey in the back and then Jerry slammed the doors, gave the top a thump and the driver pulled away.

The driver was Secret Service man Jeff Benton and as Sam managed to pull himself together, Jeff told them everything he knew, that from the direction that Kate had been shot, apparently the gunman had been in one of the darkened high-rise buildings on the left side of the street from the hotel ballroom and both local and federal agents were clearing those buildings now.

He couldn't tell them the condition of either Kate or Dan Henderson, who apparently had been shot also. He was driving them to Duke University Hospital where both Kate and Dan would be taken and were already in transport.

It was only then that Debra's brain began to process the horror. She leaned into Trey and began to silently weep, her heart aching for the entire Winston family. What should have been a night of triumph for Kate and her sons had become a night of sheer terror.

The ride to the hospital seemed to take forever. Was Kate still alive? *Please, don't take Kate,* Debra prayed as Trey held her tightly against his side. Sam, Thad and Trey needed their mother and Debra needed Kate, too. Her baby needed a grandmother. *Please, let Kate be okay.* It was a mantra that echoed over and over again in her head.

What about Dan Henderson? Had he sacrificed his life in doing his duty tonight? Four shots. There had been four bullets. One of them had hit Kate, but had the others hit Dan?

And where was Thad? Why wasn't he safely in this car with them? They should all be together right now, praying that Kate wasn't badly hurt, that nobody had been critically injured. They should all be praying that the gunman was captured and somebody could make sense of what had just happened.

She gazed down at the glittering ring on her finger and cuddled closer to the man who would be her husband. She told herself that no matter what happened tonight, she and Trey would get through the future together.

By the time they reached the hospital Trey was frantic and trying hard to hide it not just from Debra but also from Sam, who appeared to be on the very edge of his sanity.

They were led into a private waiting room with Jeff Benton stationed just outside the door. Thad was already there and he stood from the loveseat where he'd been sitting as they all entered the room. Thad looked haggard, as if the past forty-five minutes or so had sucked the very life out of him.

"What do you know?" Trey asked.

Thad gestured for Trey and Debra to sit on the loveseat and then he and Sam sank down into two straight-back chairs. "Nothing, other than the two victims have arrived and are with the doctors or whoever. I just got here a few minutes ago myself." Thad sat only a moment and then jumped up to begin to pace the small confines. Thad was tightly wound, his movements jerky with tension, his jaw taut.

Trey noted the fact that Thad had referred to their mother and Dan Henderson as the victims as if in an effort to completely divorce his emotions from the situation.

Sam had grown silent, his eyes staring unseeingly at the wall in front of him with his hands clasped together tightly in his lap.

As the oldest and the unofficial leader of the family, Trey felt helpless to do anything to help his brothers through this horrifying time. As he thought of that moment when his mother's white dress had turned red and she'd fallen, his heart felt like it stopped beating.

How could he help his brothers when he felt the open hand of utter despair attempting to grab him around the throat? The only thing keeping him partially grounded was the warmth of Debra's body next to his, the feel of her small hand gripping his so tightly and the baby that would make them a family.

Thad stopped pacing and stared at the doorway that they all knew somebody would eventually come through to give them an update. He looked as if he wanted to tear through the door to find some answers right now.

"You know, Cecily never confessed to hiring a gunman to shoot at Debra at the breakfast last week," Trey said, trying to gain Thad's attention.

"And the gunman has continued to refuse to talk about who hired him," Thad replied. "There's no way he wasn't a hired gun. His rap sheet shows him as a low-rent thug with charges of robbery and check fraud. He's not bright enough to mastermind his way out of a paper bag."

"But, after tonight, I believe his target was Mom that

day and not Debra." Trey tightened his arm around the woman he loved, remembering how frightened he'd been for her even before he'd acknowledged the love he had in his heart for her.

Thad turned back to stare at the doorway, as if he could will somebody to show up to give them some kind of a report as to what was happening with their mother.

"I wonder what's going on back at the hotel. I wonder if they've caught the shooter," Sam finally spoke, his hands curled into tight fists in his lap.

Thad looked at his brother. "I'm cut out of the loop for obvious reasons. I guess at some point we'll get an update from the Secret Service when they have something to share with us."

At that moment the door opened and a nurse stepped inside. Trey immediately recognized her as the same pretty nurse who had tended to Debra after her car accident. Lucy, that was her name. Lucy Sinclair.

"I just want to let you all know that your mother and Agent Dan Henderson are being attended to by our trauma team. Unfortunately, that's really all I can tell you at this point," she said sympathetically.

Thad took a step closer to her. "Well, that's not good enough," he said tersely. "Do you have any idea who my mother is?"

Lucy's green eyes widened a bit and then narrowed. "At the moment your mother is nothing more than a patient who needs immediate medical treatment."

"I demand to speak to the doctor in charge," Thad replied. "I'm Officer Thad Winston of the Raleigh Police Department and I want to speak to the doctor right now."

"Right now every trauma doctor we have on staff is desperately working to keep your mother and Agent

Henderson alive. They are both in critical condition." She took a step closer to Thad, her eyes flaming in aggravation. "You need to stand down, Officer Winston."

She stood toe-to-toe with him until Thad stepped back and fell back on the chair, his features crumbled in with defeat and fear.

As Lucy left the room, Trey looked at his family. Shell-shocked, that's what they were and yet despite the trauma that they were now experiencing, Trey's commitment to continue in politics only surged stronger inside him.

The bad guys didn't get to win. No matter what the outcome of tonight was, Trey intended to be on the ballot when it came time to elect the next senator of North Carolina.

One way or the other they would all survive this night. They carried Adair Winston blood inside them—they were strong and would carry on.

Debra took his hand and held tight, as if knowing what he was thinking and silently telling him that she would be right at his side.

\* \* \* \* \*

*Be sure to check out the rest of the books
in the ADAIR LEGACY miniseries:
EXECUTIVE PROTECTION by Jennifer Morey,
SPECIAL OPS RENDEZVOUS by Karen Anders
and SECRET SERVICE RESCUE by Elle James!
Available only from Harlequin Romantic Suspense!*

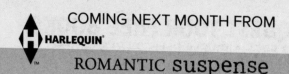

# COMING NEXT MONTH FROM

**HARLEQUIN**®

## ROMANTIC suspense

### Available May 6, 2014

#### #1799 CAVANAUGH UNDERCOVER
by Marie Ferrarella
Agent Brennan Cavanaugh's covert job in the seamy world of human trafficking turns personal when he meets the mysterious Tiana. Suddenly he's risking his life—and his heart—to save the undercover madam who's out to find her sister.

#### #1800 EXECUTIVE PROTECTION
*The Adair Legacy* • by Jennifer Morey
When his politician mother is shot, jaded cop Thad Winston gets more than he bargained for during the investigation with the spirited Lucy Sinclair, his mother's nurse. But keeping his desire at bay proves difficult when Lucy becomes the next target...and his to protect.

#### #1801 TRAITOROUS ATTRACTION
by C.J. Miller
To rescue the brother he believed dead, recluse Connor West will trust computer analyst Kate Squire. But the deeper they trek into the jungle, the hotter their attraction burns. Until the former spy realizes Kate knows more than she's telling...

#### #1802 LATIMER'S LAW
by Mel Sterling
Desperate young widow Abigail McMurray steals a pickup to flee an abusive relationship, never realizing the truck's owner, K-9 deputy Cade Latimer, is in the back. But rather than arrest her, the lawman takes her under his protection and into his arms.

---

# REQUEST YOUR FREE BOOKS!

## 2 FREE NOVELS PLUS 2 FREE GIFTS!

## ROMANTIC suspense

### *Sparked by danger, fueled by passion*

**YES!** Please send me 2 FREE Harlequin® Romantic Suspense novels and my 2 FREE gifts (gifts are worth about $10). After receiving them, if I don't wish to receive any more books, I can return the shipping statement marked "cancel." If I don't cancel, I will receive 4 brand-new novels every month and be billed just $4.74 per book in the U.S. or $5.24 per book in Canada. That's a savings of at least 14% off the cover price! It's quite a bargain! Shipping and handling is just 50¢ per book in the U.S. and 75¢ per book in Canada.* I understand that accepting the 2 free books and gifts places me under no obligation to buy anything. I can always return a shipment and cancel at any time. Even if I never buy another book, the two free books and gifts are mine to keep forever.

240/340 HDN F45N

Name _____ (PLEASE PRINT) _____

Address _____ Apt. # _____

City _____ State/Prov. _____ Zip/Postal Code _____

Signature (if under 18, a parent or guardian must sign)

### Mail to the **Harlequin®** Reader Service:
**IN U.S.A.:** P.O. Box 1867, Buffalo, NY 14240-1867
**IN CANADA:** P.O. Box 609, Fort Erie, Ontario L2A 5X3

**Want to try two free books from another line?**
**Call 1-800-873-8635 or visit www.ReaderService.com.**

\* Terms and prices subject to change without notice. Prices do not include applicable taxes. Sales tax applicable in N.Y. Canadian residents will be charged applicable taxes. Offer not valid in Quebec. This offer is limited to one order per household. Not valid for current subscribers to Harlequin Romantic Suspense books. All orders subject to credit approval. Credit or debit balances in a customer's account(s) may be offset by any other outstanding balance owed by or to the customer. Please allow 4 to 6 weeks for delivery. Offer available while quantities last.

**Your Privacy**—The Harlequin® Reader Service is committed to protecting your privacy. Our Privacy Policy is available online at www.ReaderService.com or upon request from the Harlequin Reader Service.

We make a portion of our mailing list available to reputable third parties that offer products we believe may interest you. If you prefer that we not exchange your name with third parties, or if you wish to clarify or modify your communication preferences, please visit us at www.ReaderService.com/consumerschoice or write to us at Harlequin Reader Service Preference Service, P.O. Box 9062, Buffalo, NY 14269. Include your complete name and address.

HRS13R

"Let me see, Abigail. I won't hurt you, but I need to know
bruises are the worst of it."

"That…that *crummy* button!" The words came out in
the most embarrassed, horrified tone Cade had ever heard a
woman use.

He couldn't tell whether the trembling that shook her entire
body was laughter, tears, fear, pain or all of the above. She
swayed on her feet like an exhausted toddler, and he realized
she might fall if she remained standing. He sank back onto
the picnic table bench and drew her down with him. She
drooped like a flower with a crushed stem, and it was the
most natural thing in the world to put an arm around her.
In all his thug-tracking days he'd never comforted a criminal
like this. How many of them had wept and gazed at him with
pitiful, wet eyes? How easily had he withstood those bids for
sympathy and lenience? How many of them ended up in the
back of the patrol car on the way to jail, where they belonged?

But how quickly, in just moments, had Abigail McMurray and her gigantic problem become the thing he most needed to fix in the world. He felt her stiffness melting away like snow in the Florida sun, and shortly she was leaning against his chest, her hands creeping up to hang on to his shoulders as if he were the only solid thing left on the planet.

*Now I have the truth.*

He had what he thought he wanted, yes. But knowing what had pushed Abigail to take his truck wasn't enough. Now he wanted the man who had done the damage, wanted him fiercely, with a dark, chill fury that was more vendetta than justice. He shouldn't feel this way—his law enforcement training should have kept him from the brink. He hardly knew Abigail, and the fact she'd stolen his truck didn't make her domestic abuse issues his problem.

But somehow they were.

He felt her tears soaking his shirt, her sobs shaking her body, and stared over her head toward the tea-dark river, where something had taken the lure on his fishing line and was merrily dragging his pole down the sandy bank into the water.

*Aw, hell. You know it's bad when I choose a sobbing woman over the best reel I own. Goodbye, pole. Hello, trouble.*

**Don't miss
LATIMER'S LAW
by Mel Sterling, coming May 2014 from
Harlequin® Romantic Suspense.**